Petrella at Q

A JOAN KAHN BOOK

Books by Michael Gilbert

Petrella at Q
The Night of the Twelfth
Flash Point
The 92nd Tiger
The Body of a Girl
The Family Tomb
Overdrive
Game Without Rules
The Crack in the Teacup
After the Fine Weather
Blood and Judgment
Be Shot for Sixpence
The Country-House Burglar
Fear to Tread
The Danger Within
Death Has Deep Roots
Smallbone Deceased
He Didn't Mind Danger

MICHAEL GILBERT

Petrella at Q

HARPER & ROW, PUBLISHERS
New York, Hagerstown, San Francisco, London

The characters in this book are entirely imaginary and bear no relation to any living person.   *C, 2*

"The Elusive Baby," "The Banting Street Fire," "The Death of Mrs.
Key," "Why Tarry the Wheels of His Chariot?" and "Rough Justice"
were first published in *Reveille* in 1972 and 1974; "Counterplot," "To
the Editor, Dear Sir—," "A Thoroughly Nice Boy" (under the title
"The Happy Brotherhood"), "Captain Crabtree," "The Last Tenant,"
and "Mutiny at Patton Street" were first published in *Ellery Queen's
Mystery Magazine* in 1976 and 1977. The introductory sketch, "Patrick
Petrella," was written at the suggestion of Otto Penzler for his compila-
tion *The Great Detectives*.

PETRELLA AT Q. Copyright © 1977 by Michael Gilbert. All rights
reserved. Printed in the United States of America. No part of this
book may be used or reproduced in any manner whatsoever without written permission except in the case of brief quotations embodied
in critical articles and reviews. For information address Harper & Row,
Publishers, Inc., 10 East 53rd Street, New York, N.Y. 10022.

FIRST U.S. EDITION

ISBN: 0-06-011539-4

LIBRARY OF CONGRESS CATALOG CARD NUMBER: 77-3790

77 78 79 80 81 10 9 8 7 6 5 4 3 2 1

Note

When the first of these stories was written there was no Q Division of the Metropolitan Police Area. Recently an extra Division has been carved out on the north-west outer perimeter and awarded this letter. It seemed to me that since there could be no possible confusion between this Division and the Division in which Detective Inspector (later Detective Chief Inspector) Petrella was operating during the year described in this book, I would leave it. I need hardly add that no reference is intended to any actual police officer or other person in either Division.

Contents

Patrick Petrella

WHEN LIEUTENANT OF Police Gregorio Petrella married Mirabel Trentham-Foster, their acquaintances were more than surprised; they were positively aghast They predicted disaster, rapid disillusionment and separation. The two persons concerned confounded these prophets. They lived together in love and amity, and have continued to do so until this day.

The use, in the previous sentence, of the word "acquaintances" rather than "friends" was deliberate. Both of them were solitary by nature. This may have helped to cement their happiness. When two solitary-minded people find each other their union can be very firm.

At the time of his marriage Gregorio was a Lieutenant in the political branch of the Spanish police, the equivalent, in England, of the Special Branch. It would scarcely be an exaggeration to say that he spent most of his working life keeping General Franco alive. He carried out his duties efficiently, not out of any love of El Caudillo, or even of any particular sympathy with his policies, but because it was his job, and one which he was technically well equipped to do.

For one of Gregorio's particular accomplishments, uncommon in a Spaniard, was that he was a linguist, bilingual in Spanish and French, competent in Arabic and English. This was useful since most of the hopeful conspiracies aimed at the removal of the head of the Spanish State had their origins abroad. A lot of his work took him into the country of the Basques and across the Pyrenees into Southern France.

Sometimes he went farther afield; to Tangiers, to Sicily and to Beirut. It was in Egypt that he found Miss Trentham-Foster. She was attempting a painting of the pyramids.

She had already torn up three versions in disgust and said to the friendly young Spaniard who had been watching her, "They all look so damnably conventional." Gregorio considered the matter, and said, "Might it improve them, if you painted the pyramids lying on their sides? Or even upside down?"

They were married three months later. Patrick was their only son. His upbringing accorded with his parentage. For the first eight years of his life in Spain (a country democratic with children, rigidly autocratic with adults) he spent his time running around with other boys of his own age from all classes of the community, learning things which horrified his mother as much as they amused his father. On his eighth birthday she put her small foot down. Coming as she did from an English professional family she had irreversible ideas about the proper education of male children. Captain Gregorio saw that Mirabel's mind was made up and gave way. His pay was not large, but fortunately there was family money on both sides. Prospectuses were sent for. The rival claims of different preparatory schools were carefully examined and the small Patrick was launched into the traditional educational system of the English middle and upper class.

With such an upbringing he might have found it difficult to adapt himself to boarding-school life, and it is reasonable to suppose that he was, to start with, fairly miserable; but there were factors in his favour. His temperament was, for the most part, sunny and equable. On the other hand, when he lost his temper, he lost it thoroughly; and he knew how to fight. He had not altogether wasted his time with the small *bandidos* of the slums of Madrid. His methods might be unorthodox, but they were effective.

By the time that he stepped off the other end of the educational escalator at the age of seventeen, there was nothing except the jet blackness of his hair and a slight darkness of his skin to distinguish him from any other public schoolboy.

At this point his father took a hand, and Patrick went, first to the American University in Beirut, where he learned to speak and read Arabic; then to a college of rather peculiar further education in Cairo, where he learned, among other things, how to pick locks.

His own ambitions had hardly changed since the age of eight. On his twenty-first birthday he joined the ranks of the Metropolitan Police as a Constable. A slight difficulty arising out of the question of his nationality was overcome through Colonel Gregorio's personal friendship with the then Assistant Commissioner. After he had completed his training at Peel House, Patrick's first posting was to the North London Division of Highside, and it was about his experiences here that the first stories were written.

It will be appreciated that the protagonist of a fictional series differs in a number of respects from his counterpart in real life. He is not born; he springs into being, mature, competent and armed at all points to deal with the first problem his creator has seen fit to face him with ("Oh, damn!" said Lord Peter Wimsey at Piccadilly Circus. "Hi! driver.") Such autogenesis had its dangers, even for so meticulous a plotter as Miss Sayers. A whole literature has sprung up in an attempt to reconcile the details of the earlier life of Sherlock Holmes and Doctor Watson.

There is an equally important matter which afflicts real and fictional characters alike: the matter of growing older. If Hercule Poirot really had retired from the Belgian Police Force in 1904, how old was he on his last appearance?

It may be true that readers, on the whole, care little for these niceties. For them their favourite characters live for ever in a fifth dimension where time does not wither nor custom stale. It is, however, worth noticing one point. Just as people believe that exterior circumstances occurring at the time of a child's conception (a period of happiness, a sudden shock, the conjunction of the planets or the phases of the moon) can affect the infant's character thereafter so can quite trivial occurrences on the occasion of his first public appearance affect, for better or for worse, a character destined for a long fictional life.

The fictional Patrick Petrella was conceived in church. The moment of his conception is as clearly fixed in my mind as though it had happened yesterday, not twenty-five years ago. It was a drowsy summer evening and the preacher had reached what appeared to be only the mid-point of his sermon. It was not an inspired address, and I turned, as I sometimes do in such circumstances, to the hymn book for relief. It opened on the lines of Christina Rossetti, *"Who has seen the wind? Neither you nor I. But when the trees bow down their heads, the wind is passing by."* A commonplace thought, given great effect by the rhythm and placing of the words. Then — *"Who has seen the wind? Neither I nor you. But when the leaves hang trembling, the wind is passing through"*.

And there, quite suddenly, it was. A scene, complete in every last detail. A working-class family, composed of wife and children, sitting in their front room, being talked to by a visitor (parson? social worker? policeman?) but remaining totally unresponsive to his efforts. Answering in monosyllables. Trembling. Heads bowed down. Why? Because they know, but their visitor does not, that there is a monster in the back room. Their father, a violent criminal, had escaped that day from prison and is hiding there. Certainly heads would hang and limbs be trembling. It is at that moment that their visitor (he is now quite definitely a policeman, and a youngster at that) recalls the lines of the poem and realises the truth. He bursts into the back room, and tackles the intruder, who gets the better of him, and escapes. Pursuit. Final capture.

In that short sequence, which cannot have lasted for more than a few seconds, a complete character was encapsulated. A young policeman, in his first posting (this was automatically North London, since we had lived in Highgate before migrating to rural Kent); sufficiently interested in his job, and in the people involved in it, to visit the wife of a man who was

serving a prison sentence; sufficiently acute to notice the un-
natural behaviour of the woman and her normally rowdy
children; sufficiently imaginative to deduce the reason for a
single, furtive glance in the direction of the kitchen door.
Courageous enough to go for the man, not nearly strong
enough to overpower him, but with sufficient tenacity to
continue the chase after he had been roughly handled; above
all, an unusual young man, who read and could quote poetry.

"Most police work was knowledge; knowledge of an
infinity of small, everyday facts, unimportant by themselves,
deadly when taken together. Nevertheless, Petrella retained
an obstinate conviction that there were other things as well,
deeper things and finer things; colours, shapes and sounds
of absolute beauty, unconnected with the world of small
people in small houses in grey streets. And while in one
pocket of his old raincoat he might carry Moriarty's *Police
Law*, in the other would lie, dog-eared with use, the *Golden
Treasury* of Palgrave.

*"She walks in beauty, like the night of cloudless climes
and starry skies,"* said Petrella, and, "That car's been there
a long time. If it's still there when I come back it might be
worth looking into."

Almost everything that happened afterwards was as trace-
able to that first conception as is the character of a real
person to the vagaries of his parents and the accidents of the
nursery and the schoolroom.

Other things were added later, of course.

Why was he called Petrella? A foolish question. Why are
you called Gubbins? Because it was your father's name. Why
such an odd name? Because his father was a foreigner. Then
why Patrick? Because his mother was an Englishwoman.

It was this dichotomy which produced the two opposite
strands in his character. His father was a professional policeman, who carried out a job which was not always agreeable,
in a totally professional manner. In such a situation, the end
might be held to justify the means. At the same time, since

he was a political policeman, it was inevitable that he would, from time to time, question the motives and the character of the people who gave him his orders.

From his mother, the daughter of an architect and the grand-daughter of a judge who was also an accomplished painter, he derived the cultural heritage of the English upper middle class, together with something else; an abstract notion of what was fair and what was unfair. It is a notion which is unfashionable in the materialistic win-at-any-price atmosphere of today. But curious that it should be sneered at when one considers the state in which the world now finds itself.

A Spanish temper and an English sense of equity. Such dangerous opposites were capable, from time to time, of combining into an explosive mixture capable of blowing Patrick Petrella clean out of the carefully regulated ranks of the Metropolitan Police.

At the moment of writing he is a Detective Chief Inspector, in charge of one of the three Stations in a rowdy but colourful South London Division.

His position dictates both the types of wrong-doing he will encounter and the general method of their solution. (Incidentally, it also overcomes an initial difficulty. A purely amateur detective who is also a series character has somehow to account plausibly for the extraordinary sequence of crimes with which he becomes involved. If a corpse is found in the library every time he happens to visit a country house people will soon stop asking him down for the weekend.)

To a member of the C.I.D. crime is his daily portion. It will certainly not be an undiluted diet of murder. The crimes which come his way will cover innumerable variations on the general themes of theft and violence, of arson, blackmail, forgery and fraud.

For the most part such crimes will be solved by the well-tried methods of the police. The asking of questions, the taking of statements, the analysis of physical evidence, the use of the Criminal Record Office, the Fingerprint Bank and the Forensic Science Laboratory. It is routine stuff for the most part; more perspiration than inspiration, but maybe none the less intriguing for that.

Petrella has the good fortune to belong, at a particular stage in its development, to what is, without question, the finest police force in the world. Whether he will rise any higher in it depends in part on his own efforts, in part on whether he can get along without unduly upsetting the top brass and in part on a number of imponderables about which it is pointless to conjecture.

I can only wish him well.

The Elusive Baby

AT THE SEASIDE, a heatwave can be a blessing. In August, in South London, in Detective Inspector Patrick Petrella's view, it was too much of a good thing.

"Arson, wife-beating and indecent exposure," he said to Detective Sergeant Blencowe. "Mostly the result of bad temper."

"Seasonal," said Blencowe. "Like shop-lifting and cruelty to children. We get them at Christmas. You want to count your blessings. At least we aren't lumbered with — "

What wrong-doing they were not lumbered with will never be known, because at that moment the telephone in the C.I.D. room at Patton Street rang. Petrella picked up the telephone, listened for a moment and said, "Damn and blast. All right, I'll be right over." And to Blencowe, "You'd better come with me. Someone's lifted a baby."

Baldwin Mansions was an old, but not unattractive block of council flats, arranged round an open courtyard. The flats had tiny balconies, with low balustrades. Outside the entrance to staircase E, a group of women had collected. The centre of attention was a sobbing woman. Not unattractive, thought Petrella. Middle twenties. Light hair, and a sunburned skin which was a contrast to the white cockney faces round her.

Constable Owers greeted his arrival with relief. "This is Mrs. Morgan," he said. "It's her baby boy. He was in the pram, on the balcony here." He indicated the perambulator, a new and rather expensive model, with a strip of material which acted as a sort of blind in front.

"I thought — I thought he was there," said the girl.

"You thought?"

"She means," said Owers, "that she usually keeps that sort of flap thing down in front. The child's very sensitive to sunlight."

"That's right," said one of the women. "Always down, that flap in front was."

Petrella detected a note of criticism in her voice. Maybe she was a fresh-air fiend. He said, "I suppose that means she can't tell us when he went."

"Nine o'clock she says she put him out," said Owers.

"That's right," said the girl. She started to cry again.

Petrella was remembering all the things that he now had to do. The routine was well established, but there was a lot of it. He said to Blencowe and Owers, "Start taking statements from all the women who live here. We want to know if anyone has been seen in this courtyard since nine o'clock. Any stranger. Particularly a strange woman. You know the form. I'll get back to the Station and alert Central. I'll need a description of the baby. Can anyone give me that?"

He looked round the circle, which had fallen oddly silent. It was Owers, in the end, who said, "She gave me a sort of description. It was nine months old. Dressed in a white-coloured wrap-round thing." Constable Owers was a bachelor. Blencowe said, "He means a body-binder."

"Black hair, quite a lot of it for a baby of that age. Blue eyes."

The girl stopped crying long enough to say, "He had his father's hair and eyes. He was the image of his father."

"That's enough to be going on with," said Petrella. He made his way back to the car which had brought him. As he was climbing in he noticed that one of the women had followed him. She said, "Excuse me for taking the liberty, but I'd like a word with you."

"Certainly," said Petrella. "Jump in the back, we can talk there." The woman said, "I don't want to make trouble, but the others thought I ought to have a word with you. Before you start anything."

Petrella said, "Yes," cautiously.

"It's like this. We don't think there is no baby at all, not really."

"What makes you think that?"

"That Mrs. Morgan, she's been here more'n a month now. And none of us haven't seen the baby." She added, with a depth of meaning which was not hidden from Petrella, "Nor we haven't *heard* it, neither."

Petrella, who knew something of the way life was lived in council flats, said, "I suppose it's possible. Some babies are a lot quieter than others."

"Another thing, she used to take it out in the pram, always with that flap down. Once, last week, Missus Crombie couldn't resist it no more. She said, 'I must have a peep at the little darling,' and she lifted the flap." The pause was clearly for dramatic effect. Petrella obliged her by saying, "What was inside?"

"Two packets of soap-flakes and one of corn-flakes."

"Soap-flakes," said Petrella. "Washing. Surely you'd have noticed that."

"We've seen baby clothes. A pile of them hanging out to dry. But what we said was, baby clothes don't necessarily mean a baby."

The verdict of the jury of matrons was clear. And it was a verdict which put Petrella right on the spot. He knew, none better, the necessity for speed when a baby was stolen. The whole of the police of the Metropolis and the Home Counties needed the news. Hospitals, child-welfare organisations, chemists' shops, children's clothing shops had to be alerted. A warning had to go to all Registrars. And that most useful ally, the Press, had to be briefed. He also knew that if he set all this in motion and was being fooled, he was booked for something worse than a red face.

Back at Patton Street he got on the telephone and put his divisional boss, Chief Superintendent Watterson, rapidly in the picture. Watterson said, "From what you tell me, it seems

to me we're on a hiding to nothing either way." (Some
Chief Superintendents would have said "you," not "we." It
was one of the reasons he liked working for Watterson.) He
said, "She's only been at Baldwin Mansions for a few weeks.
The baby's nine months old."

"If it exists."

"What I thought I'd do is get the girl round here for
questioning. That's natural enough in the circumstances, and
it'll keep her away from the Press. I'll find out where she
came from, get there quick. If there was a child, someone
there *must* know about it."

"We'll hope it won't be the Outer Hebrides," said Watterson, who came from those parts himself. "All right. Whilst
you're doing that, I'll alert Central, and start things moving.
But I'll warn them to keep it out of the papers for the
moment. Right?"

"Right," said Petrella. It was a relief to have some definite
action ahead of him.

An hour later, as he sat in the front seat of the police car
which Sergeant Blencowe was driving, he thought about the
story the girl had told them. It was a simple one, and it could
be true. Her husband, Evan Morgan, was a Chief Petty
Officer in the Navy, and twenty years older than her. They'd
been married for six years. During the first five years he had
had a shore-based job at Chatham and they had lived in their
caravan on a site near Cuxton on the Medway. A year ago,
two disasters had hit them at the same time. The caravan
site had closed, and her husband had been re-rated for service
on an aircraft carrier, currently in the Indian Ocean. A local
landowner, a retired Commander Fanshawe, had come to
their rescue. It was the Commander's address, the Manor
House, Cuxton, that Petrella had scribbled on a piece of
paper.

The Commander opened the door to them himself. Petrella
put him down as a man with money, who had left the service
before retiring age to look after his property. When Petrella
said, "I've come about a Mrs. Morgan. I believe she had a
caravan on your land recently," the Commander stared at

him blankly then burst out laughing and said, "Whoever said the law was slow? Fancy you getting on to it so quick."

"Getting on to what?" said Petrella blankly.

"I suppose the planning people alerted you. Mind you, I knew it was wrong, but it didn't seem to be hurting anyone. But regulations are regulations. Tell me the worst. Am I going to be put in prison?"

Petrella had at last grasped what he was talking about. He said, "You mean you didn't get planning permission for her caravan to be on your property?"

"I tucked it away, behind Long Shaw Copse. I didn't think anyone spotted it from first to last."

"That's what I really want to talk about," said Petrella, and told him the story.

"It's funny you should think that," said the Commander. "It did occur to me, from time to time, that it was rather an elusive baby. I never saw it myself, and I couldn't swear that anyone else did. Mind you, if she was fooling, she did it thoroughly. I saw baby clothes hung out to dry once or twice. And baby foods and stuff like that used to be delivered. I know that, because the trades people left the stuff here, and she collected it. They wouldn't go up to the caravan. She had a boxer bitch she used to leave in charge when she went out. A short-tempered old girl. She took a piece out of my trousers once."

"Didn't she have any friends? People who called on her? You couldn't very easily hide a baby from someone actually in the caravan."

The Commander said, speaking slowly and rather reluctantly, "There was one. I don't know that you can blame the girl. Living all alone in a neck of the woods."

"Could I have his name?"

"He's a local farmer. I don't think I'm going to tell you his name. I'm sorry I brought it up. It was only gossip really."

"All right," said Petrella. "But let's clear up one point. Her husband was posted overseas in January last year. The baby's said to be nine months old. Was it soon after he left that she got friendly with this man, because if it was — "

"All right," said the Commander. "I can do sums as well as you. Yes, it was immediately he left. She was very lonely. After the child was born, she seemed to lose interest in him. Maybe the child was company for her."

"If he existed."

"If he existed," agreed the Commander. "One way you could have found out would have been to have a word with our District Nurse. Only you can't. Six months ago she drove her car over a chalk-pit in a snow storm, on her way to a confinement. Tragic thing. However, you could try the Registrar at Chatham."

"I was planning to visit him next," said Petrella.

From Chatham, an hour later, he telephoned Superintendent Watterson. He said, "We'd better back-pedal on this. No one here ever saw the baby. And no baby of that name was registered in the last six months of last year."

"I'll talk to Mrs. Morgan," said the Superintendent grimly.

When Petrella got back, Watterson said to him, "I've had a word with the lady. I talked to her like a Dutch uncle."

"Did she admit she'd been fooling everyone?"

"Not in so many words. I thought her denials were wearing a bit thin by the end. When I told her that until we had actual proof of the child's existence we weren't prepared to pursue the case, I thought she was pretty relieved, actually."

Petrella said, "I shan't be sorry, either. It isn't as though we hadn't got enough on our plates — "

It was at this moment that Constable Owers came into the room. He laid the evening paper on the table, folding it ostentatiously so that the headline could be seen. It said, in large black letters, "WHERE'S THAT BABY?"

The police had been discreet. The inhabitants of Baldwin Mansions less so.

The next twenty-four hours was a period Petrella liked to forget. It wasn't only the reporters, although they were bad enough. A missing baby is always good for a story. A missing baby which might not exist was front-page stuff. It was when District started getting round his neck that Petrella began thinking about resignation.

Watterson did his best, but Baylis, the head of No. 2 District at that time, was a bit of an old woman. To do him justice, he was probably being prodded by Central.

On the afternoon of the second day, with the temperature in the middle nineties, Petrella put his cards flat on the table. He said, "We've got two alternatives. We can tell the world that we don't believe there was a baby. Or we can mount a search. I'd like to know which we're to do."

"So should I," said Watterson. "I put the matter in that way to Baylis myself."

"What did he say?"

"He said that I was the man on the spot, and in the best position to make my mind up."

Petrella was on the point of saying something insubordinate when the Station Sergeant opened the door and ushered in a large, aggressive, red-headed man, who said, "What's all this cock and bull about Elsie Morgan not having a baby? Certainly she had a baby. I'm his father."

Petrella said, "Might we have your name?"

"Sam Turner."

"And you farm near Cuxton?"

"That's right. Someone been telling tales out of school?"

"The person who mentioned you was careful not to name anyone. He just said that someone had been friendly with Mrs. Morgan, after her husband was posted abroad — "

"Fair enough. I'm not denying anything. I was sorry for the poor kid. Dumped down in the middle of nowhere with nothing but sheep and cows to talk to. I'm not ashamed of what I did. These things happen." He added, with a grin, "That husband of hers had been trying for five years. Perhaps he hadn't got the knack."

Petrella thought that there were few men whom he had disliked more on sight than Sam Turner. And he could understand and forgive Mrs. Morgan getting tired of him. But his mind was preoccupied with much colder and less comfortable thoughts.

Whilst he was working out this new line of speculation,

Watterson took over. He said, "I take it you've actually seen this baby?"

"Seen it? Of course I've bloody well seen it. I've had it on my knee. Piddled on me more than once, messy little bastard."

"I meant, have you seen it recently?"

An odd look came into Sam Turner's eyes. He's caught on, thought Petrella.

"I haven't seen it up in London, if that's what you mean. Soon as I read the papers I came up to have things out with Elsie. There was a bobby on the door. He wouldn't let me in. That's why I came round here."

"And this is the first time you've tried to see Mrs. Morgan since she left Cuxton?"

"Of course it's the first time. I didn't know where she was before, did I?"

"You mean she came up to London without telling you anything about it. That's rather odd, if you were the father of her child, isn't it?"

For the first time, Turner looked uncomfortable. He said, "As a matter of fact, for the last few months, we weren't quite so friendly. It wasn't any of my doing — but that's the way it was. Now I want to see her and the boy, and straighten it all out. I've got my rights."

"As things stand at the moment," said Watterson coldly, "you've got no rights at all. If you'll wait downstairs — the Sergeant will show you the way — I'll see what I can do for you."

When the door had closed behind them, he said, "What's worrying you, Patrick?"

"It's something that's been bothering me all along," said Petrella. "And I'm afraid I've guessed the answer. *If she wanted to keep the baby hidden, why on earth did she come up to London?* As long as she was tucked away, in a caravan, on private property, guarded by a dog of uncertain temper, the thing was easy. In a council flat in London it must have been almost impossible."

"All right," said Watterson. "I can see you've worked it all out. You tell me."

"I think it was because she wanted to lose the baby convincingly before her husband came home. She couldn't stage-manage it in a field in the country. No one would have believed it."

"That's possible enough," said Watterson slowly. "But if she brought the baby up with her, where is it now?"

"She didn't bring it with her," said Petrella. "It's in a hole in the ground, somewhere in Kent." He added, "Sam Turner thinks so, too. I saw him thinking it."

There was a long silence.

"It makes sense," said Watterson, at last. "We'd better alert the local talent. If she did it at the last moment before she came to London, the grave will still be fairly fresh. They've got instruments which register on freshly opened ground. They'd better get on with it." He didn't sound enthusiastic.

Petrella said, "I wonder if I ought to have a word with Mrs. Morgan first."

"We can't possibly charge her."

"*We* can't."

"What are you getting at?"

"I thought I might take Sam round with me. He already suspects the truth. As soon as he sees the child isn't there he's going to blow his top."

"Shock tactics?"

"It might work."

"I can't think of anything in Judges' Rules against it," said Watterson.

When Petrella arrived back at Baldwin Mansions he found the patient Constable Owers arguing with a thick-set, black-haired man wearing a dark blue suit and the unmistakable look of a sailor out of uniform.

"He says he's this lady's husband, sir."

"Of course I'm her husband," said the man in tones of deep exasperation. "Who the flaming hell d'you think I am? The Shah of Persia."

"I expect you have some identity documents," said Petrella pacifically.

"It's a fine state of affairs if I need a ticket to get in to see my wife," said the man. He produced a pay-book and other papers which identified him as Chief Petty Officer Evan Morgan. "I've spent fifteen flaming hours out of the last twenty in aeroplanes. Now I've got here, the police stop me seeing her."

"I think we'd all three better go in," said Petrella, with a glance at the crowd who were lapping it up. It seemed hardly the time or the place to explain who Sam Turner was.

When Mrs. Morgan opened the door to them she took a startled look at the three men, threw her arms round her husband's neck, and burst into tears. Somehow they got themselves into the living-room.

"What's all this, Else," said her husband. "I saw a lot of stuff in the papers about our baby. The Navy flew me home straight away. Where'd they dream up all that story about it not really being there at all?"

"Of course it was there," said Turner, who had been steadily coming to the boil. "I told 'em, I've had it on my knee, more than once."

"And who the hell are you?"

"If you want the truth, you'd better have it. I'm his father."

There was a moment of paralysed silence, and then Morgan, moving with surprising speed for a man of his bulk, had Turner by the throat. Turner grabbed his wrists and tried to pull them off. Then he changed his tactics and hit Morgan in the stomach. As Morgan dropped his hands, they broke apart and Petrella slipped between them. They were both bigger and heavier than he was. Before they could start the fight again they were interrupted. It was the thin cry of a baby, who has been woken up, and is annoyed about it.

Mrs. Morgan darted from the room, and came back, carrying a fat, sleepy-looking child. It had a surprising amount of hair for its age, and it was already quite undeniably russet, if not yet red colour.

"Look at him," said Turner. "Look at his hair. Look at his eyes."

"My grandfather had red hair," said Morgan. "The child's thrown back to him."

Turner growled, and sidled forward, but Petrella had had enough. He said, "If you start rough-housing again, I'll have you run in." He signalled from the window to Sergeant Blencowe, who came at the double.

"Take this man back to the car," he said, "and keep him there."

Turner looked as if he would have wished to argue, but Sergeant Blencowe had played rugby for the London-Welsh, in the second row of the scrum, and very few people argued with him.

When Turner had gone, Petrella said to Morgan, "I want to talk to you. Alone."

"We could go in the kitchen."

As they were going, the baby, who had been regarding Chief Petty Officer Morgan with a fixed, if slightly unfocused stare, suddenly smiled and said, "Da".

"There," said Morgan. "You see. *He* knows."

It hardly seemed to Petrella to be conclusive evidence of paternity, but it cheered up both the Morgans enormously.

Petrella said, "It's pretty clear, now, what happened. She was afraid you might disown the child."

"Why ever should I do that. We've been trying for one for six years."

"Quite so," said Petrella. "But she wasn't sure you'd take such a sensible attitude. And there's no doubt she'd been a bit indiscreet with that chap Turner."

"That red-headed turd. If he makes any trouble I'll fix him properly. Just tell me one thing. That child belongs to me. Right?"

"The child," said Petrella slowly, "quite definitely belongs to you. You're Mrs. Morgan's husband. It was born, I gather, ten months after you left England, but that's by no means exceptional."

"Right," said Chief Petty Officer Morgan. "That's all I wanted to know."

Petrella left the three of them together. They seemed to have arrived at a perfect understanding.

*   *   *

"Lucky his grandfather had red hair," said Chief Superintendent Watterson that evening. "I still don't understand what the hell she was playing at."

"I think I do," said Petrella. "She was nervous that as soon as her husband saw the child he'd assume she'd been fooling round with Sam Turner. Which, of course, she had. She therefore decided to ditch the child. But she couldn't bring herself to hurt it. She staged what she thought would be a convincing child stealing here in London. A black-haired, blue-eyed baby, remember? Just like his dad. As soon as the fuss died down I imagine she was going to deposit the child, warmly wrapped up, on the steps of the Town Hall. No one would have associated it with her. What she underestimated was the Press coverage. It brought Sam Turner running."

"What she underestimated," said Watterson, "was her husband's ambition to have a child, and to wipe Sam Turner's eye —"

The telephone interrupted him.

It was a fire. A garage in Banting Street.

The Banting Street Fire

WHEN PETRELLA ARRIVED, Banting Street was blocked by a line of fire engines and fire tenders. Some way ahead of him, he could see a column of billowing smoke, white where the spotlights from the tenders hit it, shot through at the base with spiteful little tongues of orange flame. Over all hung the sharp, ozone smell of the foam extinguishers; and, as he found when he put up his hand to wipe his face, a steady drizzle of black smuts.

He pushed through the crowd and ran into Bill Brewer, the Borough Fire Officer. Brewer said, "Lucky we got here as quick as we did. With this wind it could have taken out half the street. I reckon we've got it under control now."

"What is it?"

"Garage and workshop. Won't be much of it left by the time we're through." This was punctuated by a crash of falling timbers and a firework display of sparks.

"Any ideas —?"

"I'll give you my ideas in the morning," said Brewer, and hurried off. It was evident, even to Petrella's inexpert eyes, that the fire was subsiding. He went home to bed.

When he got to Patton Street next morning he found on his desk a copy of the report which had gone to Superintendent Berriman, the head of the uniformed branch. It said that the Premier Garage in Banting Street belonged to William Cookson, who had acquired it three years before. There was a workshop, which formed the whole of the ground floor, and had working space for two cars. There was a yard at the back with a small office and lean-to accommodation for four more cars, which was approached from Kentledge Road and Banting Passage. There was living accommodation over the workshop.

It was the last sentence in the report which caught Petrella's eye. This said, "The fire brigade authorities are not satisfied as to the origins of this conflagration."

Petrella was still wondering why Constable Mitchinson, who had written the report, had used a four-syllable word to describe a one-syllable event when Bill Brewer was shown in.

He said, "Sent your suit to the cleaners, Patrick?"

"I'm afraid I had to," said Petrella. "I ought to have had the sense to wear a gas-cape like you."

"Messy things oil fires. This one's messier than most, I'm afraid."

"Meaning?"

"Meaning that it certainly wasn't an accident."

"Sure?"

"Dead sure. It had three different points of origin. Two in the workshop, one in the office at the back. O.K., I'm prepared to believe a fire can start accidentally. What I'm *not* prepared to believe in is three separate accidents happening on the same premises at the same time."

"I suppose not," said Petrella.

"We'd call that conclusive by itself. But it's not all. Not by any means. There was a strong wind last night. It helped to spread the fire. But it also blew it away from one of its points of origin in the office at the back. And we found this."

He took from his briefcase an object wrapped in tissue paper, unwrapped it and placed it on Petrella's desk. It had suffered in the flames, but was still recognisable as a small alarm clock, with the frayed ends of two wires sticking out of the back.

"What does it do?" said Petrella.

"Quite a neat job. It was connected to the electric fire in the office, through the fuse box. Whoever set it up, took out

the fuse, and then turned the electric fire on. When this jig-
ger went off it restored the circuit. I don't know what had
been left in front of that fire. A pile of cotton waste soaked
in petrol or a box of old film. Whatever it was has been des-
troyed, of course."

Petrella looked curiously at the twisted, fire-stained relic.
He said, "Is there enough of it left for your experts to be
able to say when it was meant to go off?"

"Nine o'clock, they think, and that was roughly when it did
start."

"Is there any indication of how the other fires started, in
the main workshop?"

"Not a scrap. Like I said, this little fellow wouldn't have
survived if the wind hadn't got up and blown the flames
directly away from it."

He wrapped it up lovingly, and said, "I'll hand it over to
you, when I've written my report."

"I'd better be having a word with the owner," said Petrella.

He had a policeman's memory for faces, and he recognised
Willie Cookson as soon as he came into the room. He had
last seen him four years before, when he had been enquiring
into a case of organised pilfering at the Crossways Goods
Depot. Cookson, who was a large, cheerful, red-haired man,
had been one of the men he had talked to. His hair had a
touch of grey in it now, and he was not looking cheerful.

He said, "People have been talking, I hear. Saying I started
that fire. They're bloody liars. I was nowhere near the place
when it went up. If I had been, I'd have done something
about it, wouldn't I?"

"Where were you?"

"Wasting my bloody time."

"All right," said Petrella. "Tell me about it."

It was a simple, straight-forward story, and almost completely unverifiable. A man had telephoned Cookson at seven
o'clock, when he was shutting up shop. He said that he had
a five-year-old Bentley for sale and had been given Cookson's
name by a friend. It was urgent, because he was leaving the
country next day. That was why he was willing to let it go

cheap. He had mentioned a price, and Cookson had realised that if the car was in reasonable condition, this was a real bargain. The caller gave his address, a house standing in its own grounds, between Dartford and Northfleet. Cookson had said he would drive right out. The man said, don't come before half past eight, or you won't find anyone in. Cookson had arrived promptly at eight thirty. The front gates were padlocked, and there was a For Sale notice hung on them. However, a small side-gate was open, so he had left his car, and walked up to the house. No lights showing, and no answer when he rang the bell.

"I hung around until after nine," he said, "although I knew it was no good, really. I could sort of feel the house had been empty for some time, if you know what I mean."

"I do know what you mean," said Petrella. "I think it's the smell. Did anyone see you on your way out or coming back?"

"A load of people, I expect. No one I particularly noticed, though."

"I take it you're insured?"

"Of course I'm insured."

"Let's go down and look round."

"If you think you'll find anything," said Cookson. "The fire boys have been combing it over since first thing this morning."

It was a sad sight. One or two steel girders of the main structure were still there, but looked as if they might come down at any moment. The ground was knee-deep in charred woodwork, twisted metal, and the remains of what might once upon a time have been two good-looking motor cars.

Petrella climbed through to the back. Here, as Brewer had said, the destruction was less complete. The little brick-built office, which stood at the back of the yard, with a window giving on to Banting Passage, had suffered least of all. Petrella said, "When did that happen? That wasn't done by the fire."

He was looking at the window. There was a splintered break in the woodwork of the cross bar and the retaining clasp was hanging by a single screw.

"Search me," said Cookson.

"It looks as if someone has forced the window from the outside. What did you keep in here?"   •

"Papers mostly. Account books. Trade catalogues. Nothing anyone would want to steal."

"And you're certain this hadn't been done when you locked up last night?"

"Well, I'd have noticed it when I locked up, wouldn't I?"

"I suppose so," said Petrella.

He went back to Patton Street. Brewer's report arrived that afternoon. Petrella wrote his own that evening. Arson is a serious crime, so the reports went up to the Director of Public Prosecutions. In due course Cookson was charged.

On the morning of the preliminary hearing, Chief Superintendent Watterson walked down to the police court with Petrella. He said, "I'm surprised Cookson is fighting it at this stage. The normal thing would be to plead not guilty and reserve his defence."

"He's not only fighting it," said Petrella. "He's got Tasker to do it for him. I've seen him in action before. We're not going to have a walk-over."

"Do you think he did it?"

Petrella walked a few steps before answering. He said, "The circumstantial evidence is strong. The garage made a loss in its first two years. It was insured. The fire was clearly a fake. Cookson was the only person who stood to gain. But I'm not sure it adds up to proof. And I'm puzzled by that breaking in. The only person who *wouldn't* have to break in to start a fire was Cookson himself."

"That could have been a fake too."

"It could have been," agreed Petrella.

The first witness for the Crown was Brewer. He was taken carefully through his report by the solicitor for the police. When he had finished, Mr. Tasker rose to his feet. He was a big, full-jowled, black-haired man, who conducted a flourishing one-man practice near the Oval. He worked twelve hours a day for most of the year, and closed his office for the complete period of any Test Match. Mr. Tasker did a lot of the local police court work, appearing indiscriminately for and against the police in the impartial way which is so puzzling to foreigners brought up on a system of state prosecution.

He said, "I have no questions to ask Mr. Brewer. The defence accepts that the fire was caused deliberately." Then he sat down.

The solicitor for the police looked annoyed, and crossed out the names of the two experts he had been planning to call from the Forensic Science Laboratory.

The next witness, a Mr. Phipps, gave formal evidence of the existence of a comprehensive insurance policy on the Premier Garage, and added that, at the moment, his company was withholding payment on it. Mr. Tasker said, "Please tell the court when this policy was taken out."

"It was taken out three years ago, when Cookson acquired the garage."

"When *Mr.* Cookson acquired the garage," suggested Mr. Tasker gently.

Mr. Phipps blushed, and said, "That's right."

"Did you have a valuation made?"

"Yes. We agreed a valuation."

"And that was three years ago. During which time the value of all properties has gone up."

"I believe so."

"Then at the moment, the garage is under-insured."

Mr. Phipps hesitated. The Magistrate said, "Come, Mr. Phipps. That's the effect of what you've told us, isn't it?"

Mr. Phipps looked unhappy, and said, "I suppose it is."

Petrella gave evidence of having examined the garage on the following morning. He agreed that the window at the back appeared to have been forced. He was not cross-examined.

The next witness was an accountant. He produced a sheaf of papers, and told the court that the Premier Garage had lost money in its first two years, and might have been coming out level at the end of the third year.

Mr. Tasker said, "These accounts were produced to you voluntarily by the accused."

The accountant, who did a lot of work for the police, and who knew Mr. Tasker, agreed cautiously.

"I imagine that he was proud of them, wasn't he?"

"I'm not sure I understand."

"Come, come," said Mr. Tasker. "A newly established garage. A lot of initial expense to write off. Getting into the black by the third year. That's pretty good, isn't it?"

The accountant boggled at "pretty good", but settled for "fair". Mr. Tasker let it go. Some plans were produced and agreed, and the prosecution case was closed.

Mr. Tasker said, "I should be justified, sir, in asking you to rule, at this point, that the prosecution has failed to make out its case. I shall not do that, because I have some witnesses whom I think you will be interested to hear — "

Petrella and Watterson looked at each other uneasily. Mr. Tasker was famous for his surprise witnesses.

The first was an A.A. patrol, who stated, quite simply, that he had seen a car outside Cranbrook House, Northfleet, which he knew to be empty, at ten minutes to nine on the night of the fire. He had stopped to see if it was in trouble, but since it seemed to be in order, he had gone on. He had, however, made a note of the car's number in his log, which he produced. It was clearly Cookson's car. The police solicitor could think of nothing to ask him.

Mr. Tasker's second witness was a taxi driver. He said that he had parked his taxi in Kentledge Road at about half past seven for a short lay-off and a smoke. It was opposite the end of Banting Passage, and he had seen two men doing something to a window farther down the passage. Mending it or breaking it. He couldn't see which, and it wasn't any of his business. They were still there when he had driven away.

"Could you recognise them?" said Mr. Tasker.

"Not to say recognise."

"Did either of them resemble the accused?"

"Him? He'd make two of them."

"You mean that the accused is much larger than either of these two men?"

The taxi-driver agreed that that was what he meant.

The prosecution did their best but were unable to shake him.

Mr. Tasker said, "The absurdity of this charge must, by now, be apparent to everyone. First, it was suggested, if I understood the police case, that the whole story of my client's visit to Northfleet was a fabrication. In the light of our evidence, I suppose they will now say that the telephone call was invented, but that, to support his story, my client actually motored out there and hung around in a deserted garden for half an hour. Why? To establish an alibi for a fire he had arranged to start at nine o'clock? Ridiculous. If he wished to establish an alibi, why did he not go to some function — the social club run by his old workmates and friends from Crossways for instance. They had a function that evening. Then he would have produced fifty people to support his alibi."

Mr. Tasker blew his nose loudly at this point, and said, "Next, perhaps someone will explain why the accused hired two men to break into his own garage. Wouldn't it have been easier to lend them a key. This whole case is founded on a faulty premise. The Crown say, this garage was doing badly. It was insured. The accused burned it down. He was the only person who could benefit. Now we know that's not true. This garage was doing well. And going to do even better. The people who would want to burn it down — the only people with any possible motive for burning it down — were his rivals. The people he's taking business from. It's common knowledge there are too many garages in this district. There's one in the very next street. Of course, I'm not suggesting —"

"But he bloody well did suggest it," said Watterson, as they were walking back to the Station after the case had been dismissed, and a contingent of Willie Cookson's friends from the Goods Depot had cheered him all the way into the street. "Albert Rugg keeps the Octagon Garage in Kentledge

Road and everyone knows he's been losing business to Cookson."

"Albert was in court," said Petrella. "You should have seen his face."

"It's not funny," said Watterson. "We've been made to look stupid. There'll be a rocket from District about this."

"If Albert got anyone to do his dirty work," said Petrella, "I guess it would have been Stan or Les Corner. Should I pull them in and put them through it?"

"Drop it," said Watterson sourly. "The case is dead. It's finished."

But here he was wrong.

Albert Rugg, owner of the Octagon Garage, was a bachelor, like Cookson. He didn't live above his business. He had a comfortable flat, over a newsagent's shop, a quarter of a mile away. He came back to it, a week later, and had shut the flat door before he realised that he was not alone. Not only was Willie Cookson waiting for him, but he had with him three friends from the Crossways Depot.

Albert was fat, and a bit of a coward. He started to bluster, and when he had been knocked down twice, he looked fearfully out of a fast-closing right eye, and said, "What's it all about? What do you want?"

"You know bloody well what I want," said Cookson. "I want the truth."

"I don't know what you're talking about."

The larger of the men closed in again. Cookson said, "Hold it. We want him in one piece. He's going to sign a confession."

"I got nothing to confess to," said Rugg. "Just because that cunning bastard Tasker tried to put the blame on me. I ought to sue him for libel."

"I tell you what we ought to do," said the second of Willie Cookson's assistants. "I seen this on television. We tie him in a chair, and take his shoes and socks off. And we put one foot on the electric fire. It's effective, see?"

"It sounds effective," agreed Cookson. "Let's give it a try."

In no time at all they had Albert lashed to a dining-room

chair. When he started to shout they stuffed the socks they had removed into his mouth, and tied them there with a tea-towel.

At this point the doorbell rang. Cookson said, "See who it is and send them away."

One of the men went out. As he opened the flat door it came inward at him with a crash and Stan and Les Corner came in fast, supported by a cousin called Lew.

Stan Corner said, "Lucky I happened to see these bastards come in," and battle was joined. It was a lovely fight. The railway men were large, and determined. The Corner boys were smaller, but had a slight edge in skill and experience. They used for weapons whatever pieces of furniture came to hand.

The only people who took no part in the fight were Albert Rugg and Willie Cookson. Albert, because no one had time to untie him. Willie, because he was hit on the head by a small table and lost interest.

Fortunately, before anyone could be killed, a soap-stone model of St. Paul's Cathedral was thrown by Stan Corner through the window and landed at the feet of P.C. Owers, who summoned assistance on his pocket wireless and went to join the party.

"It's a funny thing," said Petrella to Watterson, "but no one seems to want to prefer charges."

"Not even Rugg? Owers says they had him tied up with his socks in his mouth."

"I think Rugg has got a guilty conscience," said Petrella.

"I suppose we could charge them with a breach of the peace."

"It was a fairly private fight," said Petrella. "Until they nearly brained Owers with that cathedral."

"We must do something about it. If we don't, we shall have a gang war on our hands."

This was the second prediction which Superintendent Watterson had made. It, too, was proved false. The final act took place, some weeks later, in Mr. Tasker's office, near the Oval.

A deed was signed by William Cookson and Albert Rugg ("hereinafter called the partners"). Cookson supplied the money, which the insurance company had now reluctantly paid up, and Rugg supplied the premises. The new garage was to be called the Premier-Octagon.

"It's called rationalisation," said Petrella, when he heard about it. He was reading a particularly unpleasant anonymous note.

The Death of Mrs. Key

THE LETTER, WRITTEN in capitals on a sheet of plain white paper, said, "How much did Fred Barron pay you to perjure yourself? I expect Scotland Yard would like to know. So I'm going to tell them. Not now. Probably next week. Think about it."

"When did you get this?" said Petrella.

"This morning," said Constable Owers. He looked half amused, half angry. "I kept the envelope. I thought you'd want it."

The envelope was a large yellow one, and Constable Owers's name and address was neatly typed on it.

"Whoever sent it," said Petrella, "can't have known a lot about police procedure."

Fred Barron had long been under suspicion of being a receiver of stolen goods, and this was the charge that the police would dearly have liked to pin on him. The Director of Public Prosecutions had studied the available evidence, and had advised against it. A summons under the Shops Act, which they could make stick, had been substituted. Constable Owers had been the main police witness, but the decision on which charge to prefer had been nothing to do with him.

"I wasn't worried," said Owers, "but I thought you ought to see it. I heard a buzz that quite a lot of people have been getting billy-doos like this."

"I heard the same," said Petrella. "I did wonder if Mrs. Key might have been getting them."

This was on Saturday. Mrs. Key had died on the Thursday. She was a frail lady, in her middle sixties, crippled with arthritis. Some time during the evening, when her companion and helper, Mrs. Oldenshaw, had departed and she was quite alone, she had wheeled herself, in her invalid chair, into the kitchen, had shut the windows and door and blocked up the gap under the door with a roller towel, and had turned on all the taps on her gas cooker.

Neighbours coming back late that night had smelled the gas and called the police.

"What makes 'em do it?" said Owers. "Send letters like that, I mean. That last bit, about waiting before reporting me. It was meant to make me sweat, wasn't it?"

"One part badness and three parts madness. If everyone was as sensible as you, and brought them straight along to us, we might have a chance of catching them. I wonder how many people have had them and kept quiet about them?"

An unexpected answer to this question was in the offing.

Sunday was not a guaranteed day of rest for a C.I.D. officer, but when the exigencies of his job allowed, Petrella liked to go to Matins or Evensong at St. Marks, which was the Parish Church of Riverside South. He enjoyed the Rector. The Reverend Patrick Amberline had been many things before, late in life, he had come to the Church. He was a man who was large in every dimension of body and mind.

On this particular Sunday evening, having heaved himself up into the pulpit like a circus elephant mounting a tub, he opened the proceedings by saying, "I have some news for you. I am — " he consulted a paper which he had in his hand, "a lecherous beast and a seducer of young girls. In fact a thoroughly dirty old man." After a moment of stunned silence, the church rocked with laughter.

When order had been restored, the Rector said, "It's really no laughing matter. I propose to pin this remarkable communication on to the notice board in the porch, so that you may see it for yourselves. The bit about my making improper advances to the ladies in the choir, you'll have to take with a pinch of salt. I'm too fat to make advances, and they're much too sensible to receive them. However, my object in mentioning this — " he paused and looked round the congregation, "was a serious one. If any of you have received these products of a sick mind, don't hide them. The answer to corruption is fresh air. Show them to everyone. Above all, show them to the police. And now, to my text — "

During the sermon Petrella cast an eye over the young ladies of the choir, and wondered which of them the anonymous letter writer had had in mind. Two rather severe ones, with glasses. Two flashy blondes, two or three who were obviously schoolgirls. One red-head, a bit older than the others, and more self-possessed. She looked the most plausible candidate.

Coming out of church, and noticing the chattering groups which had gathered at the door, he came to the conclusion that Father Amberline had done the preliminary part of the police work more effectively than they could possibly have done it themselves.

The results started to come into Patton Street Police Station at an early hour on Monday. Petrella left the scholarly Sergeant Ambrose to deal with them and walked round to Mrs. Key's little terrace house in Smarden Lane.

He found two people there. He had met Mrs. Oldenshaw before. She was a woman designed by nature to be a companion, being negative in character and accommodating in disposition. The young man with her wore large round spectacles which made him look like an owl. He turned out to be Ronald Blanshard, Mrs. Key's nephew.

Petrella said, "I don't want to bother you with a lot of questions at a time like this, but we've got the inquest on Wednesday and there are one or two points we must clear up."

The owl-like young man blinked at him and Mrs. Oldenshaw said, "I can't hardly bring myself to speak of it. She was driven to it, poor soul, that I do know."

Petrella said, "That's what I was wondering about. She didn't leave any note behind her, but it did occur to me — "

He let the sentence hang. Mrs. Oldenshaw looked at the young man, who stared sadly back at her.

"If there was anything," said Petrella gently, "we must be told."

"It was all so beastly," said Ronald. "I've seen some of the letters. The ones she kept. Mrs. Oldenshaw just showed them to me. They accused her — " he seemed to have difficulty in getting the words out, "of killing both her brothers and her husband."

Petrella stared at him.

"They were all killed in action. Her older brother, my uncle Edward, on the Somme in the first war. Her younger brother George — that was my father — he was killed in Germany in 1945." The young man paused, blinked in a very owl-like way, and added, "I can't remember him at all. To me he's just a photograph and some relics my mother keeps in a drawer at home."

Petrella said, "And her husband?"

"He was in the R.A.F. He was shot down on a bomber raid."

"But how could she possibly be blamed — "

"Read them for yourself," said Ronald.

They were detailed, ingenious and horrible masterpieces of innuendo and spite. And they all said the same thing. "You drove your menfolk to the war. They didn't really want to go. You talked them into it. Whilst you sat safely at home, they were torn to pieces by shrapnel, burst apart by high explosive, burned. Think of your husband, trapped in that bomber, roasting to death as it went down into the sea. Are you satisfied with the results? You've got all the family money now, you selfish barren bitch."

"Why on earth did she keep them?" said Petrella. "Why did she ever open them at all?"

"That was the devilish part of it," said Ronald. "They all came in different shapes and sizes of envelopes, with different sorts of typing on them. She couldn't avoid seeing them. Unless she refused to open any letters at all."

"There were telephone calls, too," said Mrs. Oldenshaw. "When she was alone here, in the evening. Whispering things to her."

Petrella swung round abruptly on his heel. He said, "I'll take all these letters. I see she kept some of the envelopes. I'll take them as well."

Back at Patton Street he found Sergeant Ambrose with a heap of papers on the table in front of him.

"Eighty-five to date," he said, "and more coming in. All hand-written in block capitals. All the envelopes typed."

Petrella said, "I want them analysed. By recipient, by the subject matter of the threats, by date, by post mark, and by typewriter. Get all the envelopes up to Central. They've a man there who can tell you the make of machine from a line or two of typescript. I want the answers as quickly as possible."

He walked out of the room as abruptly as he had come into it. Sergeant Ambrose stared after him. He had not seen Petrella angry before. However, it was the sort of job he enjoyed and he set to work quickly and neatly.

Petrella made a telephone call to Central to make sure that the expert he wanted would be available and then paid a visit to the offices of Messrs. Mellors and Rapp, Solicitors and Commissioners for Oaths, who had an office in the High Street. They were the largest firm in Riverside South. They did most of the police court work in that area. The senior partner, Mr. Charles Rapp, was tall and thin. He knew Petrella and received him without delay, in his private room, a centre-point of calm in a maelstrom of clacking typewriters, buzzing telephones and hurrying clerks.

"There's no reason you shouldn't know about it," he said when he had grasped what Petrella wanted. "As soon as we can get probate, a will becomes public property. Mrs. Key's will was very simple. She left a sum of forty thousand pounds to her nephew and only surviving relative, Ronald Blanshard, provided he survives her by one clear month. That's put in to avoid double death duties. Anything left over after payment of debts and duties and this legacy is to be invested in an annuity for her companion, Mrs. Oldenshaw."

"Will there be anything left?"

"Oh yes. I should think so. Possibly as much as ten

thousand pounds. It should provide a comfortable little annuity."

Petrella phrased his next questions cautiously. He knew that he was treading on delicate ground. He said, "Have you ever met Ronald?"

"He did come in here about a year ago, I think. To make his own will. He's an architect, I believe. He seemed a very nice young man." Mr. Rapp cocked a tufted eyebrow at Petrella.

"Oh, very," said Petrella. "I happened to run across him when I went round to the house. Do you know if he's married?

"I fancy not. But I believe he told me he was engaged. I seem to remember warning him that when he got married it would invalidate his will, and he would have to make another one."

Petrella thanked Mr. Rapp and took himself off. On the way out he thought he saw a head of hair which he recognised, bent over one of half a dozen typewriters in the general office. The typist looked up, and the impression was confirmed. It was the red-headed young lady from the choir of St. Marks.

Petrella walked back slowly to Patton Street. A picture was shaping itself in his mind. It was blurred and indistinct as yet, like a photograph taken out of focus. And it was not a pleasant picture.

Sergeant Ambrose had his first report ready. It covered ten foolscap pages of careful handwriting, and divided and subdivided the anonymous letters into every possible category, and carefully analysed each. Petrella took it home with him that evening and read it over his supper. His wife observed the bleak look on his face and refrained from asking any questions.

On the following afternoon the report on the typewriters came in from the Yard. Six different machines, it said. Two newish Lexingtons. One older and one very old Remington, one Italian Pulchrion and one German Obermark. The report added, "None of the type-faces are perfect. If a sample could be obtained from a suspect machine a positive identification would be available."

Petrella considered this, and gave Constable Owers certain instructions.

The last members of the staff of Messrs. Mellors and Rapp were usually away by six, and for the next hour the offices were handed over to the cleaners. At a quarter to seven that evening Mrs. Burgess, who was dusting round young Mr. Mellors's room, was disturbed by a loud ringing of the front doorbell. She hurried to the door and found two policemen on the step.

The older one said, "I don't wish to alarm you, ma'am, or the other young ladies, but we've had a report that a person was seen climbing into these premises by a back window."

Mrs. Burgess said, "Oh, lor, what will they get up to next?"

"There's no cause to be alarmed," said Constable Owers. "If the intruder is still on the premises, we can deal with him. But I think you ought to take these two young ladies to a place of safety."

The two young ladies, who were Mrs. Burgess's daughters, nodded vigorous agreement.

"It won't take us long to search the building. Suppose you walk across the street and have a nice cup of tea?"

This proposal was accepted with gratitude.

As soon as the ladies were clear, Owers said to his younger companion, Constable Brean, "Watch the door, Albert, and tell me if they show any signs of coming back."

He disappeared into the general office, selected six sheets of paper from the drawer of one of the desks and set to work. He was by no means an expert typist, and it took him nearly ten minutes to type out, in lower case and upper case, on each of six machines, "The quick brown fox jumped over the lazy dog," followed by, "12 x £3456–78 = 90% ?!" When he had finished he replaced all the covers carefully, and went out to reassure Mrs. Burgess and her daughters.

That same evening Petrella called on Father Amberline, who knew more about the lives, characters and intentions of his flock than most parish priests, and told him what he suspected.

He said, "You know the person concerned better than I do. Do you think they *could* have done it?"

"Before answering that," said Father Amberline, "I'd need to be convinced that it was done at all."

"I think I can convince you," said Petrella.

When he had finished, the priest said, "There are certain people of whom I could have said, with certainty, it is impossible. With this person I am far from sure. There is a streak of hardness. If the money was sufficient, they might do it."

On the Wednesday a coroner's jury returned a verdict of "suicide whilst the balance of her mind was disturbed" on Mrs. Key and Ronald Blanshard was given authority to arrange for her cremation.

On Thursday morning Petrella saw Chief Superintendent Watterson.

He said, "It's about these anonymous letters. I know now who's been sending them."

"Can you prove it?"

"I think so. If you look at these lists you'll notice two odd things. The first is that the accusations aren't vague and general. They're all quite definite. Some of them are silly things. Some dishonest. Some bordering on the criminal. In fact, just the sort of things you might expect a solicitor to hear about from his clients in the course of a day's work."

Watterson grunted. He had no great opinion of solicitors. Tiresome people who cross-examined policemen and threw dust into the eyes of magistrates.

"The second thing is that no one *except Mrs. Key* has had more than two or three. And she must have had nearly a hundred."

"You mean that all the others were cover for the attack on her?"

"That's exactly what I mean."

"And the object?"

"The object," said Petrella, "was to finish her. And it succeeded. The letters were written and the envelopes were typed out by a Miss Eileen Fairweather. She is secretary to young Mr. Mellors, junior partner in Mellors and Rapp. I'm told that she was a conscientious girl, and sometimes stayed behind to finish Mr. Mellors's letters. This gave her the run of six different typewriters in the general office. She used different machines, and different envelopes, so that Mrs. Key would be bound to open the letters."

"Clever."

"Too clever. She didn't realise that the print of a typewriter can be identified as certainly as a fingerprint."

He laid six sheets of typing paper and six envelopes on the table, and said, "Central are quite definite about it. There's not the least room for doubt. Those envelopes were typed on the six machines in the office of Mellors and Rapp."

"Why did she do it?"

"She did it for forty thousand pounds. She's engaged to Ronald Blanshard, who is Mrs. Key's only surviving relative, and inherits that sum under her will. She just couldn't wait for the old lady to die in the natural way."

Watterson brightened up. "That's better," he said. "That's something a jury will understand."

"I'm afraid it won't come to a jury."

"Why not? It seems a clear enough case."

"A case of what?"

The Chief Superintendent started to say something, changed his mind, and said, "Hmm. Murder? Manslaughter? Conspiracy to procure suicide? I see there might be difficulty there. What about demanding money with menaces?"

"She was careful never to ask for money."

"Public mischief then? Misuse of Her Majesty's mails?"

"That's more like it. A fine for a first offence."

"It doesn't seem adequate."

"It will be quite adequate," said Petrella grimly. "Once her name is mentioned in the papers there'll be fifty people round here after her blood."

Watterson considered the matter. He said, "Do we charge Blanshard as well? Do you think he was in it?"

"There's no direct evidence against him, but we'll soon know, won't we?" When Watterson looked puzzled he said,

"As soon as the truth comes out. If he *was* in it with her, you may be sure he'll stick to his guns, brazen it out, and marry her. They'll have to move away and live somewhere else. But they'll go through with it. On the other hand, if he didn't know about it, he won't touch her with a barge pole. He'll refuse to have anything more to do with her. He's got no other course open to him."

Here Petrella was wrong.

Three days after the preliminary hearing in the Magistrates' Court had been adjourned for the defence to consider the technical evidence, a patrolling policeman found Ronald Blanshard's little car parked in a quiet turning behind Woolcombe Park. Eileen Fairweather was in the front seat. She had been shot through the head. Ronald was slumped over her. After killing her, he had shot himself. He had used a German automatic which his father had brought home as a souvenir on one of his leaves from North Africa.

Woolcombe Park is not in Q Division, and Petrella only learned about it when he read it in the paper the following morning. Hard on the heels of the report came Mrs. Oldenshaw. She was so upset that it was a few minutes before Petrella could gather what she was trying to tell him.

She said, "What shall I do with it? The money, I mean. They say I shall have it all now. I don't want it."

"You'd better consult the solicitors," said Petrella. "They'll tell you what to do."

"Oh, them. They just say it's mine, and I've got to have it. I wouldn't have said 'no' to a little bit. That's what Mrs. Key meant me to have. She didn't mean me to have it all."

"If you really want to get rid of some of it," said Petrella, "why don't you give it to Father Amberline, at St. Marks."

His mind was on a very different sort of problem. In front of him on the table was a telex message. "Important. Repeated to all Stations in Q Division and for information to all other Divisions. Arthur Lamson's conviction was quashed by the Court of Criminal Appeal at three o'clock this afternoon."

Why Tarry the Wheels
of His Chariot?

THAT MORNING, BECAUSE his wife and small son were away at the seaside, Detective Inspector Patrick Petrella cooked his own breakfast. He should have been with them, but his stand-in had broken his wrist in an argument with an Irish lorry-driver and his second-in-command had mumps.

As he walked through the sun-baked streets, from his flat in Passmore Gardens to the Divisional Sub-Station in Patton Street, there was an ache at the back of his neck and a buzzing in his ears, and his tongue felt a size too large for his mouth. Any competent doctor would have diagnosed strain from over-work and packed him straight off on holiday.

The morning was taken up with a new outbreak of shop-lifting. In the middle of the afternoon the telex message was brought into his room.

"Important. Repeated to all Stations in Q Division and for information to all other Divisions. Arthur Lamson's conviction was quashed by the Court of Criminal Appeal at three o'clock this afternoon."

Petrella was still trying to work through all the unpleasant possibilities of this message when Chief Superintendent Watterson arrived.

He said, "I see you've had the news, Patrick. It was that ass Downing who did it."

He referred, in this disrespectful manner, to Lord Justice

Downing, one of the more unpredictable of Her Majesty's judges.

"I was afraid it might happen," said Petrella.

He spoke so flatly that Watterson looked at him and said, "You ought to be on leave. Are you feeling all right?"

"It's the heat. A decent thunderstorm would clear the air."

"What we want," said Watterson, "isn't a decent thunderstorm. It's a decent bench of judges. Not a crowd of nit-picking old women. I wonder if they've got the remotest idea of how much damage a man like Lamson can do."

"There'll be no holding him now," said Petrella.

Arthur Lamson was once described by the papers as the unofficial mayor of Grendel Street. He ran a gymnasium and sporting club, was a big donor to all local charities and had a cheerful word and a pat on the head for any child, or a pinch of the bottom for any pretty girl. He was also a criminal, who specialised in protection rackets, employing the youths who hung around his gymnasium to break up the premises — and occasionally the persons — of anyone who refused him payment.

Since he took no part in these acts of violence himself he had been a difficult man to peg. Indeed, he might have continued untouched by the law for a very long time if he had not fallen out with Bruno.

Bruno was a fair-haired boy, with a deceptively open face and a smile which showed every one of the thirty-two teeth in his mouth. He was a great favourite with the girls, and it was over a girl that the original trouble arose. There were other differences as well. Bruno had an unexpected streak of obstinacy. When he was not paid as much as he had been promised for a job he had done for Art Lamson he spoke his mind, and spoke it loudly and publicly.

Lamson had decided that he must be disciplined. The disciplining took place in a quiet back street behind the Goods Depot.

Whilst Bruno was in hospital, having his jaw set and the bottom half of his right ear sewn back on, he came to certain conclusions. He told no one what he proposed to do, not even

Jackie, the girl he was secretly engaged to. He went one evening to a quiet public house in the Tooley Street area, and in a back room overlooking the river he met two men who looked like sailors. To them he talked, and they wrote down all that he said, and gave him certain instructions.

A month later Bruno said to Jackie, "I don't think any of the boys know you're my girl, so you ought to be all right, but you'd better lie low for a bit. I'm going to have to clear out of London."

Jackie said, "What are you talking about, Bruno? What's going to happen? What have you done?"

"What I've done," said Bruno, "is I've shopped Art Lamson. The Regional boys are picking him up tonight. With what I've been able to tell them, they reckon they've got him sewn up."

Jackie put both arms round Bruno's neck, her blue eyes full of tears, and said, "Look after yourself, boy. If anything happened to you, I don't know what I should do."

Very early on the following morning two cars, with four men in each of them, slid to a stop opposite Lamson's house. Two men went round to the back, two men watched the front, and four men let themselves into the house, using a key to unlock the front door. Petrella was one of them. Grendel Street was in his manor and it was his job to make the actual arrest, and to charge Lamson on information received, with the crime of conspiring with others to demand money with menaces and to commit actual bodily harm.

The nature of the information received became evident at the preliminary hearing in the Magistrates' Court. It was Bruno. And it was noticed that never once, whilst he gave his evidence, did he look at Lamson or Lamson at him.

This was in March.

The trial started at the Old Bailey in the first week of June. Bruno was brought to the court, from a safe hideaway in Essex, in a police tender which had steel bars on its windows and bullet-proof glass.

On the second afternoon he gave his evidence to the Judge. Under the skilful questioning of his own counsel he repeated, even more clearly and comprehensively, the facts which he had already stated to the Magistrate. At four o'clock he had finished, and the Judge said, "It will be convenient if we break now. We can begin the cross-examination of this witness tomorrow morning."

Counsel bowed to the Judge, the Judge bowed back, the Court emptied, and Bruno was taken down a flight of steps to the basement where the van awaited him.

As he stepped out of the door, a marksman on the roof of a neighbouring building, using an Armalite rifle with a telescopic sight, shot him through the head.

"And that," said Watterson, "was that. The jury had heard Bruno's evidence, and they convicted Lamson. Of course, there was an appeal. The defence pointed out that although plenty of people had given evidence of being intimidated, the only witness who actually identified Lamson as the head of the organisation was Bruno."

And Bruno had not been cross-examined.

"How can you accept his evidence," said Mr. Michaelson, Q.C., in his eloquent address to the Court of Criminal Appeal, "when it has not been tested, in the traditional way, by cross-examination. Bear in mind, too, that the witness was himself a criminal. That he had, by his own admission, taken part in more than one of the offences with which the accused is charged. The law is slow to accept such evidence, even when it has stood the test of cross-examination — "

And so, at three o'clock on that hot afternoon in August, Arthur Lamson descended the stairs which led down from the dock in the Court of Criminal Appeal and emerged, a free man.

A considerable reception awaited him. The committee of welcome consisted of a number of reporters, mainly from the sporting papers, but a scattering from the national Press as well; one or two very minor celebrities, who didn't care where they went as long as they got into the photograph; members of the Grendel Street Sporting Club, friends and hangers on of both sexes.

The party started immediately in the bar of the Law Courts,

but this was too small to contain everyone who wanted to get in on the act. A move was made to a small club behind Fleet Street which was broad-minded about membership and seemed to observe its own licensing hours.

By six o'clock the party was larger than when it had started, and much louder. Lamson had a six-month thirst to quench, and he stood, at the centre of the noisiest group, a schooner of whisky in his large right hand, the sweat running in rivulets down his red face, a monarch unjustly deposed, returning in triumph to his kingdom.

"I got a great respect for the laws of England," he announced. "They don't put an innocent man in prison. Not like some countries I could name."

"That's right, Art," said the chorus.

"I'm not saying anything against the police. They've got their job to do, like I've got mine. If they're prepared to let by-gones be by-gones, I'm prepared to do the same."

This treaty of friendship with the police force was felt to be in the best of taste, and a fresh round of drinks was ordered.

Back in Grendel Street extensive preparations had been made for the return of the hero. Streamers had been placed in position, from top-storey windows, spanning the street, and banners had been hung out with, "Welcome Home Art" embroidered on them in letters of red cotton-wool. The two public houses, the Wheelwrights Arms at one end of the street and the Duke of Albany at the other end, were both doing a roaring trade, and the band of the Railway Recreational Club was starting on its favourite piece which was the *William Tell Overture*.

The organiser of these festivities was seated at her bedroom window, in a chair, looking down on the street. This was old Mrs. Lamson, Art's mother, the matriarch of Grendel Street. Ma Lamson was a character in her own right. She had married, out-drunk, out-talked and out-lived three husbands, the third of whom was Art's father. A stroke had paralysed her legs, but not her tongue. Confined to a wheelchair, and

rendered even more impatient by her confinement, her shrill
voice still dominated the street.

"Fix the end of that streamer, you big git," she screeched.
"It's flapping like a lot of bloody washing on a line. That's
better. My God, if I wasn't here to keep an eye on things,
you'd have the whole bloody lot down in the bloody street.
And Albert — " this was to a middle-aged man, one of her
sons by her first marriage, himself a grandfather, "clear those
buggers back onto the pavement." She indicated the drinkers
outside the Wheelwrights Arms who were sketching an in-
formal eightsome reel to the strains of *William Tell.* "We
want Art to drive straight down the street when he comes
home, don't we? He can't do it if they've turned it into a
pally-de-dance, can he?"

By eight o'clock the original party had moved from the
Fleet Street club, and re-established itself in the back room
of a public house near Blackfriars Station. Its constituents
had gradually changed. The journalists had slid away, to write
up their impressions of the event for next morning's papers.
The very minor celebrities had gone in search of the next
happening to which they could attach themselves. What remained was a hard core of serious drinkers, a few friends of
Art's, but mostly friends of friends, or those complete
strangers who seem to have a knack of attaching themselves
to any party which has reached a stage of general euphoria.

One of the few men there who knew Art personally said,
towards nine o'clock, "You ought to be getting back sometime soon. Your old lady'll be expecting you."

"That's right," said Art, "she will." He made no attempt to
move.

"She's got a sort of reception organised, I understand."

"She's a lovely person," said Art. "I'm lucky to have a
mother like that. Have you got a mother?"

The friend said that he had a mother, and she was a lovely
person, too.

Towards ten o'clock the black clouds which had been
piling up from the west had blotted out moon and stars and
the air was electric with the coming storm.

The party was showing signs of disintegrating. There were no formal farewells. People drifted out and did not reappear. For some time now, Art had been conscious of the girl. To start with, there had been quite a few girls in the party. This one had sat quietly in the background drinking whatever was put into her hand and minding her own business. Nobody knew exactly who had brought her, but nobody minded because she was a good-looking chick, with blue eyes, black hair, and lots up top. Not obtrusive, but enough to catch the eye comfortably.

Art found his thoughts centering on the girl. Drink was not the only thing he had been deprived of for the past six months. When she looked up at him and smiled, what had been vague ambition became clear desire.

How it happened, he was not clear. At one moment he was putting down an empty glass on the counter, at the next he was on the back seat of the taxi with the girl.

He slid one arm round her waist. She said, "Don't start anything here, love. The taxi driver'll sling us out. Wait till we get there."

"Where are we going?"

The girl sounded surprised. "Back to my place, of course," she said.

Art was happy to wait. He was three out of four parts drunk. One thing was puzzling him. If this chick really had been knocking back all the drinks that had been offered to her, she should have been blind drunk, but she sounded sober. A bit tensed up, he thought, but cool. Perhaps she had a very hard head. She certainly had a beautiful little body.

Her place was a surprise too. It was certainly not a tart's pad. It was on the third floor of an old-fashioned house and had the look of a working girl's flat, small but neat. She sat him down on the sofa, and said, "What about a bite of food, eh?"

This seemed to Art to be an excellent suggestion. He needed something to absorb the alcohol he had put into himself. The girl poured him out a drink from a bottle on the sideboard.

She said, "I won't be a minute," and disappeared into the small room next door which was evidently the kitchen.

Art sipped his drink, and lay back on the sofa. He had had so much luck lately that this little extra bit seemed a natural bonus. The only trouble was that he was feeling damnably sleepy. It really would be a bad joke if, with this gorgeous chick offering herself to him, he couldn't stay awake to do anything about it.

He laughed, and the laugh turned into a snort, and then into a strangled snore.

Five minutes later the girl reappeared. She picked up the glass, which had rolled on to the floor, and stared down at Art, full length on the sofa, his face red and sweating, his mouth wide open. There was no expression in her blue eyes at all.

First she moved over and shot the bolt on the door. Then she went to a cupboard in the corner of the room. It seemed to have household stuff in it. She selected what she needed, and came back.

When the storm broke Petrella was sitting in the charge room at Patton Street talking to Chief Superintendent Watterson.

"This should cool their heads," said the Superintendent. "They've been jazzing it up since opening time."

"Has the great man put in an appearance yet?"

He was answered by the telephone. It was Ma Lamson. Her voice had in it anger, vexation and an edge of fear. Petrella found it difficult to make out what she was saying.

He said, "Hold on a minute," and to Watterson, "She says Art hasn't turned up, and she's worried something may have happened to him. I can't really make out what she wants. I'd better go down and have a word with her."

"Watch it, Patrick. They all know it was you pulled him in. They'll still be hot about it."

"No one could be hot in this weather," said Petrella. The rain was coming down solidly. He drove down to Grendel

Street in a police car, stopped it at the end of the street, turned up the collar of his raincoat and went forward on foot.

The street was empty, its gutters running with water. Overhead the banners of welcome flapped, damp and forlorn. The band had cased its instruments and hurried home.

Only Ma Lamson kept vigil at her upstairs window. The rain, blowing in, had soaked her white hair which hung, in dank ropes, on either side of her pink face.

"Where is he?" she screeched. "Where's my boy? Art wouldn't let us down. Something's happened to him, I know. 'E's got enemies, Inspector. They'll have been laying for him. You've got to do something."

Petrella stood in the pelting rain and looked up at the old woman. The release of the storm had cleared his head. It had done more. It had made him almost light-headed. He felt a hysterical urge to laugh.

Restraining it, he promised that a general alert should be sent out, and made his way back to Patton Street.

He said dreamily to Watterson, "It was pure Old Testament."

"What are you talking about?"

The Superintendent knew that Petrella had a reputation for eccentricity. He had once quoted poetry at a meeting of the top brass at Scotland Yard, and had got away with it because it was Rabbie Burns, who happened to be the Assistant Commissioner's favourite poet.

"The mother of Sisera looked out of her window and cried, 'Why is his chariot so long in coming? Why tarry the wheels of his chariot?' "

"Who the hell was Sisera?"

"He was a king in Canaan. When he was on his way back to a triumphant welcome, organised by his mother, he was lured into the tent of a young lady called Jael."

"And what did she do?"

"He asked for water, and she gave him milk. She brought forth butter, in a lordly dish."

"I see," said Watterson doubtfully. "And what happened then?"

"Then she took a mallet in one hand and a tent peg in the other, and she smote him. At her feet he bowed, he fell. Where he fell, there he lay down, dead."

"What you need is a holiday," said Watterson firmly. "You're going on leave first thing tomorrow, if I have to stand in for you myself."

Five days later, when the police, alerted by worried neighbours, broke into the third-floor flat of Bruno's girl, Jackie, they found Art Lamson.

Jackie had driven a six-inch nail clean through the middle of his forehead, and had then cut her own throat. But Petrella knew nothing of this. He was helping his small son to construct a sand fort and adorn its battlements with sea shells.

Rough Justice

IT WAS A fine morning in early October when Detective Inspector Patrick Petrella became Detective Chief Inspector Petrella. The promotion had been expected for some time, but it was nevertheless agreeable when a copy of District Orders and a friendly note of congratulations from Chief Superintendent Watterson arrived together on his desk at Patton Street Police Station.

He had been six months in Q Division and had been carrying out a mental stocktaking. A few successes, a lot of routine work done without discredit, one or two undoubted flops. One of the worst had been his failure to secure the conviction of Arthur Bond. If ever anyone should have been found guilty and fined or even gaoled it was —

"A Mr. Bond asking for you," said Constable Lampier, projecting his untidy head of hair round the door. Lampier was the newest, youngest, least efficient and most cheerful of the constables at Patton Street. Repeated orders from Sergeant Blencowe to smarten himself up generally and for God's sake get his hair cut had had a superficial effect. Like brushing a puppy which immediately goes out and chases a cat through a thorn-bush.

"Mr. *Who?*"

"Bond. He's the geezer who keeps that garage. The one we didn't make it stick with that time — "

"All right, all right," said Petrella. "Don't let's conduct a post mortem. Just show him in."

Mr. Bond was not one of his favourite people. He had a big white face, a lower lip which turned down like the spout of a jug and a voice which grated more when he tried to be friendly than when he was in his normal mood of oily arrogance. On this occasion he was making no attempt to be agreeable.

He said, "You've got no right to say the things you've been saying about me. I'm telling you, I'm not standing for it."

"If you'd explain what you're talking about."

"I'll explain, all right."

He opened his briefcase and threw a document on to the table. It was a photocopy, and to Petrella's astonishment it was a copy of a report he had himself written the day before.

He said, "Where on earth did you get that?"

"Never mind where I got it. You got no right to say those things."

"I do mind where you got it. And I insist on an explanation."

"If you want an explanation, ask the editor of the *Courier*."

"I certainly will ask him," said Petrella grimly, "and I hope he's got an explanation, because if he hasn't, he's going to be in trouble."

"The person who's going to be in trouble," said Mr. Bond, his lower lip quivering with some indefinable emotion, "is you. This is libellous. I've got my rights. I'm going to take this to court. You can't go around taking away people's characters. You ought to know that."

"If you produce this document in court you realise you'll have to explain exactly how you got hold of it."

"No difficulty. The editor gave it to me."

"Then he'll have to explain."

"You don't seem to realise," snarled Mr. Bond. "It isn't him or me who's in trouble. It's you."

When he had gone Petrella telephoned Sergeant Blencowe. He said, "Yesterday I sent a batch of confidentials by hand to Central. Find out who took them, and send him up."

Five minutes later the untidy top-knot of Constable Lampier made a second appearance round his door.

"So it was you, was it?" said Petrella.

"That's right, sir."

"Then perhaps you'll explain how one of the documents got into the hands of the editor of the local paper."

"Lost the wallet, sir."

"You *lost* it."

"Had it taken."

"Explain."

"Went up by tube. Victoria Line from Stockwell. Train was very crowded."

Petrella considered the matter. So far there was an element of plausibility in it. Junior constables on routine errands usually travelled by public transport and, as he knew himself, the Victoria Line could be crowded.

He said, "What actually happened?"

"I don't really know," said Lampier unhappily. "The carriage was full. I was standing near the door. I put the wallet down on the floor, by my foot. When I got to Victoria it was gone. I made a fuss, but it wasn't any use. Someone must have slid out with it the station before."

"Why didn't you report it?"

"I did, sir. That afternoon. Soon as I got back. To Sergeant Cove."

Petrella was on the point of telephoning for Sergeant Cove when he spotted the report. It was at the bottom of his In Tray. He had been so pleased with reading about his own promotion that he hadn't got down to it.

The editor of the *Stockwell and Clapham Courier* was an elderly man with a face like a bloodhound. Petrella knew him of old as a nurser of grudges and no friend of authority. He said, "The papers were dropped in here by hand this morning. We get a crowd of people in and out of the front office. No one noticed this one in particular. If they're yours you'd better have them."

He pushed across a bundle of papers. Petrella picked them

up and looked through them. As far as he could see they were all there. He said, "Was there a covering letter?"

"There was."

"Can I see it?"

The editor hesitated. Then he said, "I don't see why not." The letter was typewritten. It said, "Dear Editor, I picked these up in a public house in Victoria Street this afternoon. I think they might interest you, particularly the stuff about Mr. Bond."

The note was unsigned.

"These are official documents," said Petrella. "You should have sent them straight back."

"How was I to know? They're not marked 'Top Secret' or anything like that."

"They're on official paper."

"Doesn't mean a thing. Anyone can get hold of notepaper."

"If you didn't know, why didn't you ring up and find out?"

"Why should I go out of my way to help the police? What have they ever done to help me?"

It was an outlook Petrella had heard expressed before, though never quite so baldly.

"All right," he said. "I agree there was no actual obligation on you to do anything. So why did you have one particular document copied, and send it to Mr. Bond?"

"Mr. Bond happens to be a friend of mine," said the editor. "I thought he ought to know about it."

"And that's the whole story?" said Commander Abel.

"That's it, sir."

"Tell me about the previous case."

"We'd heard a lot of talk about that particular garage. People who put their cars in to have a tyre changed, and when they came to collect them found the engine taken down and half a dozen things apparently needed putting right. And straight over-charging for any job that was done. It's difficult to prove. Then we thought we had got something that would stand up. This man, Mr. Ferris, put his car in for an M.O.T. test. When he went to fetch it he got a bill for nearly a hundred pounds. The point was, he'd just had the car overhauled by a garage in Southend, where he'd been staying. A complete 5,000-mile test. He lodged an official complaint. We had to take it up."

"But you couldn't make it stick."

"No, sir."

"Why not?"

"Bond had it all lined up. One of his mechanics gave evidence. A real old villain. Blinded the bench with science. Our Mr. Fairbrother's a good Magistrate, but he's not a motorist. Invoices for spare parts, all in order. Work sheets showing time spent on the overhaul. If a man came in for a test it had to be made roadworthy. He'd told the gentleman that. He'd agreed. The job had been done. Here was the evidence."

"Then what was wrong?"

"The whole thing was wrong," said Petrella slowly. "The mechanic was in it, of course. He made up his own time sheets. The spare parts were bought for cash, from car breakers up and down the borough. The sort of people who keep no records. The invoices themselves were dirty little scraps of paper. And I fancy most of them had been altered."

While Commander Abel was considering the matter the third man present spoke. Mr. Samson was the senior legal adviser to the Metropolitan Police. He said, "I'm afraid there's no doubt about it. If Bond starts an action for libel, you've got something to answer."

"But surely," said Abel, "a report like this is privileged."

"Qualified privilege."

"What does that mean?"

"It can be set aside by proof of malice."

"And just how would they prove that?"

"They'd say that this officer was so annoyed about Bond getting off last time that he made entirely unjustified allegations against him in a report. If the report had never gone outside Scotland Yard, it wouldn't have mattered. But it did. It was published to third parties."

"That's something that wants looking into, too," said Abel grimly.

"You're sure you did have that bag stolen?" said Petrella. "Dead sure, sir," said Lampier. "It happened just like I told you."

"You didn't leave it in a pub in Victoria Street?"

"Certainly not, sir."

Petrella examined the untidy young man critically. It was a long time since he had walked a beat himself. He tried to think himself back to those days. Lampier would have got to Victoria Station at about one o'clock. He probably hadn't had any lunch before he started. Would he have stopped at a pub for a drink and a sandwich? It was perfectly possible. Was Lampier a liar? That was possible too. Was it any use pressing him further? Petrella thought not. There came a moment when policemen had to believe one another. He said, "That's all right, Lampier. I just wanted to be clear about it."

Lampier, as he was going, stopped for a moment by the door and said, "Is anyone going to make trouble, sir, about that paper?"

"If they do, we'll get over it," said Petrella.

He managed to say it confidently, but it was a confidence he was far from feeling.

The next three months were not pleasant. Routine work continued. No one said anything. Even the *Stockwell and Clapham Courier* was muted. There was a brief paragraph to the effect that a local business man, a Mr. Bond, had issued a writ claiming damages against a police officer. Petrella had two further conferences with the legal Mr. Samson and could feel lapping around him, like the serpents about Laocoön, the strangling coils of the law. He knew enough about the processes of the civil courts to realise that no public servant came entirely clean out of that particular mud-bath.

Towards the end of the third conference something really alarming occurred. He began to detect, in the measured utterances of the lawyer, a suggestion that the matter might be compromised. A payment to solace Mr. Bond's wounded feelings and an apology in open court. "My client wishes it to be understood that there is no truth whatever in the statements made about the plaintiff. The plaintiff is a man of excellent character." Like hell he was. Bond was a crook.

"We're in a cleft stick," said Mr. Samson. "If we plead fair comment, we've got to show that what you said was fair. And that really means proving the charges against Bond, which was something you couldn't do in court, and certainly couldn't do now. We can run the defence of qualified privilege, but that lets them bring in all the arguments that you were prejudiced against Bond, that you didn't like him, and were sore that he'd got off."

"Which is true," said Petrella. "But it wasn't my reason for writing the report."

"If you're as candid as that when you give evidence," said Mr. Samson grimly, "the case is as good as lost."

It was a few days after this that Constable Lampier brought Nurse Fearing to see Petrella. She was a middle-aged woman, with an air of professional competence about her that was explained when he recognised her as the most senior and respected of the local District Nurses. She said, "I rely on my little car, Inspector. If it goes wrong it has to be put right. I've been driving for forty years. I know a lot about cars, and I know that this garage swindled me. The man must be brought to book."

Petrella listened, fascinated. A lifetime of dealing with nervous young mothers and panic-stricken young fathers had endowed her with a calm authority which brooked no argument. He said, "It isn't going to be at all easy, Mrs. Fearing. I hardly think you realise just how awkward it is."

"I've heard about the other case," said Nurse Fearing. "And all the lies this man, Bond, told. How anyone could get up in court and say things like that passes my comprehension, but then, I'm old-fashioned."

"All the same —" said Petrella. This was all he managed to say. For the next ten minutes it was Nurse Fearing who did the talking.

"I can't stop you," said Chief Superintendent Watterson. He sounded worried. "A member of the public has made a complaint. We're bound to follow it up. There's *prima facie* evidence. But I need hardly tell you —"

"That's all right," said Petrella. "I understand the position. If we lose this one, we're sunk. Another unsuccessful prosecution. Further proof that I'm prejudiced. Right?"

"If you don't get home this time," said Watterson, "we shall have to settle the libel case on their terms. And that won't do your prospects any good at all."

"You're understating the case," said Petrella. "I shan't have any prospects left."

"Are you going to take it yourself?"

"I may be foolish, but I'm not as foolish as that. I'm getting Mr. Tasker to handle the case."

"Tasker's good," said Watterson. "But he can't fight unless you give him some ammunition."

"We shall do our best," said Petrella.

He sounded, thought Watterson, unaccountably cheerful for a man who has placed his own head on the block.

Counsel for the defence said, "I only propose to call one more witness, sir. You have heard Mr. Bond, and seen the documents he produced. In the ordinary way I should have submitted that this evidence was quite conclusive. The solicitor appearing for the police challenged it —"

Mr. Tasker smiled blandly.

" — but was quite unable to shake it. Mr. Bond told us that he himself had purchased the new distributor —"

"Not new, reconditioned," said Mr. Tasker without troubling to get up.

"I beg your pardon," said Counsel with elaborate politeness, but a slight flush of annoyance. "I should have said the reconditioned distributor and the new set of points. He also supervised the work, which was actually carried out by his mechanic, whom I am now calling. If he corroborates the evidence already given I think you will agree that this effectively disposes of the charges which the police —" here

Counsel swivelled round and stared at Petrella, who was seated beside Mr. Tasker " — the police have seen fit to bring for the second time in three months against my client. I hesitate to use the word persecution, but in the circumstances —"

"I think we'd better hear your witness first," said the Magistrate mildly.

"If you please. Call Mr. Ardingly. Now Mr. Ardingly, I will ask you if you recall effecting certain repairs to an Austin 1100 motor car on December 28th of last year —"

Mr. Ardingly, who looked about seventeen, had blue eyes, curly hair and a shy smile, said he certainly remembered fixing a distributor to the car in question. Yes, he had done the work himself. Yes, he had filled in the time sheets which were shown to him. Yes, that was his signature at the bottom. After about five minutes of this, Counsel sat down with a satisfied smile.

Mr. Tasker rose slowly to his feet. He said, "Mr. Ardingly, this time sheet shows a record of six hours work on this motor car on December 28th and a further three hours on December 29th. Did you actually do that amount of work?"

"Nine hours to put on a new distributor," said Mr. Ardingly in tones of surprise. "Not likely."

"Then if it didn't take you nine hours," said Mr. Tasker with a look at Mr. Bond, whose white face had turned even whiter, "why did you put down that number of hours on the sheet?"

"I put down what the guv'nor told me to put down."

"It's a lie," screamed Mr. Bond, leaping up.

"I must ask you to warn your client to behave himself," said the Magistrate. "If he does not do so, I will have him taken out of the court, and held in custody."

Mr. Bond subsided slowly.

"Now Mr. Ardingly," said Mr. Tasker. "About the distributor. The reconditioned distributor, which Mr. Bond has told us he purchased from Acme Spares —"

"That's quite right. I went and fetched it for him myself. I slipped them a quid."

"One pound?" said Mr. Tasker in beautifully simulated

surprise, peering at the paper he held in his hand. "But this invoice is for twelve pounds and fifty pence."

"You know how it is," said Mr. Ardingly with an engaging smile. "They always add on a bit."

"Very satisfactory," said Chief Superintendent Watterson grimly. "Guilty as charged. Papers sent to the Director of Public Prosecutions. Charges of perjury pending against Bond. He can hardly continue his libel action against you. Would you mind explaining how you fixed it."

"Fixed it?" said Petrella.

"You're not in court now. The truth, the whole truth and nothing but the truth. How much did you pay Ardingly?"

Petrella looked genuinely shocked. "I should never have dreamed of doing such a thing. Besides it was quite unnecessary. The boy loathed Bond. He's a nasty old man, and had already made a pass at him."

"And how did you find that out?"

"He's Constable Lampier's cousin."

"I see," said Watterson. As, indeed, he was beginning to do. "No relation of Nurse Fearing, I suppose."

"He was one of her babies."

"Quite a coincidence."

"Not really. She's delivered half the borough in her time."

"I suppose there's a moral to it."

"The moral," said Petrella smugly, "is always trust your own staff."

Counterplot

MRS. PRIOR HAD had her eye on the grey-haired woman ever since she came into the shop. Not that there was anything obviously suspicious about her. Fifty-ish, Mrs. Prior guessed. Quite expensively dressed, carrying an over-sized shopping bag. It was something about her manner. The unobtrusive way she sidled into the shop; the quick look which she cast around, a look which was not directed at the merchandise on the counters, but at the people.

Melluish & Sons was the most expensive of the three shops that Mrs. Prior had to watch, and the most difficult to guard, dealing as it did in smallish luxury goods for women. They had lost a lot of stuff in the past twelve months and were beginning to talk about closed-circuit television.

Was that woman hanging about unnecessarily near the handbag counter? The attendant had turned her back to deal with another customer. A gloved hand flashed out. Mrs. Prior was too far off to see exactly what happened, but the grey-haired woman was making for the door. It was the moment of decision.

As the woman was stepping out on to the pavement Mrs. Prior intercepted her. "Excuse me, madam," she said. "I wonder if you'd mind showing me what you have in that bag?"

The standard reactions. Shock, anxiety, an assumed bewilderment. "Oh! Who are you? Why should I?"

"I am a member of the shop security staff," said Mrs.

Prior. "If I have made a mistake, I am quite prepared to apologise."

But no apology was going to be needed. She was sure of that.

Which brought Detective Chief Inspector Petrella into the story. He listened to what Mrs. Prior had to say, and to the comments of Mr. Jacklin, managing director of Melluishes, and to the few incoherent remarks of the grey-haired woman.

"We can't force you to identify yourself," said Petrella. "But you realise that if you refuse to give us your name and address we shall have to detain you until someone does identify you."

"Detain me? In prison?"

"You will be placed in charge of a woman police officer."

"Oh!"

Petrella said, in his kindest voice, "This isn't doing you any good, madam. Sooner or later we shall have to know who you are. Someone will miss you, and come along to make enquiries." He tried a long shot. "When your husband gets home from work —"

The word husband seemed to be the key. The woman broke down into a fit of gulping sobs. When she could speak, she said, "I'm Mrs. Kent-Smith. I live at Mapledurham Mansions."

"Mrs. Kent-Smith, eh?" said Sergeant Blencowe when she had been charged and sent home in a police car, the driver having instructions to bring her straight back if there was any doubt about her being who she said she was or living where she said she did. "Her old man's not going to like this. He's in business. House property and things like that."

Mr. Kent-Smith arrived just when Petrella was thinking of going out to lunch. He was a man in his middle fifties, a little paunchy, but alert enough and with a useful pair of shoulders on him. Petrella had been making enquiries, and knew that he had to deal with a formidable man. Rumour said that he had been a sergeant-major in the R.A.S.C. In the years since the war he had prospered. Starting with a bombed site at the Elephant and Castle and some luck with a war damage claim he had built up a chain of shops and offices and flats, held in a honeycomb of interlocking companies which he controlled.

"I'd like to know what all this is about," he said. "I couldn't get much out of the wife."

The sergeant-major was buried, deep down under layers of the self-made tycoon. But he was still there, thought Petrella.

He said, picking his words carefully, "A woman, who identified herself as your wife, was detected leaving Melluish & Sons this morning with one of their crocodile-skin handbags —" Petrella unlocked the drawer of his desk and took it out " — which there was no record of her having paid for. Her explanation was that she had put it into her shopping bag, meaning to pay for it, and had forgotten about it."

Mr. Kent-Smith had picked up the handbag. He said, "Silly thing to do. She could easily have bought it if she'd wanted it." The price tag was still on it. "Eighteen pounds. I understand from Jacklin that if I pay for it, he's prepared to call it a day."

"If he'd said that before she was charged," said Petrella, "it might have saved us all a lot of trouble."

"Can't you withdraw the charge?"

"We could decide not to proceed with it. But we'd only do that if there was insufficient evidence. That's not the case here. Far from it."

"Who decides on these matters?"

"In this case, I do."

"I see."

Mr. Kent-Smith was weighing him up in the thoughtful way a boxer might weigh up his adversary in the ring. He said, "I'd better explain why this means so much to me. In the ordinary way I think I'd let it go. It's a first offence, so I assume it'd be a fine and bound over. Which would teach my wife a lesson. But I can't chance it. Not at this moment. I don't know if you follow the financial Press, Inspector?"

"I don't have much time for that sort of thing."

"Well, I'm on the point of my first public flotation. You'll

see the advertisement in the papers next week. Or you would
have done."

"You mean this will stop it."

"It'll kill it. Stone dead. The whole thing depends on my
good name. It's me they're buying. If my wife's up on a
charge of shop-lifting, I might just as well call the whole thing
off."

Petrella started to say something, but Mr. Kent-Smith
raised his hand to stop him. He said, "Let me finish. Shares
in my holding company stand right now at a nominal one
pound each. They're mostly held by me and my friends. When
we get a quotation they'll go to three pounds. I can let you
have five thousand shares at par. There's nothing illegal
about it. That's the price at the moment. You could borrow
the money from your bank."

"I've been offered bribes before," said Petrella to his wife
that evening. "All policemen are. But I've never been offered
ten thousand pounds."

"What did you say?"

"I said 'no'."

"Quite right," said his wife firmly.

"I'm trying hard to think so. Actually, I'm much sorrier for
his wife than I am for him. I don't believe this is going to
stop him. He might have to put off this flotation, or whatever
it is, for six months. It'll be a nuisance, and it'll cost him more
than the ten thousand he offered me. But he'll take it out on
her. She's an odd woman. She came to see me before I left
the station this evening. Do you know why?"

"To beg herself off the charge."

"On the contrary. She came to apologise."

"Apologise? For what?"

"For giving us all such a lot of trouble. She said she knew
how overworked the police were."

"It's not true!"

"Then we had a long talk about it and about her husband.
How he's so busy with his work he never gets in until ten
o'clock at night and goes off first thing in the morning and
she never really sees him."

"This is the first evening *you've* been in before nine this week," said his wife pointedly.

"And how he seems to be growing away from her."

"What were you supposed to do about it? You're a policeman, not a psychiatrist."

"And how sorry she is she never had any children. She blames herself for it."

His wife thought about the scrap asleep in his cot upstairs who was the centre of their existence. She had nothing to say to that.

It was on the following morning that a very worried Mr. Jacklin arrived at Patton Street Police Station. The managing director of Melluish & Sons had another man with him. He said, "Yesterday evening I thought I'd make a check of our stock of handbags. I was afraid we might have lost more than one."

"And had you?"

"No, we hadn't."

"That's all right then, isn't it?"

"I mean," said Mr. Jacklin slowly, "that we hadn't even lost one."

Petrella stared at him.

"Stock purchased, stock sold, stock remaining. The items balance exactly. That's when I began to wonder. Do you mind if I look at that handbag again?"

Petrella unlocked the drawer of his desk and got it out. Mr. Jacklin took out a magnifying glass, opened the handbag, turned back the silk lining, and peered into it. He said, "Just what I thought. This isn't one of ours. We mark them with a very small symbol. It's really just a few pinpricks." He said to the other man, "It's what we thought, Sam. This is one of yours, isn't it?"

The other man took over the glass and made a brief examination. "That's right," he said. "That's our shop mark. Carson & Begg. Mr. Jacklin thought it might be us. We're the only other store in the district which handles this sort of line."

"And have you lost one?"

"Not that I know of," said the man. "But I can tell you who had that one. I sold it myself three days ago. To Mrs. Kent-Smith. She buys a lot of stuff from us from time to time."

"And she paid for it."

"Naturally."

"Then I suppose she'd better have it back," said Petrella weakly.

"And it won't be necessary to go on with the charge against her now," said Mr. Jacklin. "I'm glad about that. Mr. Kent-Smith's an important man in these parts, you understand."

Petrella said he understood perfectly.

"So," said Mr. Kent-Smith. "The whole thing was a bloody box-up. My wife gets charged with stealing something which is her own property. She's dragged round to the police station like a common criminal. *And* taken home in a police car, so that all the neighbours can get an eyeful of it."

"If she'd given her name and some evidence of identity, none of that need have happened," said Petrella.

"Why should she? She hadn't done anything."

"If she hadn't done anything," said Petrella, "why did she tell us that story about putting the handbag into her shopping bag and forgetting about it?"

"There's no mystery about that. She said it because she was scared. And who's going to blame her? Being dragged along to the police station and bullied by a crowd of louts who call themselves policemen and don't even take the trouble to check up whether something they say has been stolen has really been stolen or not before bringing charges. And if you think you've heard the end of this, Mr. Chief Inspector bloody Petrella, you can bloody well think again. I'm going straight round to my solicitor."

"I seem to be in trouble with the law again," said Petrella sadly. "Last month it was libel, now it's false imprisonment."

"Never rains but it pours," said Chief Superintendent

Watterson. "I've been accused of a lot of things myself in my time, arson, fraud, perjury. I don't know that it ever ran to libel. You'd better warn our legal chaps."

"What I really dislike about these law suits," said Petrella, "is the way they go on for months and months."

Here, however, he was wrong. It was on the following morning that Mrs. Kent-Smith called in to see him. She seemed to be in excellent spirits. She said, "I've good news for you, Inspector. My husband is dropping his complaint against you."

"That's certainly good news," said Petrella. "I wonder what made him change his mind."

"I did."

Petrella knew that this was the point at which he ought to stop asking questions, but the temptation was too great. He said, "I wonder if you'll mind me asking you. How did you do it?"

Mrs. Kent-Smith giggled. She said, "I told him that if he didn't, I'd confess to three other cases of shop-lifting. I gave him all the details. And showed him the things."

She sounded as proud as a child displaying her birthday presents.

"There was a little scarf from Simpsons. A pretty thing in pink and green. A powder compact from Greenways. Not expensive, and not in very good taste. And a cookery book from Simmonds."

"And *had* she stolen those things?" said his wife.

"I'm afraid," said Petrella, "that at that point I lost my nerve. *I simply daredn't ask her.* Luckily she changed the subject. She wanted my advice about some new curtains she had bought. She had the patterns with her. I'm not very clever about colours, so I just said I thought they were a little bright. She said she thought so too. She was going to change them."

"I see," said his wife.

"I don't know what you mean by that," said Petrella. "But if you mean that you can make some sense out of it, you're a lot cleverer than I am. Why on earth should she go through all the rigmarole of buying a handbag in one shop and pretending to steal it in another?"

"Simple. She wanted her husband to pay some attention to her."

Petrella thought about it and said, "It's plausible."

"It's obvious. Don't you remember that woman who set her house on fire because her husband didn't take enough notice of her?"

"If that's right," said Petrella, "why didn't she let him get on with his complaint against me?"

"That's easy too," said his wife. "You're the son she never had."

"Good God!" said Chief Inspector Petrella.

"To the Editor,
Dear Sir—"

IT WAS SEVEN o'clock on a misty November evening when the convoy reached the corner of Jamaica Road and Tunstal Passage. The corner block was the building belonging to Merriams, who are manufacturers of anchors, cables and other massive maritime iron-work. First came a police car, then the articulated lorry carrying the new cable press, a squat piece of machinery weighing about five tons, then Mr. Fawke, the managing director of Merriams in his private car. He spotted that there was some sort of hold-up ahead and jumped out to investigate.

The doors of Messrs. Merriam's private goods hoist were at the side of the building and opened onto Tunstal Passage. Above them there jutted out a short fixed overhead crane. The plan had been to use this crane to lift the press off the lorry and draw it into the hoist, which would then take it up to the second storey, where a gang of men waited with rollers to coax it into its final resting place. The whole plan, including a modification in the width of the press to enable it to get into the hoist, had been worked out with meticulous care.

"Wonderful, isn't it," said the driver of the lorry. Right in front of the entrance to the hoist a private car was parked.

Mr. Fawke glared at it. It was not only obstructing the doors of the hoist. It was blocking the narrow width of

Tunstal Passage and so preventing the lorry from backing down it.

"I suppose it's locked."

The car, which was a newish dark blue four-door Austin saloon, was securely locked.

"You've got keys and things, haven't you?" said Mr. Fawke to the police driver. "You use them to drive away parked cars."

"I haven't got anything with me, not personally," said the driver.

"What about a break-down van? There's one at Simmons Garage."

"The thing is, are you entitled to move it?"

"For God's sake! It's blocking my own hoist."

"We got twenty cars behind us now," said the driver of the lorry helpfully.

"Must you use your hoist?" said the constable. "What about taking it in the front entrance?"

"And up two flights of stairs?" said Mr. Fawke. "Talk sense."

Down Jamaica Road horns were beginning to sound in the mist.

"Must do something," said the constable. "If you can't get it in, you'll have to move on."

One of the men said, "What we might do, is lift the car up with the hoist. Then we could swing it out of the way, see."

Mr. Fawke said, "Good idea. Let's try it. And if it hurts the car it serves the owner bloody well right for leaving it in such a bloody stupid place. Fix the hook on the front bumper, Jim."

"I don't know as you ought," began the constable.

A figure was approaching up the passage.

"Some trouble here?" said the newcomer pleasantly. "Oh, my car in the way? If you'll ask your man to clear the entrance I'll back it out. Thank you. Thank you. Sorry to have been a nuisance. Urgent call."

They saw now that the car had a sticker on the windscreen. "Doctor. On duty."

It was only after the car had gone that it occurred to the constable, who was busy clearing the traffic block in Jamaica Road, that he had failed to get the doctor's name. He had, however, made a note of the number of his car. UGC 368M.

Detective Sergeant Milo Roughead brought in a sheaf of papers and laid them on Chief Inspector Petrella's desk with all the decorum of a butler bringing the morning mail to a ducal breakfast table. Beside the papers he placed a copy of the *Stockwell and Clapham Courier*.

Milo Roughead was a newcomer to Patton Street. When he had first arrived Petrella, who had noted from his Details of Education and Previous Service that he was an Etonian, had been prepared to dislike him, but had found him entirely disarming.

"What's this little lot about?" he said.

"Most of it's routine stuff, sir," said Milo. "There's a letter from a Mr. Raby."

"Yes, we know Mr. Raby," said Petrella.

"Then there's a copy for information, of a report from the boys in blue —"

"From the uniformed branch."

"I mean, sir, from the uniformed branch," agreed Milo unabashed. "It's about an incident in Tunstal Passage last night. It looked like being a bit of a box-up, but it came out all right in the end. Oh, and Inspector Blaikie from Junction wants a word with you."

"What's in that newspaper?"

"I thought you might like to see that. It's another letter from Mr. Mayflower."

"About us?"

"About us," agreed Milo.

Mr. Mayflower was an untiring writer to the Press. He acted as a local ombudsman, drawing attention to matters which he thought required airing. He seemed to devote a good part of his time to the police.

It is a source of amazement to me [wrote Mr. Mayflower],

that the police who, as we are constantly assured, are undermanned and overworked do not concentrate their attention on the more serious crimes. Nine-tenths of their energies appear to be dissipated in pursuing misdemeanours of no conceivable importance. Trivial offenders against parking regulations, shop opening hours and licensing laws are pursued with untiring zeal. Hours and days of police time are wasted, not only in the detection of these earth-shattering matters but in subsequent attendance at court —

It was an old complaint. And Petrella recognised that there was an element of truth in it. Particularly the bit about attendance at court. But Mr. Mayflower had chosen the wrong whipping boy. The fault did not lie with the police. They could not pick and choose which offenders they pursued. A more rational system of law and administration —

"Was there anything else, sir?" said Milo politely.

"You'd better tell Blaikie to come up. We don't want to keep him hanging about."

Inspector Blaikie was a railway policeman. Most of his work was concerned with pilfering from the two big depots in Petrella's manor. They had done a lot of jobs together, and Petrella liked the dry little man who saved the railways around twenty times his own salary every year of his working life and got few thanks for it. This time, however, it was something else.

"My man was coming back himself from the terminal at Grain," he said. "You know they travel in mufti sometimes to pick up ticket bilkers. Well, he noticed this man, who got on at Graystone Halt — that's a little station on the marsh between Cooling and Cliffe. When they reached London Bridge they both got out, and our chap heard this man say to the ticket collector, 'I'm sorry I hadn't time to buy a ticket. I got on at Gravesend.' So he intervenes, and says, 'I think you're mistaken, sir. I happen to know you got on at Graystone Halt.' Without batting an eyelid the man says, 'Exactly, that's what I said. Graystone.' "

"It would be easy to mishear it," said Petrella.

"Certainly. But they're both absolutely certain they didn't. They swear he said Gravesend, and said it distinctly. The upshot of it was, they took his name and address and reported it to me."

"What sort of man?"

"He was a doctor. Doctor Lovibond. He lives in your part of the world."

Petrella said, "Yes. I think I can place him. About sixty. Reddish brown face. Bushy grey eyebrows, grey moustache. Has done service in India."

"That's the man. Respectable citizen. Perfectly clean record."

"If your chap had waited a bit before he butted in and let him pay for a ticket from Gravesend you might have had a case. As it is, I don't believe you'll get anywhere with it."

"That's my view," said Blaikie. "We'd better drop it." He sounded relieved.

When he had gone, Petrella started on the various dockets and reports. The officious Mr. Raby, until his retirement the manager of one of the local banks, reported that a shop called Blooms Antiques in Tooley Street was selling replicas in gold of the medallion struck to commemorate the recovery of King Edward the Seventh from appendicitis.

"It appears to me," wrote Mr. Raby in the neat handwriting which had refused a thousand overdrafts, "that unless Blooms is an authorised dealer in bullion, which I beg leave to doubt, he is acting in contravention of Section 2 of the Exchange Control Act 1947. The objects relate to an incident which took place in 1901, they cannot be described, in the words of Statutory Instrument No. 48 of 1966, as coins or objects of numismatic value more than one hundred years old."

Petrella took the report and placed it firmly at the bottom of his pending tray. He felt a growing sympathy with the views expressed by Mr. Mayflower in the *Stockwell and Clapham Courier*.

The last report concerned what Sergeant Roughead had described as the box-up in Tunstal Passage. Petrella read it rapidly and was on the point of throwing it into the out-basket for filing when something struck him.

Petrella was blessed, or cursed, with visual memory. It was the sort of memory which enabled him to recall telephone numbers, dates on documents and details of that sort, usually quite unimportant. And he was certain that he had seen the number plate UGC 368M somewhere recently. He concentrated for a moment on the problem. A newish dark blue four-door Austin saloon. He saw it, in his mind's eye, parked outside a house. A house not far from his own. A house in Craven Road. A doctor's house. That was right. The car belonged to Doctor Lovibond. The man who had made a mistake about his railway ticket.

It was a mild coincidence. The sort of thing that was always happening in real life. If Petrella had had more to do that morning he would have dismissed the matter from his mind entirely. In the end the action which he did take was to extract Mr. Raby's letter from the bottom of his pending tray, and send for Sergeant Roughead. He said, "Go and see Blooms Antiques. It's a respectable little shop, as far as I know, run by a man called Friar. Find out what this is all about."

"Loosen him up a bit?"

"Certainly not," said Petrella. "You're not playing the wall game now. Just ask him where he got these medallion things from."

When Milo had departed Petrella put on his hat and coat and walked down to have a look at Tunstal Passage. Something was worrying him.

Tunstal Passage runs sharply downhill from its junction with Jamaica Road, between the flanks of two large buildings. One was Merriam's iron foundry. The other was a furniture repository. There were side doors to the yards of both these buildings, after that a length of blank wall, then a pair of wooden gates which blocked the end of the passage. On the gates, in faded white lettering, Petrella could make out, "Waterside Properties Limited".

He got one foot onto a bollard, hoisted himself up, and

looked over. Immediately in front of him was a row of shacks, the biggest being a Nissen hut, the smallest no larger than a toolshed. None of them looked habitable or inhabited. Beyond them he could see an expanse of grey flecked with flashes of white where Father Thames ran by in full flood.

Petrella came down off his perch and walked slowly back up the passage. What he was trying to work out was which of his patients Doctor Lovibond could have been calling on at seven o'clock in the evening in Tunstal Passage.

"I thought it funny myself," said Mr. Friar, "but I didn't see anything illegal in it. This lady brought along six of them in a case. Said her great-uncle used to collect them. Heavy great things. Solid gold, no fooling. I've got the last one here."

He unlocked his wall safe and brought out the medallion.

"Weighs just over five ounces. Six of them. Two pounds of gold. Worth something these days, eh?"

Sergeant Roughead examined the medallion curiously. On one side was a conventional representation of the head of Edward VII, Hanoverian nose jutting defiantly over rakish beard. On the other side the date 1901 and the words "*Pacis Amator*".

"I took one of them along to Francks," said Mr. Friar. "They looked it up for me in their catalogues. It's genuine all right. See what it says on the back. Lover of Peace. That's what they thought of him. My old father used to sing a song about that." Mr. Friar threw back his head and croaked out, "There never was a King like Good King Edward: Peace with Honour was his motter: God Save the King."

Milo was enchanted. He said, "Do you know any more verses?"

"There was one about mothers and babies. I don't recall exactly how it went."

Milo recollected that he was there on duty and said, as sternly as he could, "You realise you're not supposed to deal in gold."

"These are antiques."

"Nothing's antique until it's a hundred years old. You'd

better not sell this one until I've found out what the form is. I mean, until I've made a report."

"I suppose," said Petrella, "that one of them could be genuine and the other five could be modern copies of it. They wouldn't be difficult to make. And there's no way of dating gold. It's the only metal that doesn't age in any way at all."

"What would be the point?" said Milo. "Friar was simply selling them for their weight in gold."

"The point," said Petrella, "is that he was able to sell them at all. And that someone was able to sell them to him. If you went along to a shop with a bar of gold weighing two pounds and tried to flog it, you'd have a lot of questions to answer, wouldn't you? But take along a set of six medals, in a nice case, property of your late great-uncle, and nobody bothers. I suppose, by the way, you found out who did sell them to him."

"It was a Mrs. Smith. She gave her address as 92 Maple Avenue."

"There's no street called Maple Avenue in this district."

"The same thing struck Mr. Friar. When she left, he sent his boy after her. She had a car parked out of sight round the corner. And he got its number: UGC 368M."

It was at this point that Petrella decided to devote some real attention to the case.

He said, "Go down to Graystone Halt. It's the station beyond Cooling on the Isle of Grain branch line. Doctor Lovibond was there two days ago. To hide the fact that he'd been there he told a stupid lie and risked getting into trouble. I'd like to know what he was up to."

"If I disguised myself as a tramp — "

"Wear your old Etonian tie," said Petrella. "No one will mistake you for a policeman."

"It's an odd sort of locality," said Milo. "Flat as your hat. Cabbages and cattle. Ditches between all the fields, running down to the river. You have to pick your way. There's several places you can go in up to your waist."

"Did you?"

"No. I had a guide. A chap who's got a big house down there. He's a stockbroker, but he's mad about birds. The ones with wings and beaks I mean. He spends his time out on the marshes watching them through field glasses."

"And who did you tell him you were? A fellow ornithologist?"

"As a matter of fact I used to be his fag. I thought it was time he did something for me for a change. He gave me a damned good lunch. And we walked over the fields down to the river. He spotted a pair of goosanders — "

"It sounds lovely," said Petrella. "I suppose you remembered what you went down there for?"

"Certainly. This chap's going to be very useful. He knows all the local characters. Pays them to report the arrival of any rare birds. It's a funny part of the world. Very cliquish, if you know what I mean. There aren't many strangers, and any that come along get noticed. It used to be a great place for smuggling. The ships came up the river by night and the stuff was floated ashore and picked up at Cassibon Inlet or Egypt Bay. If there was any trouble, they used to hide it in the church at Cooling. Under the pulpit, actually. My friend's going to pass the word round. Give people the number of the car. If that doctor's up to anything they'll soon ferret it out."

Petrella said, "That sounds quite a good arrangement." It had the feel of a nice little gold smuggling racket. As soon as they got some more information they could act on it. Meanwhile other more urgent matters occupied his time.

It was on a dark day at the beginning of December, a day of drizzle which could turn later into fog, that a further instalment of Mr. Mayflower's letter-writing arrived on Petrella's desk. On this occasion he had abandoned the police and turned the searchlight of his attention onto the Immigration Service. It seemed that they were being very slow in answering enquiries from anxious relatives in India and Pakistan.

Did his readers know that there were cases where men had come to England and their families had not heard from them for eighteen months or even two years?

As he read it, a very faint prickle of alarm stirred in Petrella's mind. It was an instinctive reaction, born of experience, sharpened by the habit of joining together apparently unassociated scraps of information, which is the basis of all good police work. Somewhere, months before, he had read a report — From where, and about what? He could see himself sitting back in his chair and reading it. The hot tarry diesel-fumed smell of Patton Street had been coming in through the wide-open window. So it must have been July or August. He had thought the report worth keeping and he had filed it. Interpol. That was right. It was a routine report from Interpol.

Petrella unearthed it, and read it a second time, with the murk of December swirling down Patton Street and the sounds of life coming muffled through the tight-shut window.

A French revenue cutter, patrolling in the early morning mist, had hit a small outboard motor boat which was running without lights. By the time the cutter had succeeded in turning round and getting back to the scene of the collision the boat had sunk, but the crew of two, who were wearing life-jackets, had been rescued without much trouble. They turned out to be local fishermen. They had offered no satisfactory explanation of what they were doing, and the look-out on the cutter asserted that, just before the crash, he had seen a third man in the small craft. The two fishermen had been released after questioning as there seemed to be nothing specific they could be charged with. A fortnight later a body was recovered. It had been swept by the current into the rocks at the foot of the Nez de Joburg and wedged there. It appeared to be an Indian, in early middle age, dressed in what had, before its immersion, been a respectable suit of clothes. Under the coat, in a webbing belt worn round the waist, were twelve four-ounce tablets of gold.

Petrella sent for Sergeant Roughead and was irritated to find that he was out on an enquiry. He spent some time after that on the telephone to the managing director of Waterside Properties.

It was four o'clock, and the drizzle of the morning had turned into a thick mist, when Milo arrived back. Petrella said, "There's been a development in the gold-running business. Do you think you could get on to your pal down at Cooling and see if he's got anything to report?"

"I've had three reports from him already," said Milo smugly.

"You've had *what*?"

"Three reports. The last one was two days ago. I don't suppose — "

Petrella said, "Are you trying to tell me that you've had three reports and sat on them?"

"They weren't very conclusive — "

"Do you want to continue in the police force?" The anger in his voice was so sharp that Milo went scarlet. He found nothing to say. "There is one use and one use only for information. You share it. You don't hoard it. Or decide what's important and what isn't. Or wait till you've got everything complete and wrapped up so that you can spring it on us as a nice surprise. Do you understand?"

"Yes, sir," said Sergeant Roughead, in a very small voice.

"Then let's have it."

"The doctor has been seen down there three times. Twice he came by car and once by train to Graystone Halt, and was picked up by his wife. She'd come down earlier by car. She didn't meet him at the station actually. She waited a short distance away and he walked to the car. They've got an old farm house on the marshes. It's down a track, leading off the main road."

"Don't explain it. Just show me."

Petrella had a one-inch Ordnance Survey map spread on his desk and Sergeant Roughead put his finger on a dotted line which led out over the marshes and stopped just short of the river. A building was marked at the end of it.

"It's called Barrows Piece," said Sergeant Roughead. He seemed to have recovered some of his spirits. "A farmer called

Barrow built it, and committed suicide in the barn. It's pretty lonely. The Lovibonds seem to use it as a weekend cottage."

Petrella had picked up the telephone and dialled a number. Before he could speak, a recorded voice at the other end said, "Doctor Lovibond will not be available until Monday morning. If you have a message would you speak it slowly, beginning now."

Petrella replaced the receiver and looked out of the window. The mist was thickening into fog. He said, "Tell Anderson I shall want his car, with him driving it. He'd better have a set of chains with him. I shan't be starting before ten o'clock."

Milo said, "Right, sir. Anderson plus car chains at twenty-two hundred hours." He looked like a dog who is not certain if he is going to be taken for a walk or not.

"All right," said Petrella. "You too."

As the car crept through the fog Petrella said, "The main outline's clear enough. Dr. Lovibond had a medical practice in Pakistan. A lot of wealthy clients and a lot of contacts. He was just the man to run this end of a high-class illegal immigration service. When a rich Pakistani is taken on — one at a time probably — he's told to bring most of his portable wealth with him in gold. He comes overland to the north coast of France and is run out by the fishermen to a small cargo boat, which times its run to arrive off Tilbury in the early hours of the morning. At some point before they reach Tilbury the passenger is put ashore near Barrows Piece. The pay-off is in gold. We've found out that the doctor has a small workshop on that Waterside Properties lot. That's where he turns the gold into different saleable objects. Then his wife disposes of them for him. We've traced three of her outlets besides Blooms Antiques. When we get down to it we shall probably find a lot more."

"What did he do with the Pakistanis after he got them to Barrows Piece?" said Sergeant Roughead.

Petrella said to the driver, "You fork left here, Andy. Just before you get to the bridge." And to Sergeant Roughead, "That's what we may be going to find out. The doctor's down there and a fog like this is just the job for them."

It was past midnight when they reached the track, and drove slowly up it, chains churning the mud. It twisted and turned, between high hedges of thorn, going downhill all the time. Then they were out in the open, with nothing ahead of them but a wall of white mist.

"It can't be too far now," said Sergeant Roughead, who had a torch on the map and his nose down over it.

"All right. We'll leave the car here," said Petrella. "See if you can turn it without getting bogged, Andy. You come with me, Sergeant."

A hundred yards, and the house loomed ahead of them. At first they thought it was deserted, but as they came nearer they could see that there was a chink of light in one of the downstairs windows. Petrella touched Sergeant Roughead on the arm and went forward alone. His feet grated on a gravel path and he stood very still. But the window ahead was tightly shut and now he could hear, through it, the sound of music.

He crept forward again, treading through a flowerbed, and peered through the gap in the curtains at a scene of innocent domesticity. Doctor Lovibond was sitting in one wicker chair in front of the fire, smoking a cheroot and reading a newspaper. His wife, in the other chair, was sewing. The portable wireless set on the table stopped giving out music and a voice made an announcement. The doctor lumbered to his feet and left the room. Petrella heard a door opening on the far side of the house. He wondered exactly what he was going to say if the doctor came round with a torch and found him kneeling in his rose-bed.

After a few minutes the doctor came back again. Whatever he was waiting for, it had been a false alarm. Petrella crept back to Sergeant Roughead. He said, "They wouldn't be sitting about at one o'clock on a winter morning for fun. They're waiting for something all right. We'll get back to the car and wait there. It's got a heater."

Sergeant Roughead said, "G-g-good."

It was nearly four o'clock when they heard it. The moan of a foghorn and the thump-thump of a diesel engine. A small,

single-screw boat, Petrella guessed, coming up slowly against
the stream. They climbed out of the car. During the time they
had been sitting there a light wind had got up and was
starting to roll away the fog.

When Petrella reached the window he saw that Mrs.
Lovibond was alone. She had her back to him and was doing
something with a bottle and glasses at the sideboard. The
beat of the engine was quickening again as the boat picked
up speed. The woman half turned her head to listen, and
Petrella saw her face for the first time. Piled grey hair, a beak
of a nose, a deep cleft down each side of an unsmiling mouth,
a strong firm chin. It was a face that had built empires. A
face that had ruled a thousand Indian servants. The face of
a pukka mem-sahib. The back door banged and Dr. Lovibond
came in, carrying a heavy portmanteau in one hand, his
other hand on the arm of a tall, thin Indian, enveloped in a
greatcoat, the astrakhan collar turned up to his ears, a woollen
cap pulled down over his head.

The doctor prodded the fire into a blaze, whilst his wife
helped the newcomer to take off coat and cap and sat him
down in one of the chairs in front of the fire. Doctor
Lovibond produced some dry socks and a pair of slippers
which the man put on. Mrs. Lovibond had gone across to
the sideboard, where three glasses stood ready. She selected
one of them carefully, brought it back, and handed it to their
guest. The smile which she switched on as she did so raised
her lips away from her teeth.

Petrella put one shoulder to the flimsy casement, which
broke inwards with a splintering of wood and glass. As he
got one knee on to the sill to climb through, he said, "I
don't think I should drink that."

The first to move was the woman. She put down the glass
on the table, took a quick step back to the sideboard, snatched
up one of the bottles standing there, and aimed a blow at
Petrella's head. Petrella ducked. The bottle missed his head,
flew out of her hand and hit the wall just beside Sergeant
Roughead, who was climbing through the window. Petrella
got his arms round the woman, who was screaming at the top

of her voice. They rolled on to the floor together. The two men had hardly moved. The newcomer seemed paralysed with shock. The doctor looked, without any expression on his face at all, at his wife, rolling on the floor, at Sergeant Roughead, at the police driver who was climbing through the shattered window. Then, before they guessed what he was going to do, he picked up the glass on the table and swallowed the contents. As his body jack-knifed forwards on to the floor, the woman started howling.

"Strychnine," said the police doctor. "I suppose the whisky would have disguised the taste long enough for the visitor to have got some of it down. One mouthful would have finished him. Your face could do with a bit of patching."

It was nine o'clock and the sun was shining over a landscape which had turned white with frost. Petrella said, "It was her nails."

They had taken away Nora Lovibond, strapped to a stretcher. Through the gap in the window Petrella saw the Chief Constable and went out to have a word with him.

He said, "We've found the place. It's just behind the barn. They're opening it up now."

The digging was being done by a constable and Sergeant Roughead. They were uncovering a pit. A dapper figure, in a neat fawn coat, watching the operation, was Dr. Summerson, the Home Office Pathologist. He said, "Careful now. It would be better to take the last earth away with your hands." He looked doubtfully at Milo, whose face was grey. "That is, if you don't mind. Perhaps I'd better get my coat off and give you a hand."

"That's all right," said Milo. He got down into the pit and started to scrape away the last of the earth.

There were six bodies, each wrapped in a coat, seeming to huddle together in their earthen bed as if to make room for more.

"Peace with Honour," said Milo. He climbed out of the pit, turned away and was sick.

A Thoroughly Nice Boy

THE GRANTS LIVED in Kennington. Mr. Grant worked in an architects' office in the City and had inherited the small terrace house in Dodman Street. It was convenient, since he could reach the Bank Station in ten minutes on the Underground. But it was not a neighbourhood which he found really congenial. There was Mr. Knowlson, who worked in insurance and lived two doors up. But most of the inhabitants of Dodman Street were uncouth men, with jobs at one or other of the railway depots, who went to work at five o'clock in the morning and spent their evenings in public houses.

Mr. Grant had often spoken to his wife of moving out to the suburbs, where people went to their offices at a rational hour and spent the evenings in their gardens and joined tennis clubs and formed discussion groups. The factor which tipped the balance against moving was Timothy. Timothy was their only child and was now fourteen, but with his pink and white face and shy smile he could have been taken for twelve. After a difficult start he was happily settled at the Matthew Holder School near the Oval, and sang first treble in the choir of St. Marks.

"It would be a pity to make a change now," said Mrs. Grant. "Timothy's easily upset. I've put his dinner in the oven; I hope he won't be too late back from choir practice. If his dinner gets dried up he can't digest it properly."

At that moment Timothy was walking very slowly down the road outside St. Marks. He was walking very slowly because, if the truth be told, he had no great desire to get home. When he did get there, his mother would make him take off his shoes and put on a dry pair of socks and would sit him down to eat a large and wholesome meal, which he did not really want, and he would have to tell his father exactly what he had done in school that day and —

A hand smacked him between the shoulder blades and he spun round. Two boys were standing behind him, both a bit older and a lot bigger all round than Timothy. The taller one said, "It's a stick-up, rose-bud. Turn out your pockets."

Timothy gaped at him.

"Come on, come on," said the other one. "Do you want to be duffed up?"

"Are you mugging me?"

"You've cottoned on quick, boyo. Shell out."

"I'm terribly sorry," said Timothy. "But I've actually only got about tenpence on me. It's Thursday, you see. I get my pocket money on Friday."

He was feeling in his trouser pocket as he spoke and now fetched out a fivepenny piece, two twopenny pieces and a penny and held them out.

The taller boy stared at the money, but made no move to touch it. He said, "How much pocket money do you get every week?"

"A pound."

"So if we'd stuck you up tomorrow, we'd have got a quid?"

"That's right," said Timothy. "I'm terribly sorry. If you're short tonight I could show you how to make a bit perhaps."

The two boys looked at each other and then burst out laughing.

"Cool," said the tall one. "That's very cool."

"What's the gimmick?" said the second one.

"It's the amusement arcade, in the High Street. There's a big fruit machine, tucked away in the corner, no one uses it much."

"Why no one uses that machine is because no one ever makes any money out of it."

"That's right," said Timothy. "It's a set-safe machine.

I read about this in a magazine. It's a machine that's organised so that the winning combinations never come up. A man comes and clears the machines on Friday. By this time it must be stuffed with money."

"So what are you suggesting we do? Break it open with a hammer?"

"What I thought was, it's plugged into a wall socket. If you pulled out the plug and broke the electric circuit *whilst it's going* the safety mechanism wouldn't work. It'd stop at some place it wasn't meant to stop. You'd have a good chance."

The two boys looked at each other, and then at Timothy.

He said, "It'd need three people. One to distract the attention of the attendant. You could do that by asking him for change for a pound. The second to work the machine and the third to get down behind and jerk out the plug. I could do that, I'm the smallest."

The tall boy said, "If it's as easy as that why haven't you done it before?"

"Because I haven't got — " said Timothy and stopped. He realised that what he had nearly said was, "Because I haven't got two friends."

"We'd better go somewhere and count it," said Len. Their jacket pockets were bursting with twopenny bits.

"That bouncer," said Geoff. He could hardly get the words out for laughing. "Poor old sod. He just *knew* something was wrong, didn't he?"

"He was on the spot," agreed Len. "He couldn't very well say that machine's not meant to pay out. He'd have been lynched. Come on."

Since the "come on" seemed to include Timothy he followed them. They led the way down a complex of side streets and alleyways, each smaller and dingier than the last, until they came out almost on the foreshore of the Thames. Since the dock had been shut, two years before, it had become an area of desolation, of gaunt buildings with shuttered windows and boarded doorways. Len stopped at one of these

and stooped down. Timothy saw that he had shifted a board, leaving plenty of room for a boy to wriggle under. When they were inside and the board had been replaced Geoff clicked on a torch. Stone stairs, deep in fallen plaster and less pleasant litter.

"Our home from home," said Len, "is on the first floor. Mind where you're treading. Here we are. Wait whilst I light the lamp."

It was a small room. The windows were blanked by iron shutters. The walls, as Timothy saw when the pressure lamp had been lit, were covered with posters. There was a table made of planks laid on trestles, and there were three old wicker chairs. Timothy thought he had never seen anything so snug in the whole of his life.

Len said, "You can use the third chair if you like."

It was a formal invitation into brotherhood.

"It used to be Ronnie's chair," said Geoff with a grin. "He won't be using it for a bit. Not for twelve months or so. He got nicked for lifting fags. They sent him up the river."

"Your folks going to start wondering where you are?"

"No, that's all right," said Timothy. "I can say I went on to the club after choir practice. It's a church club. The Vicar runs it."

"Old Amberline? That fat poof."

Timothy considered the Reverend Patrick Amberline carefully and said, "No. He's all right in that way. You have to keep an eye on one of the vergers though."

Mr. Grant said, "Timmy seems very busy these days. It's the third night running he's been late."

"He was telling me about it at breakfast this morning," said Mrs. Grant. "It's not only the choir and the boys' club. It's this Voluntary Service Organisation he's joined. They're a sort of modern version of the Boy Scouts. They arrange to help people who need help. When he leaves school he might even get a job abroad. In one of those depressed countries."

"Well, I suppose it's all right," said Mr. Grant. "I used to be a Boy Scout myself once. I got a badge for cookery too."

They were busy weeks. For Timothy, weeks of simple delight. Never having had any real friends before, he found the friendship of Len and Geoff intoxicating. It was friendship offered, as it is at that age, without reserve. He knew now that Len was Leonard Rhodes and Geoff was Geoffrey Cowell and that Len's father was a market porter and Geoff's worked on the railway. He had enough imagination to visualise a life in which you had to fight for anything you wanted, a life which could be full of surprising adventures.

The first thing he learned about was borrowing cars. This was an exercise carried out with two bits of wire. A strong piece, with a loop at the end, which could be slipped through a gap, forced at the top of the window, and used to jerk up the retaining catch which locked the door. Timothy, who had small hands and was neat and precise in his movements, became particularly skilful at this. The second piece of wire was used by Len, who had once spent some time working in a garage, to start the engine. After that, if no irate owner had appeared, the car could be driven off and would serve as transport for the evening. Timothy was taught to drive. He picked it up very quickly.

"Let her rip," said Geoff. "It's not like you were driving your own car, and got to be careful you don't scratch the paint. With this one a few bumps don't signify."

This was on the occasion when they had borrowed Mr. Knowlson's new Ford Capri. Timothy had suggested it. "He's stuck to the television from eight o'clock onwards," he said. "He wouldn't come out if a bomb went off."

The evening runs were not solely pleasure trips. There was a business side to them as well. Len and Geoff had a lot of contacts, friends of Geoff's father, who seemed to have a knack of picking up unwanted packages. A carton containing two dozen new transistor wireless sets might have proved tricky to dispose of. But offered separately to buyers in public houses and cafés and dance halls, they seemed to go like hot cakes. Len and Geoff were adept at this.

The first time they took Timothy into a public house the girl behind the bar looked at him and said, "How old's your kid brother?"

"You wouldn't think it," said Geoff, "but he's twenty-eight. He's a midget. He does a turn on the halls. Don't say anything to him about it. He's sensitive."

The girl said, "You're a bloody liar," but served them with half pints of beer. Mr. Grant was a teetotaller and Timothy had never seen beer before at close quarters. He took a sip of it. It tasted indescribable. Like medicine, only worse. Geoff said, "You don't have to pretend to like it. After a bit you'll sort of get used to it."

Some nights they were engaged in darker work. They would drive the car to a rendezvous, which was usually a garage in the docks area. Men would be there, shadowy figures who hardly showed their faces. Crates which seemed to weigh heavily would be loaded on to the back seat of the car. The boys then drove out into the Kent countryside. The men never came with them. When they arrived at their destination, sometimes another garage, sometimes a small workshop or factory, the cargo was unloaded with equal speed and silence and a wad of notes was pushed into Len's hands.

The only real difference of opinion the boys ever had was over the money. Len and Geoff wanted to share everything equally. Timothy agreed to keep some of it, but refused any idea of equal sharing. First, because he wouldn't have known what to do with so much cash. More important, because he knew what it was being saved up for. One of the pictures on the wall of their den was a blown-up photograph of a motor-bicycle. A Norton Interstate 850 Road Racer.

"Do a ton easy," said Len. "Hundred and thirty on the track. Old Edelman at that garage we go to down the docks says he can get me one at trade prices. How much are we up to?"

As he said this he was prising up a board in the corner.

Under the board was a biscuit tin, the edges sealed with insulating tape. In the tin was the pirates' hoard of notes and coins.

"Another tenner and we're there," said Geoff.

Timothy still went to choir practice. If he had missed it his absence would have been noticed, and enquiries would have followed. The Reverend Amberline usually put in an appearance, to preserve law and order, and on this occasion he happened to notice Timothy. They were practising the hymn from the Yattenden hymnal, *O quam juvat fratres.* "Happy are they, they that love God." The rector thought that Timothy, normally a reserved and rather silent boy, really did look happy. He was bubbling over, bursting with happiness. "Remember now thy Creator," said the Reverend Amberline sadly to himself, "in the days of thy youth." How splendid to be young and happy.

That evening, Detective Chief Inspector Patrick Petrella paid a visit to Mr. Grant's house in Dodman Street. He said, "We've had a number of reports of cars being taken away without their owner's consent."

"That's right," said Mr. Grant. "And I'm glad you're going to do something about it at last. My neighbour, Mr. Knowlson, lost his a few weeks ago. He got it back, but it was in a shocking state."

"Yesterday evening," said Petrella, "the boys who seem to have been responsible for a number of these cases were observed. If the person who observed them had been a bit quicker, they'd have been apprehended. But she did give us a positive identification of one lad she recognised. It was your son, Timothy."

"I don't believe it," said Mr. Grant, as soon as he had got his breath back. "Timothy would never do anything like that. He's a thoroughly nice boy."

"Can you tell me where he was yesterday evening?"

"Certainly I can. He was with the Voluntary Service Organisation."

"The people at Craythorne Hall?"

"That's right."

"May I use your telephone?"

"Yes. And then I hope you'll apologise."

Three minutes later Petrella said, "Not only was he not at Craythorne Hall on Wednesday evening, but he's never been there. They know nothing about him. They say they only take on boys of seventeen and over."

Mr. Grant stared at him, white-faced.

"Where is he now?"

"At choir practice."

"Choir practice would have been over by half past eight."

"He goes on afterwards to the youth club."

Petrella knew the missioner at the youth club and used the telephone again. By this time Mrs. Grant had joined them. Petrella faced a badly shaken couple. He said, "I'd like to have a word with Timothy when he does get back. It doesn't matter how late it is. I've got something on at the Station which is going to keep me there anyway."

He gave them his number at Patton Street.

The matter which Petrella referred to was a report of goods, stolen from the railway yard, being run to a certain garage in the docks area. It was out of this garage, at the moment that Petrella left Dodman Street, that the brand - new, shining monster was being wheeled.

"She's licensed and we've filled her up for you," said Mr. Edelman, who was the jovial proprietor of the garage. "You can have that on the house." He could afford to be generous. The courier service which the boys had run for him had enriched him at minimal risk to himself.

"Well, thanks," said Geoff. He was almost speechless with pride and excitement.

"If you want to try her out, the best way is over Blackheath and out on to the M2. You can let her rip there."

Geoff and Len were both wearing new white helmets, white silk scarves wrapped round the lower parts of their faces, black leather coats and leather gauntlets. The gloves, helmets and scarves had been lifted the day before from an outfitters in Southwark High Street. The coats had been bought for them by Timothy out of his share of the money. Len was the driver. Geoff was to ride pillion.

"Your turn tomorrow," said Geoff.

"Fine," said Timothy. "I'll wait for you at our place."

"Keep the home fires burning," said Len. "This is just a trial run. We'll be back in an hour."

"And watch it," said Mr. Edelman. "There's a lot of horse-power inside that little beauty. So don't go doing anything bloody stupid."

His words were drowned in the roar of the Road Racer starting up. Timothy stood listening until he could hear it no longer, and then turned and walked away.

Petrella got the news at eleven o'clock that night.

"We've identified the boys," said the voice on the tele-phone. "They both lived in your area. Cowell and Rhodes. I can give you the addresses."

"Both dead?"

"They could hardly be deader. They went off the road and smashed into the back of a parked lorry. An A.A. patrol saw it happen. Said they must have been doing over ninety. Stupid young buggers."

The speaker sounded angry. But he had seen the bodies and had sons of his own.

The Cowells' house was the nearest and Petrella called there first. He found Mr. and Mrs. Cowell in the kitchen, with the television blaring. They turned it off when they understood what Petrella was telling them.

"I warned him," said Mr. Cowell. "You heard me tell him."

"You said what nasty dangerous things they were," agreed his wife. "We didn't even know he had one."

"It was a brand-new machine," said Petrella. "Any idea where he might have got it from?"

"Tell you the truth," said Mr. Cowell, "we haven't been seeing a lot of Geoff lately. Boys at that age run wild, you know."

"We've brought up six," said Mrs. Cowell, and started to cry softly.

Mr. Cowell said, "He and Len were good boys really. It was that Ronnie Silverlight led them astray. Until they ganged up with him we never had no trouble. No trouble at all."

It was one o'clock in the morning by the time Petrella got back to Patton Street. The Desk Sergeant said that there had been a number of calls. A Mr. Grant had rung more than once. And a boy who said he was Len Rhodes's brother was asking for news.

"How long ago was that?"

"About ten minutes ago."

"That's funny," said Petrella. "I've just come from the Rhodes'. And I don't think Len had a brother. What did you tell him?"

"I just gave him the news."

"What did he say?"

"Nothing. He just rang off. I think he was speaking from a call box."

At this moment the telephone on the desk rang again. It was Mr. Grant. His voice was ragged with worry. "It's Timothy," he said. "He's not come home. You haven't —"

"No," said Petrella, "we haven't got him here. Is there anywhere else he might have gone? Has he got any friends?"

"We don't know anyone round here. He wouldn't just have walked out without saying anything. His mother's beside herself. She wanted to come round and see you."

"I don't think that would do any good," said Petrella. "We'll do what we can." He thought about it and then said to the Desk Sergeant, "Can you turn up the record and find out what happened to a boy called Ronald Silverlight. He was sent down for petty larceny, about two months ago. One of the Borstal institutes. See if you can find me the warden's telephone number."

In spite of being hauled from his bed the warden, once he understood what Petrella wanted, was sympathetic and co-operative. He said, "It's a long shot, but I'll wake Ronnie up and ring you back if I get anything."

Ten minutes later he came through again. He said, "This might be what you want. I gather they were using some derelict old building down in the docks area. It wouldn't be easy to explain. The best plan will be to send the boy up in a car. It'll take an hour or more."

"I'll wait," said Petrella.

It was nearly four o'clock before the car arrived, with a police driver and Ronnie Silverlight and a warder in the back. Petrella got in with them and they drove down, through the empty streets, towards the river.

"You have to walk the last bit," said Ronnie.

Petrella thought about it. There seemed to be too many of them. He said, "I'll be responsible for the boy. You two wait here."

When they got to the building Ronnie said, "We used to shift the bottom board, see, and get in underneath. It'll be a tight squeeze for you."

"I'll manage," said Petrella.

He did it by lying on his back and using his elbows. When he was inside he clicked on the torch he had brought with him.

"Up there," said Ronnie. He was speaking in a whisper and didn't seem anxious to go first, so Petrella led the way up.

When he opened the door the first thing that caught his eye was a glow from a fire of driftwood in the hearth which had burned down to red embers. Then, as his torch swung upwards, the white beam of light showed him Timothy. He had climbed on to the table, tied one end of a rope to the beam, fixed the other in a noose round his neck, and kicked away the plank.

Petrella put the plank back and jumped up beside him, but as soon as he touched the boy he knew that they were much too late. He had been dead for hours.

He must have done it, thought Petrella, soon after he had telephoned the Station and heard the news. And he made up the fire to give him some heat and light to see what he was doing.

"It's Timmy Grant, isn't it?" said Ronnie. He sounded more excited than shocked.

"Yes," said Petrella. "It's Timmy." He was thinking of all the things he would now have to do, starting with the breaking of the news to his parents.

"He was a good kid," said Ronnie. "Geoff wrote me about him."

Petrella's torch picked up a flash of white. It was a piece of paper which had fallen off the table. On it was written, in Timothy's schoolboy script, two lines. Petrella recognised them as coming from a hymn, but he did not know, until Father Amberline told him long afterwards, that they were from the hymn that the choir had been singing that evening.

> And death itself shall not unbind
> Their happy brotherhood.

Petrella folded it up, and slipped it quickly into his pocket. It was against all his instincts as a policeman to suppress evidence, but he felt that it would be brutal to show it to Mr. and Mrs. Grant.

———————

The Cleaners

PART I

Inquest on the Death of Bernie Nicholls

"SAY IT AFTER ME," said the Coroner's officer, eyeing the jury as a drill-sergeant might eye a batch of recruits. "I will diligently enquire into and a true presentment make —" The jury did its best. "Of all matters given into our charge concerning the death of Bernard Francis Nicholls. And will without fear or favour a true verdict give according to the evidence produced before us" — "According to the evidence," said a bright-looking girl, three beats behind the choir and in a very clear voice, "produced before us."

The Coroner's officer looked at her suspiciously and replaced the printed card on the shelf in front of the jury box. The Coroner said, "Well now — " and Police Sergeant Underhill of the Thames Division of the Metropolitan Police took the oath and explained to the Coroner that, being on duty on the morning of January 1st, he had been passing Malvern Steps and had observed what appeared to him to be a body lying on the foreshore below the Malvern Jetty and just above the high-water mark.

"What time of day was this, Sergeant?"

"Approximately half past seven, sir. Just beginning to get light."

The Coroner made a note. He was a nice little man and

Petrella, who was at the back waiting to be called in the next case, knew him for a breeder of canaries and an unreliable bridge player. A sound enough Coroner, though, who went by the book when it suited him and stood no nonsense.

"I directed the police launch to the steps and climbed down onto the foreshore. I found the body of a man lying head downwards, that is to say with his head towards the water. Since he had quite clearly been dead for some time I did not disturb the body. I observed a broken portion of wooden railing near the body and I saw that there was a break in the railing which ran along the edge of the quay about six feet above him. I therefore deduced —"

"That's all right," said the Coroner. "You thought he'd fallen through the railing; very probably he had."

A man, with thick black hair and a thick white face, rose to his feet, said, "The point will be disputed, sir," and sat down again.

The Coroner said, "Good gracious. Mr. Tasker. I didn't see you. Do you appear in this case?"

"I represent Mr. Mablethorpe, the owner of the premises and of the quay," said Mr. Tasker.

"And I represent the deceased," said a thin, sad-looking man.

The Coroner peered at the second speaker over the top of his glasses, identified him, and said, "Very well, Mr. Lampe. Some dispute about liability, no doubt. Looks as though we shall be here for some time. I expect that's all you can really tell us, isn't it, Sergeant? Any evidence of identity?"

Mr. Lampe rose once more to his feet and said, "I am able to identify the body. The man was employed in my office and his name —"

"Better have this formally. For the record, you know."

Mr. Lampe accordingly moved from his seat on the solicitors' bench to the witness box and told the court that he identified the deceased as Bernard Francis Nicholls aged fifty and employed by his firm, Messrs. Gidney, Lampe and Glazier, as a legal assistant.

"Not a qualified solicitor?"

"No sir. But a very experienced conveyancing clerk. He had been with us for five years."

"When did you see him last, Mr. Lampe?"

"When I left the office at about six o'clock on the night of December 31st."

The Coroner's officer said, "There is a witness who saw him later that evening."

"Very well," said the Coroner. "But let's hear the doctor first. I'm sure he wants to get away. Doctors always do."

Dr. Pond said that he had examined the body, both *in situ* and later at the Kentledge Road Mortuary. There were minor abrasions, consistent with a fall from the quay on to the foreshore, a distance of about six feet. There was also one large depressed fracture, on the crown of the head, a little right of centre. He placed his own hand on top of his head to demonstrate the position. The Coroner nodded and said, "He could have hit his head, I suppose, when he fell."

Dr. Pond said, cautiously, that there were several large stones embedded in the mud of the foreshore and he understood that the police had removed one of them for further examination.

"Yes, doctor?"

"I examined the contents of the stomach," said Dr. Pond, with the relish with which pathologists always seem to discuss this topic, "and I discovered what appeared to be the remains of a meal taken shortly before death consisting principally of ham and bread. It was also apparent that the deceased had consumed a substantial quantity of whisky in the last hours of his life. There was evidence, from the degeneration of the liver and the spleen, that this indulgence may not have been of recent origin."

Observing the jury looking baffled, the Coroner said helpfully, "That's the doctor's way of saying that he had been a heavy drinker for some time. Would you have said an alcoholic, doctor?"

"It would be difficult to be certain."

"And in your opinion the blow on the head was the cause of death."

Dr. Pond hesitated for a moment and then said, "It was certainly one of the causes."

"One of the causes?"

"It is possible that the blow on the head rendered him unconscious and that the proximate cause of death was exposure. You will bear in mind, sir, that the night of December 31st was a very cold one. There was a short fall of snow around midnight and there was snow actually on the body when I saw it."

The Coroner said, "Yes, I see," and the jury tried to look as though there was some point which they ought to be thinking about. "Were you able to arrive at any conclusion as to the time of death?"

"In the circumstances it was not easy to be definite. But when I saw the deceased at nine o'clock that morning I judged that he had been dead at least eight hours. More probably ten or twelve."

The young lady juror said, "If there was snow on the body and none underneath it, it would mean that he was there before the snow started at midnight, surely."

"That would be a logical conclusion," said the Coroner blandly. "Thank you, doctor."

The next witness, a big red-faced bald-headed man, said that his name was Saul Elder, and that he was licensee of the Wheelwrights Arms in Sutton Street. He knew the deceased well by sight. He regularly patronised the Wheelwrights Arms and had been there on the night in question. He had eaten two rounds of ham sandwich and had consumed three double and two single whiskies.

"Was that a normal evening's intake?"

Mr. Elder said that it varied. Sometimes Mr. Nicholls drank more than that. Sometimes less. It was about average. He had left about eleven o'clock.

"Did he seem to be in normal spirits when he left?"

For a moment Petrella, who knew Mr. Elder well, thought that he was going to make some gruesome play on the word spirits, but he evidently recollected where he was and confined himself to saying that Mr. Nicholls looked much as usual.

The last witness was Detective Chief Inspector Loveday, in whose manor Malvern Steps lay. (A hundred yards downstream and it would have been Petrella's headache.) He said that he had been called to the scene at half past eight. Some photographs had been taken, which he could produce. He had taken charge of a large piece of stone and had submitted it to the Forensic Science Laboratory. He could also produce their report. The point of interest in it was that they had found a quantity of blood on the stone, and embedded in the blood some small splinters of bone. The blood was of the same group as the deceased and the splinters were quite clearly from his skull.

The Coroner said, "The jury can see the photographs if they wish. But I don't imagine that they add anything to your evidence, Inspector."

The witness agreed and said that the jury might find some of them a bit unpleasant. The foreman, after collecting nods, said he thought they could arrive at a verdict without seeing the photographs.

Inspector Loveday was about to step down when it was observed that Mr. Tasker was on his feet. He said, "Tell me, Inspector, was one of them a photograph of the broken piece of railing we heard about?"

"Yes."

"Of the railing itself?"

"Yes."

"I'd like the jury to see that one."

"Perhaps you have a spare copy for me," said the Coroner.

Spare copies were produced with such speed that Petrella guessed that Loveday must have been warned what to expect.

Mr. Tasker said, "I'd like you to observe that the railing is comparatively new, and is formed of stout upright posts, approximately five inches square, set in concrete. The railings themselves are bars of wood four inches by three. I shall be calling Mr. Mablethorpe who will tell you that it was erected, under his personal supervision, less than two years ago. The wood is oak, which is not —" here Mr. Tasker bared a fine set of white teeth, "a notably fragile material."

"I've no doubt it was a very fine fence," said the Coroner. "But the fact is that one of the bars broke."

"Quite so," said Mr. Tasker. "The question is, who broke it, and how did they do it?"

It was extraordinary, thought Petrella, how the whole atmosphere of the court had suddenly changed. The jury were no longer apathetic, but were crowding together to look at the photographs. The Coroner had his head on one side, like a blackbird sighting a promising worm. His colleague, Jack Loveday, was looking resigned.

"I would ask the jury," said Mr. Tasker, "to look particularly at the first photograph. A very good and detailed photograph, if I may say so. They will observe three overlapping circular depressions, of approximately four inches in diameter, close to the fractured end of the rail. It is not easy to judge from the photograph, but I have been allowed to examine the railing itself, and I can assure them that they vary from a quarter to a full third of an inch in depth. In my view they were made by a very heavy sledge-hammer, applied with considerable force —"

"Well," said Loveday, "he got his adjournment, which is what he was angling for. The rail and post have gone up to the lab for a report."

"What's it all about?" said Petrella. They were having a quick beer at the pub opposite the court.

"He came in originally to look after old Mablethorpe's interests. If the fence had been rotten, there could have been a hefty claim for damages by Nicholls's wife. Now he's seen the photographs he's taking it a lot farther."

"Yes," said Petrella. He knew Mr. Tasker for a man who never left a promising hare unhunted. "But what exactly is in his mind?"

"I wish you'd find out," said Loveday. "You know him better than I do, and his office is nearer you than me."

Petrella, who was aware that Loveday was involved in a particularly unpleasant child-murder case, said, "All right. I'll take it on and let you know what happens. O.K.?"

"O.K.?" said Loveday. "And thank you."

Mr. Tasker ran a one-man solicitor's practice from an office near the Oval. He appeared in the local Magistrates' Courts indiscriminately for and against the police. Petrella had found him to be astute, but fair, in both rôles.

He said, "I saw you at the back of the court, Inspector. I guessed you might be round to see me."

"I wanted to hear a bit more about this railing."

"Have a look at this sketch. It'll show you the point I was trying to make. The end of each rail was countersunk into the post on the *inner* side. You see what that means?"

"It means that it couldn't have been knocked off by someone falling against it. The top of the post would be in the way. Right?"

"Correct. And each rail is fastened to the post by three six-inch nails driven right through and turned flat on the other side. You won't shift them in a hurry."

"Then the only alternative is a flaw in the wooden rail."

"Right," said Mr. Tasker. "That's the only alternative. But in this case it isn't true. I've had the rail examined by my own expert. He'll say that it's as sound a piece of oak as you'll find anywhere in England."

Tho two men looked at each other in silence for several seconds. Then Petrella said, "So what's your idea about all this?"

"I think it's fairly obvious."

"Let's have it, all the same."

"Someone wanted Nicholls out of the way. It was more than one person probably. It's got the feel of a gang job. All they had to do was follow him home from the pub. They knew he'd go past Malvern Steps and they knew he'd be full of whisky. One of them has already got hold of a handy chunk of rock from the foreshore. He walks up behind him, and slugs him on top of the head with it. Didn't it strike you as odd that the fracture should have been on *top* of his head. If you broke through a railing and fell six feet you might land on your face or you might land on your bottom, but you wouldn't land on top of your head."

"It did strike me as a bit odd," said Petrella. "You suggest they just pitched him down and put the chunk of rock back beside him. And broke the rail and threw that down too."

"That's right. And that rail took some breaking. They had to hit it three times with a fourteen-pound sledge-hammer to crack it."

"Can you think of any reason why anyone should want to get rid of Nicholls?"

"Search me."

"Did you know him professionally?"

"We were sometimes on opposite sides in a house sale or purchase. He acted for Lloyds."

Petrella was aware that in that part of South London if someone mentioned Lloyds they meant neither the well-known City outfit nor the bank. They were referring to Lloyd and Lloyd, who were the largest and busiest local firm of property dealers specialising in sales of small houses, flats and one-man businesses. Petrella knew them well. He had bought his own flat from them.

Mr. Tasker said, "Nicholls brought them all the Lloyds business. He knew old Jimmy Lloyd from army days. Now Nicholls has gone, the business will go somewhere else. Lampe's got no one capable of handling it."

"Hasn't he got any partners? What about Gidney and Glazier?"

"Gidney's dead. Glazier's retired. Lampe ought to have retired too. Probably can't afford to. Poor old sod."

A more cheerful aspect of the matter occurred to Mr. Tasker. He said, "Come to think of it, if he loses Lloyds' business, I might get it."

"You realise that makes you the number one suspect," said Petrella. As he was going he added, "If you do hear anything about Nicholls, you might pass it on and we'll look into it. It'll help you to get the verdict you want if you can suggest some sort of motive."

"You scratch my back, I'll scratch yours," said Mr. Tasker cheerfully.

The offices of Messrs. Gidney, Lampe and Glazier were in Kentledge Road, opposite the mortuary. There was a sad air of mortality about them, too. The unmistakable odour of decay.

Mr. Lampe received Petrella in a room which was lined on one side with deed boxes and on two sides with books. Neither boxes nor books looked as though they had been opened for some years. Mr. Lampe said, "I saw you in court, Inspector. Do I understand that you are now in charge of this matter?"

"I'm giving Inspector Loveday a hand," said Petrella. "Temporarily. I thought you might be able to tell me something about Nicholls."

"Ah," said Mr. Lampe. "Yes. Well — he was a very able conveyancer. Before he came to me he had been many years with a firm in Lincoln's Inn. But he found the daily journey across London tiring. As we grow older, Inspector, bodily comfort becomes more and more important."

"He was a native of these parts."

"He has lived here all his life. And married a local girl. I am doing what I can to look after her, poor soul."

"Is she hard up?"

This direct question seemed to disconcert Mr. Lampe. He said, "You'll understand that I haven't had time to look closely into Nicholls's private affairs. But I never got the impression that he had a great deal of money to spare."

"It would seem," said Petrella, "that any money he did have to spare went on whisky."

"I find that remark uncalled for."

"When you took him on, did you know that he was an alcoholic?"

A flush spread over Mr. Lampe's pale face. He said, "There is no truth in that at all. I was surprised that the Coroner let the question stand. I shall take the first opportunity at the adjourned hearing to protest very strongly. Mr. Nicholls liked a drink after the day's work was over. If that makes him an alcoholic, there must be a great number of them about —"

"I'm afraid I put the old boy's back up," said Petrella to

Sergeant Roughead. "A pity, because after that he stood on his professional dignity and I couldn't get anything out of him at all. We shall have to tackle this from the other end. You'd better go along and have a word with Saul Elder at the Wheelwrights. I'd like to know who Nicholls was drinking with that evening."

Sergeant Milo Roughead, late of Eton and the ranks of the Metropolitan Constabulary, accepted the assignment with enthusiasm. He had always found Mr. Elder friendly, and drinking in pursuit of information was the sort of duty which appealed to him.

The Wheelwrights Arms, though full to suffocation on most evenings, was little patronised by day. He found the saloon bar empty and Mr. Elder, with his sleeves rolled up, polishing glasses. He drew a pint for Milo and a half pint for himself and said, "And what may we do to help the cause of law and order, Sergeant?"

"You can tell me something. Who was here with Nicholls on the night he was killed?"

When Mr. Elder froze into sudden immobility, Milo realised that he might have been indiscreet. There was a long silence. Then Mr. Elder slowly resumed his polishing. It was a full minute before he said, "Killed, eh? So that's what Tasker was getting at. I thought it might be."

He examined the glass, holding it up against the light, then put it down and picked up another one.

"It's not certain, by any means," said Milo. "But we're looking at it that way for the moment."

"So you want to know who was drinking with Nicholls?"

"That's right."

"Difficult to say. He had a lot of friends. Not friends really. Acquaintances. People who would always take a drink off him, and sometimes stand him one back. Charlie Cousins, the bookmaker. Phil Green, who drives a taxi. You know him. Sam — I don't know his other name — works in the Goods Depot. I could give you a half dozen names if I thought hard enough. They was all in here that night, and more besides. We had an extension up to midnight, seeing as how it was New Year's Eve."

"But you don't remember anyone in particular?"

"No. First one, then the other."

"Did anyone leave with him?"

Mr. Elder thought hard about this. Whilst he was thinking the door of the small bar at the back opened and two men came out. Milo could see them quite clearly in the mirror behind the bar. Both of them were big men, who carried themselves like soldiers. Both had the pug faces of fighters, short noses, small eyes and unobtrusive ears. The one in front had smooth black hair. The other had thick reddish hair which grew to a peak on his forehead and ran down either side of his face in long side-boards.

They walked out without speaking and the street door swung softly shut behind them.

"I got a few names," said Milo, "and I can check up on them, but I don't fancy we shall get much out of them. It was a New Year's Eve crush, everyone standing drinks to everyone else. There was one thing, though. Did we ever connect the Wheelwrights with the crowd from the Elephant — Les Congdon's lot?"

"The Elephant? No, I don't think so. They usually stick to their own patch of the jungle."

There had been a dynasty of gangs centred on the Elephant and Castle; known at different times as the Elephant boys, the Mahoots or the Jumbos — or simply by the name of the man who happened to have taken over the leadership. They were the mercenary soldiers of the South Bank, happy to sell their services to the best paymaster; dispersed when some gross outrage had roused the police to action; re-forming as soon as the dust had settled.

"Why do you ask?"

"I thought I spotted two of them coming out of the private bar. Chris Mason, I'm sure was one of them. I recognised that widow's peak."

"If that's right," said Petrella, "the black-haired one was probably his brother, Len."

"They didn't look like brothers."

"Their father was Buster Mason, who used to box at the Blackfriars Ring. He was married four times — officially. Died of a brain haemorrhage some years ago. Chris and Len are bad boys. I'll have a word with Loveday. They're his homework, not mine." He was wrapping a scarf round his neck as he spoke and buttoning up his raincoat. The weather was vile. Rain alternating with sleet, driven by a wind which was blowing from the North Sea. "I'm going to have a word with Jimmy Lloyd. Private business. You can look after the shop until I get back."

James Lloyd was sixty-five. The years since the ending of the war had brought him a lot of money. They had also added unnecessary pounds to his weight, an inflated paunch and a troublesome digestion. It was hard to believe that he had once played wing-threequarter for Aberavon.

He said, "Shouldn't be too difficult to find a buyer. Everyone's looking for small flats. You'll be after something bigger, I take it?"

"We'll need one more room at least," said Petrella, "when the second child does decide to put in an appearance. Preferably a spare room as well."

"Two living, three beds, usual offices." Mr. Lloyd made a note on his pad. "What did you put down when you bought this one?"

"I paid seven hundred pounds for a gas-stove, two tatty carpets and some pelmets which we pulled down as soon as we got in."

"Usual swindle," said Mr. Lloyd. "Much more honest to call it a premium and have done with it. You didn't throw the pelmets away, I hope."

"We've got them stowed away somewhere. *And* we've put in a new gas-stove."

"Lovely," said Mr. Lloyd. "Present state of the market, should be able to get you a thousand. Of course, you'll have to lay most of it out again when you get a new flat. Tom Adams will keep his eyes open too. Right, Tom?"

This was to a tiny, bird-like man who had come into the room without knocking.

"My head accountant, Tom Adams," said Mr. Lloyd. "I don't think you know Detective Chief Inspector Petrella, do you?"

"I haven't had the pleasure," said Mr. Adams in a thin piping voice.

"The Inspector wants to move into a larger flat. Three beds. Must do our best for him. Got to keep on the right side of the law, boy."

Mr. Adams looked doubtful. He said, "It's a very popular size. I'll certainly keep my eyes open." He paused. "If you're busy now, I can easily come back."

"That's all right," said Petrella. "I've finished."

When he got back to Patton Street Station he sent for Detective Sergeant Ambrose, and said, "There's a job I want you to look into. It was a long firm fraud. About ten years ago up at Highside. I've forgotten the name of the man concerned. It wasn't my case. He was an unqualified accountant who worked for a firm of builders. Sent down for five years by Arbuthnot at the Bailey. See if you can find me the name and a photograph."

Sergeant Ambrose accepted this vague assignment calmly. He was a painstaking and methodical person and had no doubt that he could unearth the information without too much difficulty.

The inquest on Nicholls was resumed a fortnight later. Photographs and reports were produced to the jury. Mr. Lampe's strong protest about the description of the deceased as an alcoholic was duly noted. The Press, who had been alerted to the possibilities of the case, were there in force. The Coroner summed up at length and the jury, after discussion, returned a disappointing verdict; that there was insufficient evidence to show how Bernard Francis Nicholls had come to his death.

Chief Superintendent Watterson, at Division, read the report of the inquest and said to Petrella, "I suppose you'd better keep the file open. Something might turn up." Which was as good as saying, "Forget about it and get on with your own work. You've got plenty of other things to do."

A week later Nicholls was cremated, the principal mourners being his wife, who seemed to be bearing up reasonably well, and a sister who came down from Lancashire for the occasion. Mr. Lampe made the arrangements and attended the ceremony.

On the following day Petrella heard the good news. Mr. Lloyd had found a flat for him. He went round with his wife to see it and they both liked it. It had three bedrooms and a large cupboard which could, with imagination, be described as a fourth bedroom. Mr. Lloyd said, "Had a bit of luck there. Man who lived in it is working for the Electricity Board. He's been moved up to Scotland. Got to get out quick. Prepared to take five hundred."

A week later Petrella was installed in his new flat and had received the sum of four hundred and twenty-five pounds, in notes, from Mr. Lloyd, this being the difference between the thousand pounds which he had duly got for the gas-cooker, two threadbare carpets and the hastily re-fixed pelmets, the five hundred he had paid for an electric water-heater and an old sofa in the new flat, and Mr. Lloyd's commission on the double deal.

It was on a Monday, a week after the move, that Sergeant Ambrose laid a photograph on Petrella's desk. He said, "I think this is the man you were enquiring after, sir. Named Thomas Anderson. Five years for fraudulent trading. Twelve other cases taken into consideration. Released after serving three years and four months. Nothing known since."

They were clear photographs, taken from the front and in both profiles. There was not the least doubt that it was Tom Adams, head cashier at Lloyd and Lloyd.

Petrella gave the matter a lot of thought. On the one hand, he had personal reasons for feeling grateful to Mr. Lloyd. On the other hand, it looked as though Adams had been going straight since he came out of gaol. If he did say anything to Lloyd, and Adams lost his job, would he not be guilty of persecuting an innocent man who had fought his way back from crime to respectability? It was the twelve other cases that made him hesitate. Could a man who had committed such a systematic series of frauds ever really be trusted to look after someone else's money?

It was while he was thinking about it that the telephone rang. It was Superintendent Watterson. He said, "You're wanted at District tomorrow at ten o'clock."

"What on earth for?"

"No idea," said Watterson. "But you'd better brush your hair and put on a clean collar. It's the old man who wants to see you."

The head of C.I.D. in No. 2 District, at that time, was Commander Baylis. He was not popular with his subordinates, although he seemed to satisfy his superiors well enough. He had come to his appointment through the specialised branches at Central, having risen from the Criminal Record Office, via control of the Fraud Squad to a quiet Division on the respectable western fringe of London. Watterson had once described him to Petrella, in an unguarded moment, as an old woman. Petrella's occasional encounters with him had done nothing to dispel this impression.

When he was shown into the Commander's office he was surprised to see a third man, whom he recognised from past dealings over pension contributions as Mr. Rose, an assistant in the office of the secretary.

Baylis said, "Sit down, sit down. I'm sorry to drag you all the way up here, but a point has come up on which I thought I ought to have a word with you personally."

The words were polite enough, but Petrella felt a faint tremor of disquiet.

"Perhaps you'd be good enough to explain to the Inspector, Mr. Rose."

Mr. Rose said, "As you know, Inspector, we go to great lengths to monitor the bank accounts of police officers. The commonest form of attack, by people who want to get the police into trouble, is to suggest that illicit payments have been made to them, very often directly into their bank accounts."

Petrella said, "Yes." He was aware of the system. Like all police officers of a certain seniority he had signed an authority to his own bank opening his account to inspection.

"We made one of our periodical checks on your own account yesterday. You had paid in a rather large sum, in notes. Four hundred and twenty-five pounds."

Petrella said, the relief in his voice evident to the two men, "That's quite all right. It was a balance which was due to me when I changed flats; apparently two-bedroom ones are more saleable than three-bedroom ones. You can check it all up with Lloyd and Lloyd."

Mr. Rose looked at Commander Baylis, who said, "Yes, yes. I see. That explains how the money came into your hands. It doesn't explain why thirty of the ten-pound notes were part of the proceeds of a recent wage snatch."

PART II

A Lively Night at Basildon Mansions

When he had got his breath back, Petrella said, "Which particular wage snatch was that, sir?"

"At Corinth Car Parts. Last November."

"Two months ago."

"Fourteen months ago."

Petrella nearly said, "I should hardly describe that as recent." It was the sort of thing he would have said to Watterson without a second thought. Something told him that Baylis might not take it well. Mr. Rose, obedient to a slight inclination of the head, had slid out of the room.

Baylis said, "You may be excused for not knowing much about it, Inspector. For better or worse, it was handed over to the Serious Crimes Squad. And we all know the secrecy with which the S.C.S. like to wrap up *their* operations."

Petrella did know it. He was also beginning to understand the acrimony in Baylis's voice.

Since their formation two years before, the Serious Crimes Squad had done a lot of good work. They had also upset the regular hierarchy of the C.I.D.; a hierarchy which linked the Detective on the job, the Detective Inspector in charge of the Station, the Detective Superintendent or Chief Superintendent at Division and the Commander at District in an orderly and well-understood chain of command. The S.C.S. by-passed all of these and was answerable only to the Assistant Commissioner at Central. Districts and Divisions were given periodical reports of their operations, but had no executive control over them.

Petrella said, "How much did they get?"

"Ninety thousand pounds. Corinth is a big outfit, but it wouldn't have been anything like that if it hadn't been the last week in November, when they hand out the Christmas bonus."

"We had another big one in April," said Petrella. "G.E.X. Engineering in Deptford."

"There have been two since then. G.E.X. was in April. Costa-Cans in September. That adds up to three major unsolved wage snatches in my District. In my opinion — "

What indiscretion Baylis was on the point of committing was not to be revealed. Mr. Rose had sidled back into the room. He nodded his head.

Petrella knew what he had been doing. He had been telephoning Lloyd and Lloyd and checking up on his story. He took no umbrage. He would have done the same in Baylis's place.

"Although we aren't allowed to interfere in an S.C.S. operation," said Baylis, "I hardly think the powers that be could object to your following up an obvious lead of this sort, do you?"

The atmosphere had become noticeably more friendly.

"I certainly think I ought to follow it up, sir. After all, we don't know that it had anything to do with the Corinth job. The money may have passed through half a dozen hands. It's simply a case of a firm being found in possession of stolen property. A routine enquiry."

"Exactly," said Baylis. "They can't expect *all* detective work in the District to come to a grinding halt just because the S.C.S. has been engaged — and not too successfully engaged if I might say so — in investigations in our manor, can they?"

"I've got the reports here, if you'd like to look at them," said Watterson. "Most of the banknotes taken in the Corinth job were ordinary small denomination stuff, used notes, impossible to trace. It was just that the directors thought it would be a nice idea to give each of their senior employees a ten-pound note in their bonus packet. They were the new Florence Nightingale issue. So they drew this packet of two hundred tenners and the bank kept a note of the serial numbers which were in sequence. It's thirty of those notes that have ended up in your pocket. It doesn't prove anything against Lloyds of course. Most of their transactions are on a cash basis. Sale of small businesses and stock-in-trade, as well as flats and houses."

"I imagine the Inspector of Taxes would like a sight of their books."

"They don't keep books. They keep a bank account. The money goes in one end and out at the other. All the same, Mr. Lloyd might be able to help. It can't be every day that he gets paid in new ten-pound notes. Why don't you ask him?"

"I'd do just that," said Petrella. "But I'm not sure that he could tell us."

"Oh?"

"The man who looks after the cash is a Mr. Adams."

"Then ask him."

"That might be counter-productive," said Petrella. He told Watterson about Mr. Adams, alias Anderson. Watterson scratched his pointed chin and said, "I see. Yes. This begins to have an interesting sort of smell about it. If Adams *is* bent, do you think someone might be using him to dispose of some of their hot money?"

"It seemed possible. The only thing is, if it's right, ought we to tackle it ourselves?"

Watterson said, in almost exactly the same tones as Baylis, "The S.C.S. can't expect us to suspend all work in the Division just because they've got interested in two or three jobs round here."

"Actually," said Petrella, "couldn't we have handled those jobs just as well as the S.C.S.?"

"I'm not sure," said Watterson. "I don't get as up-tight about it as Fred Baylis. Those three snatches were real professional efforts. It wasn't so much the snatch itself. That was a case of using plenty of muscle. Hitting hard and running fast. All very tightly planned no doubt, but there've been plenty of others as good. It was the intelligence work that was outstanding. They've always struck when there was a maximum of money available. In the G.E.X. case in April they were actually paying out a three weeks' supplement, all in one go, on the settlement of a round of wage bargaining. In the Costa-Cans case the company knew that it was a heavy pay-out that week and took special precautions. The security team went to the bank in their usual van and collected a dummy pay-roll. Satchels full of old newspapers, actually. The real money went out of the back door of the bank in a private car. *That* was the car they hit. You can see what I mean by organisation. It's all in the reports. Take them away and read them."

As Petrella was going he said, "Who was that expensive-looking lady in the expensive-looking car that I saw waiting outside District Headquarters?"

"That," said Watterson, "would be Mrs. Baylis. A second reason for Fred's ulcers."

Petrella said, "We've got a job on, and it's going to need very careful handling, because there are a lot of toes that haven't got to be trodden on."

His audience consisted of Detective Sergeant Blencowe,

large and impassive; Detective Sergeant Milo Roughead, tall and dressed in a manner nicely calculated to compromise between a country house upbringing and life in the ranks of the C.I.D.; Detective Sergeant Ambrose, looking his normal neat and efficient self, and probationary Detective Lampier, recently promoted to the plain-clothes branch and looking, if it were possible, even more untidy out of uniform than he had looked in it.

"Another thing," said Petrella, "this is something outside the ordinary day-by-day stuff. We can't have routine entirely disrupted by it. It'll have to be tackled as and when we can manage it. Along with all our other stuff."

His audience tried to look enthusiastic. Only Detective Lampier succeeded convincingly. He was new to the job.

"What we want to find out is whether there's any connection between Lloyd and Lloyd and the villains who pulled these three snatches. You can be certain that if there *is* any connection it's carefully organised. These aren't the sort of people who leave letters lying around or make incautious telephone calls. The way I propose to tackle it, we'll make a two-pronged attack. I've no real reason to think that Lloyd himself is involved, but Blencowe can chat him up and see if he can get anything useful. He knows you used to play for London Welsh and he used to play for Aberavon years ago. It'll make a point of contact."

"I'm not sure that it'll be tactful to remind him," said Blencowe. "When we played Aberavon last year one of their forwards got his ear bitten — mind you, it was his fault; he should have kept his ears to himself."

"Why not bite Lloyd in the ear," said Petrella. "It should break the ice beautifully. The rest of you concentrate on Adams. He's the real lead. We've got a friend with an upstairs room we can use. Lloyds shut at half past five and I imagine Adams is away fairly promptly. You can take it in turns, one evening each. Just follow him. Don't breathe down his neck. All I want to know is, if he goes anywhere except straight home."

When Petrella spoke of a "friend" he meant someone who,

without being an informer, was prepared to help the police in small ways, reckoning to have it counted in his favour next time he happened to run into trouble. Mr. Grandlund, who lived over his wireless shop opposite the offices of Lloyd and Lloyd, was a friend; and it was in his front room, comfortably seated in a chair opposite the window, with the net curtains drawn, that Sergeant Ambrose spent Tuesday evening and Detective Lampier Wednesday evening.

On neither occasion did the following of Mr. Adams present any difficulty. He took a bus from the corner, rode out in it to Blackheath, where he had a flat in one of the large houses on the heath, went straight in and turned on the television. The watcher, having been told not to make an all-night job of it, left him to it.

Manfred Tillotson got to his feet, moved over to the circular table in the corner, and poured himself out a drink. He put three fingers of brandy into a tumbler and added an equal quantity of dry ginger-ale and a single cube of ice. All his movements were neat and precise.

Carrying the tumbler, he went out of the room, down the hallway to a door at the end, his feet making no noise on the thick grey carpeting on the floor.

It was a bathroom, and there was a girl lying in the bath with her back to the door. Manfred reflected that you could never really judge a girl's age until she had her clothes off. Dressed in the style she affected, Julie would have passed for sixteen. Undressed, it was clear that she was older, though not, perhaps, very much older.

Hearing the click of the door opening, the girl turned her head.

"You should never lie in a strange bath with your back to the door," said Manfred. "There was a man called Smith who finished off three wives, just because they were foolish enough to do that."

The girl blinked at him. She said, "Why did he do it, for God's sake? And how?"

"Why was for the insurance money. How was by putting

one arm under their knees and lifting them. Their heads went under and they drowned."

"They must have been daft," said Julie. "If I'd been one of them, do you know what I'd do?" Manfred took a sip from his drink and stood looking down at her. He said, "I'm sure it would be something original."

"I'd hook out the plug with my foot. All the water would be gone long before I drowned."

Tillotson said, "I wonder why none of the Mrs. Smiths thought of that. You'd better get dressed, sweetie. My brother's coming in at six."

"So what?"

"Samuel doesn't entirely approve of our arrangements. He says I'm mixing business with pleasure."

"I could never see what was wrong with that," said Julie. "But then I'm an old-fashioned girl."

"I'll pour you an old-fashioned drink."

They were both finishing their drinks when Samuel Tillotson came in. He was older and greyer than his brother, but with the same thickness in the neck and body and the same length of arm and breadth of shoulder. Julie was more afraid of him than of Manny. She finished her drink quickly and said, "Well, I'll be off."

Samuel followed her out in silence, shut the front door behind her and came back into the room.

"Don't say it," said Manfred.

"Don't say what?" said Samuel.

"That it's a mistake to mix business and pleasure. What will you take?"

"A small whisky and water. With that girl, it might be. You know how she came to us?"

"Through Ma Dalby."

"Right. She arrives from Liverpool. Young and broke. Ma Dalby picks her up. Boards and lodges her. And offers her the usual line of employment."

"Which she accepts."

"For a time. Until it occurs to Ma that she's an intelligent girl. A cut above the average runaway. And happens to have taken a secretarial course in her last year at school. So she offers her to us."

"Where she has given great satisfaction."

"I don't doubt it," said Samuel. "More water, if you don't mind. Satisfaction in the office. Satisfaction in the home."

"Then what are you beefing about?"

Samuel Tillotson tasted his drink again, found it to his satisfaction, and swallowed a mouthful. Then he said, "You know Ma's routine. She likes to know the real name and real address of her girls. They always give her false ones at first, but she has ways of finding out. With Julie it was easy. She had a suitcase with a twopenny lock. As soon as she was out of the house Ma had it open. There was a packet of letters. From an ex-boy friend. She thought it must have been an ex-boy friend. Some of them were quite — intimate."

"So what," said Manfred. "Girls carry things like that about with them."

Samuel didn't seem to hear him. He was gazing into the heart of his drink. Swirling it round gently and peering at it, as though it had some secret he could unlock. He said, "The letters were all handwritten. One of them was still in its envelope. The name and address on the envelope were typed and the envelope had been torn open so roughly that the stamp and postmark and part of the girl's name were gone. But the address was there. 138 Colefax Road, Liverpool. Ma made a note of it before she put the letter back."

"Well?"

"There is a Colefax Road in Liverpool. But there is no number 138. The numbers go no higher than ninety."

Manfred thought about it. He said, "It doesn't prove anything. Julie would know that Ma liked to have their names and addresses. The other girls would have told her. So she faked up the envelope. Right?"

"That's what I mean by the dangers of mixing business and pleasure," said Samuel. "You're saying that because you want her to be what she says she is. A little Liverpudlian, hungry for money and sex. I can think more dispassionately about her."

"And what does your dispassionate thinking tell you?"

"It tells me that we are up against some very clever people. And it tells me that, with our plans for the fourteenth, this isn't a time when we can afford to be careless. She must be watched."

"I don't mind her being watched. But nothing must be done to her until I am convinced."

Samuel pinched his brother affectionately in the muscles of his forearm. He said, "Dear Manny, no step shall be taken until we are unanimous. As always."

On Thursday evening a wind of near gale force, non-stop from Siberia, was hitting the East End of London, slinging bucketfuls of frozen rain horizontally down the street. Milo Roughead had put on two extra pullovers and brought with him an oilskin coat borrowed from a boating friend.

"Nasty night to be out in," said Mr. Grandlund. "I'll get you a cupper. Warm the inner man."

Milo was half-way through the cup of tea when he put it down, snatched up his coat and bolted down the stairs. Mr. Adams was on the move.

He was battling down the street, head lowered against the wind. He passed the bus stop. His objective turned out to be the Underground station. Milo gave him fifty yards, then followed him, in time to see him disappearing down the moving staircase. He bought himself a ticket to the end of the Northern Line. The station was an old-fashioned one, with emergency stairs. Milo went down them fast. He could hear a train coming. He reached the platform in time to see Mr. Adams get in, two carriages farther up. This suited him well. He jumped in after him. The train was on the Bank switch and was nearly empty. They had reached Essex Road before Mr. Adams moved. Fortunately three other people got out with him. They all travelled up in the lift together. When they reached the street Mr. Adams and the three other men turned right. Milo turned left and walked away from them. Out of the corner of his eye he saw Mr. Adams cross the New North Road and make off up Northampton Street. He reversed smartly and followed.

The weather helped. It was the sort of night in which a pedestrian kept his head down and ploughed steadily forward without much regard to what was happening around him. It was quite a long walk, up Alwyne Road and Willow Road, then left again. His knowledge of London geography told Milo that they must be getting close to Canonbury, that much bombed area which had blossomed into fashion after the war, and was now full of tarted-up Georgian houses and blocks of new and expensive flats.

"He can't be walking for pleasure," said Milo to his sodden feet. "Must be getting somewhere soon." At this moment Mr. Adams turned to his left up a shallow flight of steps and disappeared into the building.

Milo slowed down, wiped some of the rain out of his eyes and read, above the doorway, in golden letters, "Basildon Mansions".

What now?

There was no sign of the porter. Presumably he was down in his own snug basement with his nose glued to the television and a glass of something in his hand, lucky sod.

Through the glass of the swing door Milo could see a board with the numbers of the flats and the names of their occupants. There were twelve flats, starting with 1a and 1b on the ground floor and running up to 6a and 6b. It was clearly out of the question to knock on twelve different doors and if he waited in the hall he was going to be much too conspicuous when Mr. Adams finished his business and came out. On the other hand, having followed him so far he wanted to finish the job. The flats were new and expensive; too expensive for the sort of income earned by a cashier in a firm of estate agents.

A thought occurred to him. He walked across and inspected the lift. The tell-tale above the gate showed that the last person to use it had taken it up to the fourth floor. This was interesting, but not conclusive. If Mr. Adams had been making for a flat on the ground floor, or even possibly on the first floor, he might not have used the lift at all.

Milo had a further thought. Each of the flats clearly ran

the whole way from the front to the back of the building, one on either side of the central hallway. It was a fair bet that the main living-room would be in front, overlooking the street, with the bedrooms at the back. He turned up the collar of his coat and went out again. The front door of an office building opposite afforded a certain amount of shelter. Milo started to count windows. The top two floors were unlighted. Below that a light showed on the left but not the right. That must be 4a. On the next floor down both sides were black. 2b on the right showed lights, but not 2a.

It was at this point in his observations that Milo realised that he was not alone. Three men were closing in on him, one from either side coming slowly, blocking escape; the third coming straight at him and coming fast.

He had very little time to think. Groping behind he felt for the handle of the door. It was not that he expected it to be open. He wanted something to give him purchase. As the man in the centre launched himself at him he half turned, holding on to the big handle, and kicked. His foot landed low down in the man's stomach. The man gave a sharp gasp, more anger than pain, and folded forward. Milo hurdled his body and made for the doorway of Basildon Mansions. As he reached it, the door opened and a very large woman came out. She was wearing a fur coat and a fur hat, and was attached to a small furry animal. Milo slid past her, kicking the animal as he did so. The woman said, "Really — " and at that moment received the full impact of the first of his pursuers.

By this time Milo was inside the lift and had latched the outer grid. There were two men in the hall. The front one was doing what looked like a slow waltz with a grizzly bear. The second was trying to get past. Milo pressed button number 6. As the inner door slid shut he noted both his opponents making for the stairs.

By the time the lift reached the top floor Milo had done some thinking. Much depended on whether he had put number three out of action. If he had, the simplest plan would be to take the lift down again and bolt for the street. But he rather doubted it. Number three, he guessed, was no worse than winded. If he was now guarding the front hall he could certainly block him until the other two got down. And since it was clear that they knew he could identify them, and were prepared to risk it, this led to a conclusion which was far from comfortable. What he wanted was a place of refuge with a telephone and a more reliable witness than the woman in the fur coat. He had an idea where he might find all three, but it was going to need luck and split-second timing.

He waited, with the inner door of the lift open and the grid shut until the leading pursuer reached the top landing. It was, as he had thought, Len Mason and he guessed that the second one was his brother Chris. Milo was glad to see that both of them had bellows to mind. As they reached the lift he pressed button number 2.

Flat 2b, which had been showing a light, was the flat on the opposite side of the landing. As soon as the lift had stopped, Milo wrenched open the grid, dived across, and leaned on the bell.

He could hear the men clattering down the stairs. Also footsteps inside the flat. It was going to be a very close thing.

The door of the flat opened. Milo leaped inside, slammed it behind him and fixed the chain on the door. The occupier of flat 2b was a thin elderly man with silver-grey hair and a placid expression.

He said, "Is somebody chasing you?"

There was a thud on the front door.

Milo said, "I'm afraid that's right, sir."

"Do you think they are going to break down my door?"

"I think they'll try," said Milo. "Have you got a telephone?"

"I have a telephone," said the grey-haired man, "but I fear it is not operative. It has been out of order for a week. The Post Office allege that they are short of staff."

The assault on the door was increasing in fury. The men seemed to have got hold of some sort of battering ram and were smashing it against the wooden panels.

"They'll have the whole door down in a minute," said Milo. "Have you got a back entrance?"

"I have," said the man, "but I have no intention of using it. I intend to defend my domicile."

"I admire your spirit," said Milo, "but these are violent men."

"Then we are entitled to adopt correspondingly violent measures. One moment." He went into the nearest room and reappeared holding a pair of very large old-fashioned pistols.

"I keep them loaded and primed," said the man.

"Have you got a licence for them?"

"Quite unnecessary. They are genuine antiques. See Section 14 of the Firearms Act."

The top part of the door disintegrated and the head and shoulders of Chris Mason appeared. The grey-haired man said, "I was a magistrate for many years in India and I always held to the view that the law allowed a man to employ a *reasonable* amount of force in countering an unprovoked attack. I am told, by the way, that this weapon throws high."

There was a shattering roar of sound and a jagged hole appeared in the lower panel of the door.

The head and shoulders of Chris Mason disappeared. Sirens sounded at the end of the street.

"That sounds like reinforcements," said Milo. "Let's see if we can get what's left of that door open."

There was a trail of blood on the stairs. When they got down to the hall the Masons and their colleague had disappeared. The open door at the other end of the hall indicated the way they had gone. The fur-coated lady was sitting on the floor with her back to the wall, recovering from a fit of hysterics. The small dog was helping her by washing her face.

"Quite a lot of blood," said the grey-haired man. "Do you think I winged him?"

"More likely splinters from the door panel," said Milo. "If you'd actually hit him with a bullet out of that gun it'd have taken his leg off."

It was the porter who had summoned the police. He now reappeared cautiously from the basement and said, "What's going on here?" The uniformed sergeant from the leading police car said the same thing a moment later. Milo did his best to explain.

"They must have had a car parked somewhere round the back," said Milo. "They got clean away. But I recognised two of them. We could pick them up easily enough."

It was nine o'clock on the following morning. The storm had blown itself out in the night and a pale yellow sun was lighting, but not warming, the streets of South London.

"I expect we could," said Petrella coldly. "And all three of them will deny it and produce convincing alibis for the whole evening. I don't imagine Mrs. Mapledurham will be a very convincing witness, and the porter didn't see them. It'll be your word against theirs."

"I suppose so," said Milo. He was trying to suppress the father and mother of a sneeze.

"And it won't be very good publicity, will it? A police officer being chivvied up and down stairs by a party of hooligans. Someone will have to pay for that door, too."

Milo felt that he was being unfairly treated, but had been a policeman long enough to know that this happened. Petrella glared round at Blencowe, Ambrose and Lampier as if daring them to say something. They were all sensible enough to keep their mouths shut. He said, "I think it's time we stopped playing cowboys and Indians and used our heads. First point, how did they pick you up so quickly?"

"I suppose Adams spotted me and telephoned for help."

"Unlikely," said Petrella. "And the timing's much too quick."

"I'd guess one of them was watching Adams," said Blencowe. "Just to make certain he wouldn't be followed, or to take the necessary steps if he was."

"I think so, too," said Petrella. "So that brings us to the next point. It must have been important to someone that Adams *wasn't* followed. And I don't believe that 'someone' lives in Basildon Mansions. Adams was using the front-door-back-door technique. He walked straight through and out at the back. Leaving you to be attended to."

"Yesh, arashoo!" said Milo. "Sorry."

"That leads us to a third conclusion," said Petrella. "If they were prepared to go to those lengths to knock you off, it means that the man Mr. Adams had come to see must be living fairly close. If he'd been two miles away, Adams would simply have left you standing where you were, catching a cold, and wandered off without bothering about you. I had a look at the area this morning. There are three other blocks of flats. Ashburton Mansions, Chesterfield Court and Devonshire Court. I want a run-down on *all* the people in them. Ambrose and Lampier, you can tackle that. You'll have to do it quietly and tactfully. The best line will be to see if the landlords will help. They must have taken references from their tenants when they moved in. Blencowe, you keep as close to Lloyd as you can. And you" — he turned round on Milo — "had better go home and put your feet in a mustard bath."

When they were back in their own room Lampier said, "What's eating him? I've never seen him like this before."

"He feels personally involved," said Ambrose. "It's the hot money Lloyd palmed off on him. He's not forgotten that."

Milo said, "Arashoo. I think I'll take him at his word."

It was at ten o'clock that same morning that Mr. Adams called at Patton Street Police Station and asked for Petrella. If he knew anything about the events of the night before he showed no signs of it. He perched himself on the chair in front of Petrella's desk, accepted the cigarette that was offered to him and said, "Mr. Lloyd sent me along to see if we could interest you in a proposition."

Petrella said, "Yes?"

"You know a lot of people in this district. People who need flats and other premises from time to time. People who have property to dispose of. If you'd be prepared to keep your ears open and pass these people on to us — you needn't be involved in any other way, except for just mentioning our name — we'd be prepared to pay you a retainer. It's quite a usual arrangement."

"What sort of sum had you in mind?"

"We thought of twenty-five pounds a week. If any business resulted from your introduction there'd be a commission on top of it."

"It's very kind of Mr. Lloyd," said Petrella. "But I fear I shall have to say 'no'."

"Think it over."

"I've done all the thinking I'm going to do."

Mr. Adams seemed unabashed. He rose to his feet, and turned once more at the door to say, "Think about it."

When he had left, Petrella switched off the tape recorder under his desk. He was smiling, but not agreeably.

Part III

The Peripatetic Birds

The methodical Sergeant Ambrose laid a pile of notes on Petrella's desk and said, "I think we've got them all now, sir. You can read the detailed reports if you like, but in my view there really are only two possibles. Manfred and Samuel Tillotson. They have flats opposite each other, 6a and 6b on the top floor of Chesterfield Court. They're the most expensive flats in the block. They've both got sun terraces. The landlord says they've had the partition between the two terraces removed. That means they have a private access to each other's flats."

"A nice example of brotherly togetherness," said Petrella. "What do the brothers do when not sunning themselves on adjacent terraces?"

"They have a business in the City. Tillotson (Middle-East) Agencies, Barnaby House, Moorgate. It's in the London telephone directory. All quite open and above-board."

"If so open and above-board, what makes you think they might be villains?"

Ambrose said, "I've seen both of them. They seemed to me — " he was picking his words with care " — to be the

only people there of the calibre to be running the sort of show
we have in mind."

"In other words," said Petrella, "you're backing instinct.
I'm not saying you're wrong. It can be a better horse than
science."

On the following morning he took the Underground to the
Bank Station and walked down Moorgate. It was nearing the
lunch hour and men and girls were pouring out onto the
pavements into the mild February sunlight, making the most
of their sixty minutes of freedom. Barnaby House was a
smallish building on the west side of the road. Petrella spent
some time strolling along the opposite pavement, keeping an
eye on the door. He noticed three very attractive-looking girls
come out together and make off down the street. Then a
couple of paunchy middle-aged men, a severe lady in glasses
and a group of young men.

When it seemed clear that most of the inhabitants were
out of the building he ventured into the hall. A board gave
him the information he wanted. Tillotson (Middle-East)
Agencies occupied the first floor. The ground floor was
Cranmer and Cranmer, Chartered Surveyors, and the remaining floors were occupied by Benjamin Dalby and Partners,
Solicitors and Commissioners for Oaths.

Petrella made a note of the names and took himself back
to the Oval. He found Mr. Tasker in his office, lunching off
sandwiches and bottled Bass.

"Dalbys," said Mr. Tasker, picking his teeth to extract a
shred of ham. "Yes. I know them. Nice little firm. Shouldn't
have said they'd touch anything crooked."

"I wasn't thinking of them as being crooked. It's their
neighbours I'm interested in. Do you happen to know any of
the partners?"

Mr. Tasker consulted the Law List and said, "As a matter
of fact I do. Young Buckle used to be an articled clerk here.
Lazy young devil. I could give him a ring. Have to tell him
some sort of story."

"Tell him the truth. Say I'm interested in one of the parties
who uses the building."

Mr. Tasker looked at his watch. He said, "We won't catch him at the office now. Never took less than two hours for his lunch when he was articled here. Probably takes three now he's a partner. I'll ring him this afternoon. There are plenty of good pubs in the City. Offer him lunch at one of them tomorrow."

Young Mr. Buckle turned out to be an entertaining lunch companion. He said several disrespectful things about Mr. Tasker, but obviously admired him. When Petrella brought the conversation round to Tillotsons, Mr. Buckle said, "As soon as I heard you were interested in someone in the building I guessed it must be them. They're a mystery outfit, they really are."

"In what way?"

"Well, they've got an expensive set of offices and a super line in staff, but they never seem to have any customers. And what's more — you can't help noticing these things when you work in the same building — they never seem to get any mail."

"Maybe they do all their work by telephone and telex."

"It's possible. But in that case, what do you suppose those lovelies do all day? Sit on their boss's knee?"

"Would they be the three girls I saw coming out of the place yesterday?"

"If they were worth a second look, they must have been. Cranmers seem to go in for an all-male staff and we haven't got a female in the place under forty. The idea being to keep our minds on our work I imagine."

"Those three were certainly worth looking at," agreed Petrella.

"And I'll tell you another odd thing about them. They go away and come back again. Did you notice one of them, a brunette with a snub nose and a page-boy haircut?"

"Yes. She was the one in the middle. What about her?"

"She disappeared just after Christmas. Not this Christmas, the one before. Then she came back, sometime in May, and the red-head took off. She was back in October."

Petrella listened, fascinated. He said, "Is anyone missing now?"

"I'll say. It's the blonde. Pick of the bunch. Shoulder-length hair and green eyes. She went off about the time the red-head came back."

"You seem to keep a close eye on their comings and goings."

Young Mr. Buckle said, without a blush on his downy cheeks, "I'm a devoted bird watcher."

Petrella returned thoughtfully to Patton Street. He felt certain that he had his hand on one of the threads, one of the clues to the labyrinth, but he could not yet disentangle it. Why should two business men keep three or four attractive and presumably expensive girls in an office, doing nothing all day. Unless, of course, they had insatiable sexual appetites, but then, surely, it would be cheaper, rents in the City being what they were, to have installed them in flats. Maybe they had got a perfectly genuine tie-up with the Middle East. There was plenty of money there and a smashing girl would be a useful maker of contacts. But somehow he doubted it. Like Sergeant Ambrose, he was guided in such matters more by instinct than by reasoning.

He said to Lampier, "You've got one of those candid-camera arrangements. I want you to photograph three young ladies. You can probably get them all in one shot as they come out for lunch. Only for God's sake don't be caught doing it. Then have the three faces screened and enlarged."

A few evenings later Samuel strolled across to talk to Manfred. He found his brother listening to the long-range weather forecast. He said, "It seems that we are to have more than the average amount of rain this month. Some high winds to start with, dying down later, with possibilities of fog. No ice."

"It sounds just what the doctor ordered," said Samuel. "A few fog patches on the fourteenth, but no ice on the road. It will suit us down to the ground."

"Eight days to go."

Samuel said, "I saw an advertisement in the Sunday papers. I've been making some enquiries about it. A villa in the hills to the east of Beirut. Twenty thousand pounds sterling, or the equivalent in local currency."

"Are you thinking of buying it?"

"I've made an offer."

"I see," said Manfred. "So you have decided it is time we retired?"

"Our local contacts could organise the transfer of our funds. We should lose fifteen per cent on the transaction, but it would be worth it."

"Is something worrying you?"

"A lot of little things. There seem to have been one or two people, with nothing to do, on the pavement outside Barnaby House lately. It could be my imagination."

"And?"

Samuel said slowly, "I am not happy about Julie."

"You needn't worry about her. I have traced her family. It wasn't difficult. They live in the Liverpool suburb of Litherland. Until Julie came to London she had spent all her life there. The envelope was obviously planted for Ma Dalby. But she's not a police spy."

"A greedy little girl who knows too much could be more dangerous than a police spy," said Samuel. "Remember also, she has never actually done a job for us yet. That leaves her free to talk if she wants to."

"What are you suggesting?" said Manfred. He was beginning to sound angry.

"Nothing drastic. I suggest we get the boys to throw a scare into her. Enough to keep her quiet until after the fourteenth. That's all."

Manfred thought about it. He said, "I agree that we don't want to take any chances at this particular time. But if you do what you suggest, I think you will be making trouble where none existed before."

"Let's sleep on it," said Samuel. He looked at his watch. "Adams should be ringing."

"He's usually very punctual," said Manfred. "Have a

drink." He was half-way to the drink table when the telephone rang. He picked up the receiver, and conducted a one-sided conversation which consisted chiefly of grunts on his part. Finally he said, "I'll pick you up in my car at the road junction in the middle of Blackheath at seven o'clock tomorrow."

His brother said, "Has there been some development?"

"Yes and no. I asked Adams to find out if there was any particular reason why he should have been followed the other night. He thinks he has found the reason. I am going to discuss it with him. If he is right, we may have to think very carefully about it."

"I leave the thinking to you," said Samuel, "with every confidence." He put an arm round his brother's broad shoulders and gave him an affectionate squeeze.

Petrella sat up in bed and said, "Of course."

"Of course what?" said his wife sleepily.

"It must be the answer."

"Go to sleep," said his wife.

Ideas which arrive at two o'clock in the morning sometimes turn out to be chimeras, but at breakfast time the idea still looked solid. As soon as he got to Patton Street he sent for Sergeant Ambrose. He said, "Go round to these three addresses, see the managing director first and then get hold of the chap who's in charge of hirings and firings."

"The personnel manager."

"Right."

"And what do I ask him?"

"I've written down two dates opposite each name. I want to know if a girl was taken on around the first date and quit around the second."

"They're all fairly large outfits."

"Certainly. But I'm not talking about a girl in the factory. I mean someone who had a job in the executive office. Secretary or P.A. to one of the top bods. Something like that."

"And if they say yes?"

"Show them the photographs."

*　　　*　　　*

The long-range weather forecast had got away to an accurate start. A cold, heavy rain was coming straight down out of a black sky. Mr. Adams turned up the collar of his coat and cursed Manfred Tillotson for choosing such a desolate spot for his rendezvous.

A Vauxhall Magnum drew up to the kerb. Manfred said, "Get in. Take your coat off and throw it on to the back seat."

The car heater was on and the interior was warm and comfortable. Manfred said, "There's a flask in the pocket beside you. Help yourself." They drove on for a few minutes in silence. They seemed to be making their way down off the heath, towards the river.

At the bottom of Maze Hill Manfred swung the car into a side turning, drew up, and said, "Well, what's the answer?"

"I'm afraid Mr. Lloyd's getting careless."

"In what way?"

"When he paid one of our customers in cash he gave him thirty of the new tenners from the Corinth job."

"Thirty?" said Manfred thoughtfully. "He might have thinned them out a bit more than that. Still, it's all part of the system, isn't it?"

"It wasn't the number of notes, it was the person he gave them to. Chief Inspector Petrella."

"He did *what*?"

"That's right. Petrella's our local gaffer at Patton Street."

There was a long silence whilst Manfred thought this over. Then he said, "We all know the Yard keeps an eye on senior officers' accounts. That must be how they spotted it." He was silent again, thinking out the ramifications of this new development. It had been worrying when he had not known why Adams had been followed. Now that he had the explanation it was less alarming. But there was a possibility that had to be checked.

"Is there any chance," he said, "that Lloyd did it on purpose?"

Mr. Adams turned his head. The car had been carefully parked half-way between lamp posts. There was not enough light for him to see Manfred's face clearly. He said, "I *think* it was just a slip-up."

"But you're not sure. Why?"

"He's been seeing a lot of one of the sergeants from Patton Street. A Welshman called Blencowe. They talk rugby football."

"All the time?" said Manfred. "Or just when anyone else is listening."

"It's in the Wheelwrights. They have a couple of beers there most evenings. I didn't think — "

"That's right," said Manfred. "You didn't think."

But he was thinking, turning over possibilities, making plans against a contingency which ought to have been foreseen and now had to be dealt with. He was silent for so long that, in the end, it was Mr. Adams who spoke. He said, "The fact is, he's getting old. And tired. I don't think he means to tell them anything, but if they keep hammering at him, he might fall apart."

"Don't upset yourself about it," said Manfred. "It's not your problem. I'll drop you at your flat."

When Julie left Chesterfield Court at about seven o'clock, two evenings later, she had in her handbag a letter from her mother. It had reached her by a roundabout route, through the good offices of a friend of a friend. Mrs. Marsh was not a great letter-writer. The four pages were punctuated with exclamation marks and scored with underlining, but their message could have been put in two words, "Come home".

Julie considered the proposition coolly. There had been moments, in the last week, when she had sensed undercurrents of distrust in the curious little circle into which she had fallen. Nobody had said anything. Possibly what had worried her were things which would have been said before and weren't being said now. On the other hand, the conditions were easy and the pay was fabulous. She had a sudden picture of home. The streets of Litherland. Men and girls trooping off at eight o'clock on a grey morning to a day's work and trooping back again in the evening tired, but planning a night out at the

local with a crowd of boys; boys with unsuccessful moustaches;
boys who smelled of beer and cigarettes and talked about
nothing but soccer. It was familiar and it was safe; but my
God, it was dull.

She was still thinking about this when she got off the train
at Borough Station and started to walk home to her top-
floor flat in Manciple Street. She was half-way there when
the car drew up just ahead of her and a man got out. She
had seen him twice before with Manfred, but didn't know
his name. He said, "Hop in, chick, we'll take you home."

"Not worth it," said Julie. "It's only two streets on."

"Come on."

"What do you think my legs are for?"

"I could give you one or two answers to that," said Mason
coming closer. "But don't let's stop here all night discussing
it. Just get in."

"I told you, no."

Mason came so close to her that she had to step back. She
found herself up against railings. Mason said, lowering his
face towards her, "In my book, little girls do what they're
told. If they don't, they're apt to lose things. Like, say, bits
of their face."

She saw the bright gleam of steel in his right hand, held
down by his side. She also saw that a man was coming along
the pavement towards her.

She screamed out, "Leave me alone."

The newcomer rolled to a halt. He was as big as Mason
and was smiling in a good-natured way. He said, "Phwat
goes on here?" The lilt in his voice proclaimed an Irishman.

"I should advise you to keep walking, chum," said Mason.

"Would you now," said the newcomer. "And suppose I
were to ask the little lady if she was in trouble."

"He's trying to get me into that car," said Julie.

"If you don't care to go with him," said the newcomer
judicially, "then there's no reason you should. No reason
at all."

By this time the driver had got out of the car. Mason

said, "For the last time, if you don't keep your fucking nose out of our business, you'll get fucking-well hurt."

The newcomer gave a long whistle, apparently of surprise. He said, "Hey, Patrick. Would you believe it. I'm being intimidated."

A second man had appeared on the scene. He said, "Whadder you know?" He had approached very quietly. Mason could see a third figure in the shadows behind him. He sensed that there might be others. He was outside his own territory. It was no moment for taking chances. He swung round, signalled to the driver and climbed back into the car.

The three men on the pavement watched in silence as the car drove off. The first one said, "We could use that taxi of yours, Len."

"It's just round the corner. I'll fetch it."

"You do that. The little lady's had a bad fright. I can see that."

"It's very good of you," said Julie faintly. Her legs seemed to be in danger of giving way under her.

"Think nothing of it," said the first man. "It's a sad world if we can't spread a little light and happiness. You go with Len. He'll take you home right enough."

Julie said, "It's only three streets away. It's hardly worth bothering." But she got in.

"You come from Liverpool, I guess," said Len. "There's a coincidence, for it's my own home town."

As they drove off, Julie was coming to a decision. All her money and her important possessions were in her handbag. There was nothing in her flat that she couldn't replace. She opened the glass partition and said, "I've changed my mind. Do you think you could drive me to Euston?"

Len seemed unsurprised. He executed a tight U-turn and set off in the opposite direction. When they got to Euston his kindness was not exhausted. He parked the taxi against the kerb, put a glove over the meter and said, "I'll come along with you whilst you find your train. That is, if you've no objection."

He was a square, solid comforting sort of person. Julie

smiled at him and said, "I'd like that, Len. Are you sure you won't get into trouble leaving your cab there?"

"No trouble I can't get out of," said Len.

They found that an Inter-City train was leaving for Liverpool in ten minutes, which gave them time to buy her a ticket and some newspapers to read.

Len waved to her in a fatherly way as the train drew out. Then he moved off to the nearest telephone box —

"Get round to her place, then, and wait for her," said Manfred.

"We did that," said Mason. "We waited more than an hour. She never turned up. I think she's scarpered."

"Scarpered where?"

"Back home to Liverpool would be my guess."

"Did you hurt her?"

"We didn't touch her. Never had a chance. This other lot turned up. Paddies. Four or five of 'em."

Samuel, who had been listening on an extension line, said, "What makes you think she's gone back to Liverpool?"

"She'd been talking about it to the other girls. I think she had a letter from her mum."

"One of you had better watch her flat. Take it in turns. If she shows up, report back. But no further action until we tell you."

When he had put down the receiver he said, "I don't like it."

"What's wrong with it?" said Manfred. "We told the boys to throw a scare into her and they've done it. Not quite the way we intended, I agree. But if she really has gone home to mum, that's what we wanted, isn't it?"

"*If* she keeps her mouth shut."

"She knows what'll happen to her if she doesn't."

"Maybe," said Samuel. "I still don't like it. It happened too conveniently. Those men being on the spot."

"There are a lot of Irishmen in that area. They work in the leather market and the goods depot at Bricklayers Arms."

"I know," said Samuel. "I know."

Manfred looked at him curiously. He had a respect for his brother's instinct, but on this occasion he seemed to be stretching it. He said, "We know Julie's address and we've got friends in Liverpool. Why don't we ask one of them to go out to her house tomorrow? He'll find out soon enough if she's there."

By the time the eight-twenty Inter-City train from Euston reached Lime Street Station, Liverpool, Julie was three parts asleep. She stumbled out on to the platform and wandered down it, trailing behind the other passengers. She was trying to work out exactly what she was going to say to her mother and how she was going to explain her arrival in the middle of the night equipped only with the contents of one large handbag.

It was some seconds before she realised that the man with grey hair was speaking to her. He said, "You are Miss Marsh, aren't you? I'm Detective Inspector Lander. This is my warrant card. Oh, and the policeman in the booking hall will identify me, if that'll make you happier. A lot of people don't know what a warrant card looks like anyway."

"I'll believe you," said Julie. "What do you want?"

"We thought it might be useful if you'd agree to come along to the Station and make a short statement. After that we could run you home. You won't find it too easy to get a taxi to take you out to Litherland at this time of night."

It took Julie only five seconds to make up her mind.

It was at about six o'clock on the following evening that Sergeant Milo Roughead said to Petrella, "I think I've got it, sir."

"Measles, the D.S.O., or a ticket to the Police Federation Ball?"

"None of those," said Milo. He was relieved to note that Petrella's customary good humour seemed to have returned. "It's an idea."

"I'll buy it. But it had better be good."

"This idea is absolutely top line. Do you think that Lloyd and Lloyd might have been set up as cleaners?"

"Come again."

"It's an idea the Mafia developed in America. They get hold of a lot of hot money through narcotics and prostitution and gambling and things like that. But they also control a few absolutely straight businesses as well. Places that keep books and have bank accounts. They feed the dirty cash into them and it comes out the other end on a nice clean respectable bank statement."

Petrella thought about it. He said, "How exactly would it work in this case?"

"If the people at the top are in the wage-snatch game they must be lumbered with a lot of banknotes. Not always new, like those tenners they passed off on you. Usually old small-denomination stuff. All the same, they can't just turn up at a bank with a sackful of them and say, 'Credit this to my private account'. Not without a few questions being asked. So they pass it on to Lloyd and Lloyd. They do most of their buying for cash. That means the stuff gets well spread out. When they sell, they take a cheque in the ordinary way and pay it into their bank. How to wash your money whiter than white in two simple processes."

"Then you think Lloyd's in it himself?"

"I think he must be, sir. And another person who'd have to be in the know was the chap who did the legal work of buying and selling. If he wasn't in the game he'd be bound to ask why all the purchases were for cash and the sales were paid for by cheque."

"Bernie Nicholls," said Petrella. In the march of events during the last six weeks he had almost forgotten that body, face downwards on the frozen foreshore of the river.

"What about Adams?"

"I should think he was put in by the Tillotsons to keep an eye on Lloyd. I don't mean that they actually distrusted Lloyd. But it must have been handy to have their own creature in the organisation too. He'd be under their thumb, because they knew about his record."

The more Petrella thought about it, the more sense it made. He said, "I'm not sure how we're ever going to prove it, but I think you're right."

"Can we tie the Tillotsons to it?"

"We can tie the Tillotsons to the wage snatches all right," said Petrella. "We can tie them with three sweet little clove hitches. Their names are Sandra, Avril and Jayne. They all work, or pretend to work, for Tillotsons (Middle-East) Agencies. Let us suppose that you are the personnel manager of Corinth Car Parts. You need a secretary to work in the accounts department. You advertise. Past experience has shown you that you won't get many applicants and will probably have to fall back on paying an exorbitant fee to an employment agency. However, to your surprise and delight an applicant turns up who has every qualification, is prepared to accept the wage you offer without quibbling, and, as an extra which must appeal to a susceptible personnel manager, happens to be a very attractive-looking girl. What do you do?"

"I hold my breath," said Milo, "and ask for a reference from her last employer."

"Her last employer is Tillotsons (Middle-East) Agencies. They give her a glowing reference. They are very sorry to lose her. She is only leaving them because she finds the journey to work difficult."

"And did this actually happen?"

"It happened three times. Sandra, who is a blonde with shoulder-length hair and green eyes, joined Corinth Car Parts in the autumn of the year before last. They lost a large wage packet in early November of that year. She was back at Tillotsons by Christmas time. At about that date Avril, a brunette with a snub nose and a page-boy cut — you'll find her photograph, it's numbered 1, in that folder —"

Milo examined the photograph with appreciation. He said, "Let me guess. She joined G.E.X. and left them shortly after their wage snatch in April."

"Absolutely correct. And Jayne — she's the red-head — No. 2 photograph, joined Costa-Cans in May, and was back in the nest by October."

"Who's Number 3?"

"Her name is Julie and she comes from Liverpool. I think she must be on probation. As far as I know they haven't loosed her on British industry yet. They must be saving her up for the next job."

Milo was examining the three photographs. He said, "Those are the three girls who are currently at Tillotsons, I take it."

"Correct. Lampier photographed them as they were coming out to lunch last week."

"Then where is Sandra?"

"If we knew that," said Petrella, "we should know where the *next* big wage snatch was going to take place." On these words Petrella's desk telephone gave a buzz and Station Sergeant Cove said, "I thought you might like to know, Superintendent Watterson's on his way up. He's got the top brass with him."

Petrella said, "Thanks, Harry." And to Milo, "I don't suppose they've come to give us a Valentine. You'd better clear out."

Commander Baylis came straight to the point. He said, "The general manager of G.E.X. Engineering put in a report that one of your men had been round at his place asking questions. He wanted to know what it was all about. So do I."

Petrella said, "You might have had similar reports from Corinth Car Parts and Costa-Cans, sir. Sergeant Ambrose visited all three."

"Would you mind explaining why."

Petrella did his best.

"And who authorised you to investigate these three wage snatches?"

Petrella said, "I wasn't investigating the wage snatches. I was investigating two men called Tillotson. I arrived at them in the course of an enquiry into the affairs of Lloyd and Lloyd, which was authorised by you personally."

Watterson said, "You remember, sir. This arose indirectly out of the death — suspected murder — of a man called Nicholls."

"Precisely," said Baylis. He said it in the pleased tone of a small man about to score a small point. "Correct me if I'm wrong, Superintendent; but I understood that the body in question was not found in this Station area at all."

"You're right," said Watterson. "By a matter of a hundred yards. It belonged to Loveday, at Borough."

"Then will you please hand it back to him."

Petrella was now as angry as Baylis. Disregarding a warning look from Watterson, he said, "Since Lloyd and Lloyd *are* in my area I assume I'm allowed to continue my investigation into their affairs."

"Then you assume wrongly. To the best of my knowledge, and I have had quite a lot to do with them, Lloyd and Lloyd are a perfectly respectable firm. It is not my job to allocate your duties, but if I was in Watterson's place I'd instruct you to attend to more serious matters — confining your attention to your own Station area."

He stalked out, leaving Petrella and Watterson staring at each other.

"What on earth's biting him?" said Petrella.

Watterson blew his nose in the peculiar trumpeting manner which Petrella recognised as meaning that he wanted time to think. He said, "If it was just the wage snatches, Patrick, I could understand that. They're S.C.S. jobs and he's not even allowed to touch them himself. So you can imagine he wouldn't be too pleased at you butting in. But warning you off Lloyd and Lloyd just doesn't make sense."

Sergeant Blencowe put his head round the door and said, "Sorry to interrupt, but I thought you ought to have this at once. Owers just found Mr. Lloyd in an alley off the Cut. Head smashed in. Whoever did it dragged the body into a doorway and covered it with sacks. Owers spotted his boots."

"Well now," said Watterson. "That's different. It's in your area, isn't it?"

"It certainly is."

"Then I don't see how anyone can object if we investigate this one, do you?"

Part IV

St. Valentine's Day

St. Valentine's Day was cold, but bright.

By nine o'clock Petrella was at the Kentledge Road Mortuary. The Coroner's officer took him through the public offices, into the long back room with overhead fluorescent lighting where the body of Jimmy Lloyd, stripped of all clothes and all human dignity, lay on a slab.

Dr. Summerson came out of a room at the back wearing a white surgical gown and pulling on a pair of thin rubber gloves.

He said, "Good morning, Patrick. Q Division are keeping us busy these days." And to the mortuary assistant, "Hand me those scissors, would you, Fred. I'd like to get some of the hair away. Then we can take a proper look at the damage."

Petrella watched him at work, snipping away the dank grey strands of hair and swabbing off the blackened blood. He had watched too many post-mortems to be badly upset, but it usually took a minute or two for his stomach to settle.

"Not much external bleeding. A very deep impacted fracture, about an inch to the right of the centre of the rear occipital dome. Did you get that, Lucy?"

Petrella realised that he was speaking to his secretary, who was in the back room taking notes. She said, "How many 'c's'."

"Two for preference," said Dr. Summerson. "Wonderful girl, but can't spell her own name. I am removing a number of splinters of bone and will place them separately in an envelope marked L/A. I can now see into the wound which seems to me — " a pause for probing, " — to be just over two inches deep at its point of greatest penetration. Would you care to have a look at it, Patrick?"

Petrella peered cautiously into the cavity. He presumed

that the grey matter at the bottom of it was brain tissue. He said, "What do you suppose did it?"

"It wasn't anything very sharp. Nothing like an ice pick, for instance. More like the blunt end of a hammer. Judging from the point of impact and the direction of the blow the man who hit him was several inches taller than Lloyd, right handed and standing almost directly behind him. We may know a bit more when the laboratory has finished with these bone fragments. They'll pick up traces of rust, things like that."

When Petrella came out, the Coroner's officer had the contents of Mr. Lloyd's pockets arranged on the table. A packet of Senior Service cigarettes and a Ronson lighter. Three felt-tipped pens, one black, one red and one green. A cheque book. A fat black wallet with a rubber band round it. Two dirty handkerchiefs, a bunch of keys and a pile of loose coins. In the wallet, fifteen pounds in notes, a number of different credit cards, two uncashed cheques for small amounts, a new book of stamps, with one stamp missing, and a photograph of two small girls with the words, "For Grandfather" written on the back.

"Better list them and let me have a copy," said Petrella. There was an odd-looking coin among the loose change. When he picked it up he saw that it was a polished metal disc with a hole in the middle.

"Shove ha'penny," said the Coroner's officer. "Poor old Jimmy. He must have been pretty pissed if he put that in his pocket in mistake for a tenpenny piece."

"I'd better give it back to its owner," said Petrella. His next call was at the Wheelwrights Arms, where he was let in by the side door. Mr. Elder identified the metal disc as his property and said, "Poor old Jimmy. I wouldn't have been surprised if he'd walked off with the dart-board actually."

"Was he as drunk as all that?"

"He wasn't drunk. He was just — I don't know — he wasn't with it at all."

"What exactly do you mean?"

"Well — he came in about eight o'clock and asked for a

double Scotch, and took it over to a table in the corner, and put it down and seemed to forget about it."

"You mean he just sat there?"

"That's right. Until Charlie Cousins went over to talk to him. Then he seemed to remember it was there and drank it off quickly. Charlie came back to the bar for another round and said, 'What's up with old Lloyd? He isn't making much sense at all.' However, as I said, he wasn't drunk. One or two other people went across to chat him up and they got him playing on the shove ha'penny board. He seemed to be going a bit better at that point. Then, quite suddenly, right in the middle of a game, he said, 'I'm sorry, lads. This isn't my night,' and walked straight out."

"What time would that have been?"

"About half past ten."

"Did you get any idea what was wrong with him?"

"Not from anything he said. It did put me in mind of Jimmy Wilson. You wouldn't remember him. It was before your time. He came in here one evening and behaved just like that. Walked out at closing time and threw himself off Tower Bridge. Of course, we only found out afterwards his wife had been killed in a car smash that afternoon."

The telephone at the back of the bar rang. Mr. Elder lifted off the receiver, listened for a moment and said, "It's for you."

It was Sergeant Blencowe. He said, "I'm round at Lloyd's office. The girls are in a bit of a flap. Adams hasn't put in an appearance."

Petrella said, "I'll be right over."

When he got there he found the two girls in the outer office twittering with the pleasurable sort of excitement which is produced by a crisis for which you have no sort of responsibility. In the inner room Sergeant Blencowe was talking to the sad solicitor, Mr. Lampe. Mr. Lampe said, "I heard the shocking news about James Lloyd and I came straight round. I really don't know what to do. Since Nicholls died I've been handling Lloyd's business myself. There were half a dozen outstanding matters which had to be cleared up. My conveyancing is a bit rusty, but luckily they were none of them too complicated. Straight sales and purchases. One of them was due to be completed this morning. The purchase of the stock of a sweet shop and tobacconist."

"For cash?" said Petrella.

"Why, yes. It was for cash. Most of Mr. Lloyd's purchases seem to have been made that way. I confess I thought it rather curious."

"And you were coming round here to collect the money from Mr. Lloyd."

"Mr. Adams usually dealt with matters like that."

"I see," said Petrella. It was confirmation. "I suppose the cash was kept in some sort of safe."

"It's next door," said Blencowe. "And some sort of safe is right." They all went into the adjoining room. The green and gold monster was set solidly into the brick-work of what had once been a fireplace.

"You wouldn't open that with a bent hairpin," said Blencowe.

"Who's got the keys?"

"I asked the girls," said Blencowe. "Old man Lloyd had one set. Adams had the other."

"Nip down to the mortuary," said Petrella. "There was a bunch of keys on Lloyd. I'll give them a ring from here and tell them you're coming."

Blencowe was back in ten minutes. There was only one key that looked like a safe key. Petrella slid it into the lock with an odd feeling of anticipation. It turned smoothly. He pulled down the handle and swung the heavy door open.

There were three shelves which held a few bundles of deeds and leases, carefully tied in red tape. The space under the bottom shelf was occupied by a locked steel drawer.

"That's where the cash was always kept," said Mr. Lampe, who was peering over his shoulder. Petrella found the right key pulled open the drawer. It was empty.

He said to Mr. Lampe, "You were coming round here, you told us, to collect the cash to complete this purchase. How much was it?"

"Nine hundred pounds."

"And you've had cash from here before."

"Oh yes. Several times. Once nearly two thousand pounds. I told Mr. Lloyd that it was foolish to keep it all here, even in a modern safe like this. The insurance companies are apt to make trouble about that sort of thing."

"How much do you suppose he had here at a time?"

"It's difficult to say. I remember Nicholls telling me that he once paid out five thousand pounds in five-pound notes."

"The cupboard's bare now," said Blencowe.

Petrella said, "Take a car and go straight out to Blackheath. You know Adams's address. If he's there, invite him to come back with you to the Station. If he won't come, telephone me. But don't let him out of your sight."

"And if he isn't there?" said Blencowe.

"I'd like to know that, as soon as possible."

There was something else at the back of his mind. It was connected with the bunch of keys. Something which might be important. It was no good trying to force it. Either he would think of it, or he wouldn't.

Manfred looked at his watch, and said, "Five past eleven. He isn't often late on a time call."

"He may have been held up," said Samuel. "Any news of that girl?"

"Nothing but good news. She hasn't been out of the house this morning."

"She might have been talking on the telephone."

"She might have been," said Manfred. "*If* the house was on the phone, which it isn't. I told you you were worrying about nothing."

"I don't worry about nothing," said Samuel. "What I worry about is things I can't understand."

"Such as — ?"

"Such as what happened yesterday evening. I had a word with young Mason. He was driving the car and he got out to help his brother. He was a bit more honest than Chris. It wasn't five or six Paddies. It was just three of them."

"Three?"

"That's what he said."

"And they walked away from them. Why?"

"What he said was, he thought his brother was right to pull out. He said, suppose we'd started something, and the police had turned up and we'd all been pulled in, who was going to handle the job today?"

"Justifiable."

"Justifiable," agreed Samuel. "But quite untypical. Those boys hit first and think afterwards."

"You've got some idea in your head about it," said Manfred patiently. "Let's have it."

"People like the Masons, who live by violence, get a sort of instinct about the opposition. Either it's amateur or it's professional. If it's amateur, they go in happily and knock hell out of it. If it's professional, they think twice."

Manfred was about to say something when the telephone rang. He said, "That'll be Adams. And about time too."

It wasn't Adams. A woman's voice said, "Is that the Water Board?"

"I'm afraid you have the wrong number," said Manfred. The woman was still apologising when he rang off.

"He's gone," said Blencowe. "Packed up late last night and pulled out. It's one of those old houses, carved up into flats. The sort of place where everyone knows what everyone else is doing. The old codger on the second floor says he heard him arrive about eleven o'clock, by taxi. What really interested him was that Adams kept the taxi waiting. For about half an hour, he says, whilst he banged about upstairs. Then he came out, with a suitcase in either hand, climbed into the taxi and drove off. The lady on the first floor heard him, too. He woke her child up when he slammed the front door. She was very cross about it."

"I don't suppose, by any chance," said Petrella, "that anyone heard where he told the taxi to go to."

"Certainly they did. They all had their windows open by that time. He told him to go to Victoria."

Petrella said, "I think we've got enough to put out an all stations call."

"Could be out of the country by now."

"I don't think so," said Petrella. "He wouldn't find a boat train at that time of night. I think Victoria was bluff. He's gone to earth somewhere."

He rang through to Division, found Watterson there, and explained what had happened. Watterson listened carefully and then said, "If that solicitor is prepared to say that there was normally a very substantial amount of cash kept in that safe, of which Adams had the only other key, and if he's disappeared and the safe's empty, we should be able to justify a general call. They have to alert the various exit points as well. It's quite an elaborate operation. I'll get the wheels turning."

Petrella put down the telephone and started to work out timings. Adams had decided to quit, no doubt, because he saw himself going the same way as Bernie Nicholls and old Mr. Lloyd. He had grabbed whatever money was in the safe and left his flat. So far, so good. But what had happened next?

There was no train with a cross-Channel connection after ten o'clock at night. On the other hand, there were night flights from Heathrow. If Adams had made his preparations in advance — and he was the careful sort of man who might well have done so — he could by now be almost anywhere in the world.

It was at this point in his reflections that Petrella's sub-conscious got through to him with its message. It might have been some vague connection between "all the countries in the world" and a stamp album he had possessed in his youth, or it might have been simple coincidence. A new stamp book, with one stamp missing. He said to Blencowe, "What time did you leave your flat this morning?"

"Eight o'clock," said Blencowe.

"Had the post come?"

"Doesn't arrive till half past eight earliest."

"Telephone your wife and ask if there's a letter for you."

Blencowe looked surprised, but went out to his own room.

He was back in a few minutes and said, "Bang on the nail, Skipper. Local postmark. Timed seven o'clock last night. What's in it — a bomb?"

"Something of the sort," said Petrella. "Get hold of it quickly. Take the car."

They were finishing reading the letter when Watterson arrived. They showed it to him and he read it in silence. It was two sheets of Mr. Lloyd's office paper covered on both sides with Mr. Lloyd's cramped handwriting and it contained a full and exact description of the money cleaning activities which he and Adams had been carrying out for the Tillotsons during the past five years. Names, dates, the lot.

Watterson was silent when he had finished reading. Something seemed to be worrying him. Petrella said, "When he wrote that he knew he was for it. And he just bloody well didn't care." There was a further moment of silence. Petrella said, "I hope they catch Adams before he gets out of the country."

Watterson said, "I had to put your request for an all stations alert through District. They turned it down."

Petrella felt himself going red. He said, "Baylis turned it down? What the hell's he playing at?"

Watterson looked at Blencowe, who removed himself quietly from the room. Then he said, "That's right. Baylis turned it down personally. Half an hour ago. That's what I came to tell you."

"He realised that Adams was most probably leaving the country?"

"He had all the relevant information."

"And he doesn't want him stopped?"

Watterson didn't answer this immediately. He had known Petrella for a long time, and had worked directly with him for nearly a year. He knew him to be a cool and controlled person, persistent where persistence was needed, but not stupidly obstinate. A man who would be guided, ninety-nine times out of a hundred, by reason and not by passion.

But he also knew that Petrella's father was Spanish, being high up in the Spanish Intelligence Service; and that there was, deep down inside Petrella, normally kept under lock and key, a black Iberian demon. He himself had seen it in action only once. It was a sight he had not forgotten.

Since Petrella seemed to be waiting for an answer to his last question he said, "All I can tell you is that District refused to sanction your request for a general alert and a port watch. And that the refusal came personally from Commander Baylis."

"No reason given."

"Not to me."

Petrella said, "I see." His voice was controlled again, but it was the control of a fury which was now cold rather than hot. He thought for a moment, and then said, "A short time ago Adams came into this room and offered me a bribe. It was a large bribe and well wrapped up. He said that if I kept my eyes and ears open for possible clients for Lloyd and Lloyd he would pay me twenty-five pounds a week, with commission on top. He seemed surprised when I turned it down. What he didn't know was that the whole conversation was taped. You can hear it if you like."

"I'll take your word for it. What does it lead to?"

"It leads me to wonder how much he was paying Commander Baylis."

Watterson said, without any inflection of either surprise or anger in his voice, "The fact that Adams tried to bribe you doesn't prove that he succeeded in bribing Baylis."

"It doesn't prove it," said Petrella. "But consider the facts. First, he's got a very expensive wife. You told me so yourself. Second, he personally blocked any further investigation into the affairs of Lloyd and Lloyd. A very respectable firm he called them; you remember?"

"Did you tape that conversation as well?"

"No. But you heard it. And wouldn't, I imagine, deny it."

"Go on."

"Finally he's stopped us taking the most obvious and elementary steps to catch Adams. Why? There can only be one reason. He doesn't want him caught. Because if he's caught, he'll talk. And now that Lloyd's dead, Adams is the only person who can incriminate Baylis."

There was a long silence, in which they heard a car in the street outside run into another car and a furious row start up. Neither man so much as glanced at the window.

At last, Watterson gave a sigh which seemed to let a lot of air out of his lungs. Then he said, "What do you propose to do about it?"

"There's only one thing we can do. We shall have to go over his head."

"When you say 'we' are you proposing that I should support you?"

"I don't need your support. I only ask you to forward my request."

"You realise that you're putting your own head on the block. Unless you can prove what you're saying, prove it to the hilt, you're finished in the police."

"I don't think," said Petrella coldly, "that I should care to remain a member of a force that could let Baylis get away with this sort of thing."

"Always supposing that you're right."

"I'm right," said Petrella. "And you know that I'm right."

"What makes you think that?"

"If you hadn't known I was right, you'd have started shouting the odds long ago."

Watterson managed a faint smile. He said, "An application to see the top brass normally takes time. But it can be expedited. I'll see what I can do."

Petrella walked from Waterloo Station, down York Road, through the deserted forecourt of County Hall and over Westminster Bridge. He found the action of walking useful when he wanted to think.

A message had come through at midday. It simply said that the Assistant Commissioner would see him at ten minutes to three that afternoon. Petrella had spent most of the interval putting the case against Commander Baylis into logical order. In the form of notes, it now covered two sheets of foolscap, neatly folded and slipped into the breast pocket of his coat. He was under no illusions as to what lay ahead. The man he was going to deal with had been a barrister before he became a policeman. He had a coldly logical brain and a tongue which was feared from one end of the Metropolitan Police to the other.

This was the reason for the notes. Not that Petrella had any intention of producing them and reading from them. He had learned them by heart. They were in his pocket as a form of talisman.

As he reached Parliament Square, Big Ben showed twenty minutes to three.

The Tillotsons sat together in Manfred's drawing-room. It was five minutes since either of them had opened his mouth. Then Manfred said, "You're still worried about something. Is it that girl?"

"Julie?" said Samuel. "No. I don't think she can do us any harm now. I was wondering about Adams."

"If he knows what's good for him," said Manfred, "he'll be out of the country."

Silence fell again. Samuel looked at his watch and said, "They should be going in now. We'll hear, one way or another, inside fifteen minutes."

A moment later, when the bell rang, he instinctively put his hand out for the telephone. Then he realised that it was the door bell.

"Were we expecting visitors?" said Manfred.

"Not to my knowledge," said Samuel. "I'd better go and see who it is."

His brother said, "It's probably the lady who thought we were the Water Board."

"You're to go straight up," said the uniformed Sergeant in reception. "Lift to the second floor. Someone will be waiting for you when you get there."

Someone turned out to be a girl with a severe hair style and the sort of look which defied anyone to take liberties with her in business hours. He followed her obediently.

The room they went into was a surprise. It was certainly

not the Assistant Commissioner's office. It had more the look
of an operations room in an army or air force headquarters.
There were two policemen with telephone headsets on. They
were seated on high stools in front of a very large plan moun-
ted on a board, and occupying most of one wall. As far as
Petrella could see from where he stood it covered a short
length of road and the approaches to some sort of building.
It might have been a factory. There were a number of dif-
ferent-coloured counters attached to the plan; eight or ten of
them were blue, one rather larger one was green and there
were three red ones in a row along the bottom. When one
of the policemen moved a blue counter, apparently in answer
to a telephoned instruction, he saw that they must be
magnetised.

There was also a wireless installation, with a loudspeaker,
which crackled suddenly and said, "The opposition is arriv-
ing. Three small vans, two coming in from the main road on
the west. One from the side road on the south-east."

The policeman moved the three red counters into position.

The Assistant Commissioner, who was seated in a swivel
chair at the head of a long bare table, said, "No blue car
to move until I give the word. The green can come in now to
the main entrance and start normal unloading."

The wireless operator said, "Green move up and unload."

"Blue four, five and six close up gently to Point 'A'."

The men on the board were using both hands now to shift
the counters.

It was like the moment in Fighter Command headquarters,
thought Petrella, remembering a film he had seen. The
moment when all forces were committed.

Two of the three red counters had closed on the green
and the other was coming up fast.

"All blue cars move now," said the Assistant Commissioner. "And the best of luck to all concerned."

One of the policemen on the telephone said, "They seem
to be putting up a fight, sir."

"Splendid," said the Assistant Commissioner. "I never mind
a fight when the odds are three to one in our favour." The

policeman grinned. There was a general relaxation of tension. The Assistant Commissioner seemed to notice Petrella for the first time. He said, "I'm afraid you caught us at a busy moment. Come along to my office."

When Samuel reached the front door he took the precaution of looking first through the small viewing glass. A large tweedy lady was standing in front of the door with a sheaf of papers in her hand. She put up her hand and rang the bell again with a touch of impatience. Samuel opened the door and had started to say, "What can I do for you," when the lady placed one of her sensible shoes in the opening to prevent him closing the door and two men, who had been standing flat against the wall on either side of the door, jumped forward, knocked the door open and surged through.

The Assistant Commissioner said, "That job you were watching was at Warfields, the big building contractors. I expect you know their place out on the M4. It would have been a record haul if they'd got away with it. Warfields have a big Middle-East job on and the money was to pay off the wages of all the English sub-contractors."

Petrella said, "It seemed to go very well, sir."

"Very well indeed. Two of our men were hurt. Four of theirs. Nobody killed. However, that's by the way. What I really wanted to tell you was why I blocked your request for an all stations call and port watch for Adams."

Petrella nearly said, "So it was you who blocked it," but realised, in time, that he was on very thin ice.

"There was no need for anyone to look for Adams. We have him in very safe custody. He's working for us. I don't mean that he's a policeman in disguise. We bought him, three months ago. We had to pay quite highly to secure his allegiance. But I think it was worth it. For instance when he joined us last night he brought with him, from Lloyds' safe, the total proceeds of the Costa-Cans snatch. A lot of it is new notes and some of the other notes have bank markings on them. First-class evidence."

Petrella said, "Yes. I quite see that."

"I've read Superintendent Watterson's report."

Now for it, thought Petrella.

"I'm always telling our people that you can't keep criminal investigation in tidy pigeon holes. This sort of thing is always happening. You approach a matter from one direction. The S.C.S. approach it from another. There's bound to be overlapping. It's the price we pay for specialisation. However, I think we can clear up both ends now. We've not only got Adams's evidence available to us, we've got a very useful statement from Miss Marsh in Liverpool. That's one of the advantages the S.C.S. enjoy. They aren't starved of manpower. They had forty men on the job, at one time and another. All Tillotson girls were under constant supervision. That's how we knew in advance about the Warfields job, of course."

Petrella said, "I suppose both the Masons were involved in it."

"Certainly. They had ten men taking part. We had thirty. Now that the Masons are inside, some of the others will start talking. We may even be able to pin the Nicholls and Lloyd killings on to them. It'll be a long hard fight once the lawyers get going. But I fancy we shall get there in the end."

This seemed to be the cue for Petrella to leave; but the Assistant Commissioner had something else to say. He seemed to be picking his words very carefully.

He said, "I should not have bothered to explain all this to you personally, Inspector, if I had not had a very good report about you from Superintendent Watterson at Division and Commander Baylis at District. You understand?"

"I understand perfectly," said Petrella. "And thank you very much."

As he was walking back across Westminster Bridge he took out two sheets of foolscap paper and tore each of them into sixty-four pieces. Then he threw them over the parapet. A brisk St. Valentine's Day breeze caught them and fanned them out and the tiny paper snowflakes floated down and landed on the broad bosom of the Thames.

Captain Crabtree

IT WAS THE moment when spring turned into summer. The showers of April and the warm sun of May had brought up a bumper crop of weeds along the roadways and wharves of what had once been a busy dock.

"The union found new jobs for the dockers," said Petrella. "The lesser characters had to shift for themselves. The gatemen and clerks and tea-boys and runners." He was talking to Detective Sergeant Milo Roughead. Once Petrella had got used to the attitude of disenchantment with which Eton cloaks its pupils he found himself discussing many of his problems with him. Lower Dock was a problem.

"So what did they do?" said Milo.

"A lot of them went back to sea. As deck-hands, engine room assistants, stewards, or cooks. It was the family tradition. In their own way, sailors are just as cliquish as miners and dockers."

"And the ones who didn't go back to the sea?"

"There was an alternative occupation open to them," said Petrella sadly. "Crime. Not so much the actual lifting. The disposal of the proceeds. If you hand the stuff over to a fence, what's the going rate? Twenty-five per cent of the value, if you're lucky. And always a chance that the fence will shop you, to save his own hide."

"You sound like a disillusioned burglar," said Milo. "What's the alternative?"

"Ship it abroad. You can get good prices in Ostend,

Amsterdam and the Hague, for the sort of stuff they were lifting; jewellery, gold, old silver, watches, guns, cameras. And less chance of discovery all round. It only needed organising."

"Do we know the organiser?"

"I know his name," said Petrella. "He's a gentleman called Captain Crabtree. And that's all anyone does know about him."

"How do we know that much?"

"About six months ago someone lifted a collection of gold coins and medals from Carfews. It was shipped abroad, no question about it. The insurance reward was so big that if the stuff had been in this country someone would have 'found' it for sure. The night after it happened three young tearaways got lit up in a pub down by the docks. One of them — his name was Fred Carling — said, 'No one's going to see that little lot again. Captain Crabtree's looking after it.' One of our snouts was in the bar and heard him."

"It sounds a bit thin to me," said Milo.

"You haven't heard the end of the story. Next day when Fred turned up at work, he had two lovely black eyes and a tooth missing. Now, the point is that Fred is a pretty fair lightweight boxer. To mark him like that would have needed several people. Say, two to hold him and one to hit him. *And Fred never made any complaint to anyone.* He accepted his punishment and he accepted it without a squeak."

"Just like a public school, really," said Milo.

Captain Crabtree came under discussion at the conference which was held every Monday at District Headquarters. Chief Superintendent Watterson was in the chair.

"He's running a regular export agency," said Petrella. "There are dozens of ways of getting round the Waterguard and the Docks Police. They can't search every member of the crew every time he goes on board. And if they don't want to run even that risk, there's nothing to stop them postponing delivery until the ship's been cleared and is lying off, waiting for the tide. Run a small boat out to her. If all the crew are in the game the officers won't know a thing."

"What makes you think it's organised on that scale, Patrick?"

"Our fences are beginning to squeak."

Watterson guffawed. He found it difficult to get upset over the troubles of receivers of stolen goods.

"They've probably got a union," he said. "Why don't they go on strike?"

"It's no laughing matter, sir," said Petrella. "You know as well as I do there are only two ways we catch thieves. Either someone squeaks and there's not much chance of that here — "

"They're a tight-lipped crowd," agreed Chief Inspector Loveday, who looked after the Borough.

" — Or we trace the actual goods back to them. But if the stuff's all going abroad, we lose that chance as well."

But Watterson was in too good a humour to allow himself to be depressed by Petrella. He said, "There's a third way of catching them, Patrick. Luck."

It happened that same evening.

The two boys had taken a lot of trouble over getting into Mr. Plowman's pawnbroking establishment. Barry had a brother who had worked there for a few months, and had found out all about the alarms on the doors and windows; alarms which sounded in the charge room at Patton Street Police Station, two hundred yards away. Rex had had the idea. There was an empty office above the dry-cleaning establishment two doors along from Plowmans. They had broken into this in the quiet hour before the pubs shut and had then waited patiently. They knew that the police patrol went past at one o'clock and again at five. It gave them four hours.

A trap door at the head of the stairs took them up on to the roof. After they had watched the one o'clock patrol go by they crawled along the leads, fastened the rope they had brought with them to a pipe and climbed down again to first-storey level. This brought them opposite the window of Mr. Plowman's office, which was over the shop. They had to take a chance on whether an alarm had been fixed to this window. There hadn't been one when he was there, Barry's

brother said, and he was usually reliable about things like
that. Barry kicked in the glass with his foot, slipped the
catch and they climbed through. The door into the passage
was locked, but since the lock was on the inside this was no
great obstacle. Five minutes later they were in the shop itself.

Here there were drawers and locked showcases to be dealt
with. The work was slow because they had to keep out of the
direct line of sight from the shop window, which was brightly
lit all night; a form of advertisement which Mr. Plowman
thought worth the electricity bills he incurred.

It took three hours to fill the satchels they had brought with
them. Rex said, "What about that little lot, eh? Just for
finishers."

It was the window display. Engagement rings, ladies'
watches, earrings and brooches. All good stuff, guarded only
by a sliding glass panel, held in place by a tiny lock.

"Pity to leave it," said Barry. It had been half an hour
since anyone had gone past in the silent street outside. "Break
the glass, grab what we can and scarper. Right?" He swung
the heavy case-opener which he had been using.

This was when their luck deserted them. The breaking of
the glass set off one of the alarms. They heard the car coming.

"Out," said Rex.

They raced upstairs, slinging the heavy satchels round their
shoulders as they went, climbed out of the office window and
dropped into the yard behind the shop at the moment that
the police car squealed to a halt in front of it and three men
tumbled out.

Sergeant Blencowe, who was an experienced man, said,
"Two of you round the back, quick." He then got busy on
the car wireless and called up two more cars.

What followed was a game of chess. The boys knew the
board, but Sergeant Blencowe knew the moves. Ten breathless minutes later one of the three police cars cruising along
West Road spotted two figures scuttling down East Bank
Street, alongside the Creek.

"Got 'em now," said the driver and spoke briefly on his
wireless. The area between the Creek, the river and the

abandoned dock was, as he knew, a cul-de-sac. Two of the cars blocked the only two roads in as the third shot down East Bank Street in pursuit.

But the boys had disappeared.

Ten minutes later, when Sergeant Blencowe was scratching his bald head and swearing, a launch of the Thames Division on routine patrol saw two objects bobbing in the water. The Sergeant in charge swung his spotlight and identified them as two sleek heads.

"Odd time to have a bathe," he said.

"No law against it," said Barry as he was hauled aboard. They were taken to Leman Road Police Station and searched. Nothing was found on either of them.

"All the same, we're taking you in," said the Sergeant. He had been listening in on the Q Division net.

On the following afternoon, Petrella strolled down East Bank Street with Milo Roughead.

"We had to let them go," he said. "No one got a clear identification. All they could be charged with was midnight bathing, which isn't a crime yet."

"I suppose they dumped the stuff in a friendly house," said Milo. "They'd just have had time if they were quick."

"I expect they did," said Petrella. "And if we could get two hundred search warrants, we might find it. Or again, we might not." He stopped to watch a game of hopscotch that was being played on the pavement under the generalship of a red-haired girl of nine. None of the children took any notice of them.

Petrella said, "As a matter of fact, I'm not so interested in where they put the stuff. What I'd like to find out is where they went into the river. They hadn't got time to do anything elaborate like picking locks or cutting their way through barbed wire. The launch picked them up off the East Quay, a few minutes after they were seen running down this street. They must have gone almost straight into the water and it can't have been much lower down than this. The tide was on the ebb. They couldn't fight current and tide. They'd just go down with it and pretty fast. They must have gone in two or three hundred yards *above* where they were picked up."

"Not many possibilities," agreed Sergeant Roughead. The strip of ground on their left, between East Bank Street and the Creek, belonged to a marine engineering works. It had a high wall topped with broken glass. When they reached the point where the Creek ran into the river, the road swung to the right. On their left was a line of derelict houses, guarded by a fence of corrugated iron sheets, the tops cut into points, an awkward obstacle to surmount even in daylight and with the help of a ladder. A hundred yards along were the railings of the deserted dockyard, topped by a treble row of barbed wire.

"We've come too far," said Petrella. "If they did go in here, the current would have carried them a lot farther down. We'll go back."

At the point where East Bank Street turned through a right angle and ran along the river there was a gate in the wall which they had overlooked, with a board on the wall beside it. The lettering was weather-worn and was difficult to read.

"The Church of St. Barnabas, Lower Dock. Holy Communion on Sundays at 8 a.m. Evensong at 6.30 p.m." And underneath, "Arthur Sabine M.A., Rector."

"Good Lord. Yes," said Petrella. "That's old Sabine's church. Let's have a look at it."

They pushed open the gate, which had neither lock nor bolt, and saw in front of them, on the rising ground, at the point where the Creek ran into the river, a space of well-mown grass and in the middle of it a small, neat building topped by a disproportionately high spire. The construction was red brick, weathered to the colour of old burgundy, with ashlar-work corners.

"One of Wren's pupils, wouldn't you say?" said Milo.

"My knowledge of church architecture is as slight as I guess yours is," said Petrella coldly. "Anyone who put up a church in these parts three hundred years ago would be certain to copy Wren."

"Some of it isn't three hundred years old," said Milo, unabashed. "That ashlar work's been renewed lately. Must have been an expensive job. Good endowments, do you think?"

"Or a generous congregation," said Petrella.

The west door swung easily on its hinges. There was nothing dim and religious about the interior. The word which came into Petrella's head was "ship-shape". The windows, which had evidently suffered in the Blitz, were plain glass with a few coloured lozenges let into them. Through them the afternoon sun glinted on the brasswork and was reflected from the well-polished woodwork of the pews. Some of the memorial tablets on the walls were old, but the armorial devices and the lettering had been freshly picked out in black and scarlet and gold.

"I hope that the brightness of the colouring does not offend you."

The Reverend Sabine had come in very quietly. His appearance matched his church. His white hair was neatly brushed, his face glowing with a serenity which was firm and secure but not soft.

"I had an expert here from Winchester recently. He persuaded me that the tablets and effigies in our churches were originally all brightly and cheerfully coloured. By the time the colours wore off people had forgotten what they once looked like. Or perhaps they associated bright colours with Roman Catholicism. At all events, they let them fade. An epitome of our lives, wouldn't you say? When we are young, everything is bright. As we grow older, things turn to grey."

Petrella said, "I like the colours very much, sir. I like the whole church. Is it very old?"

"It was built in 1670."

"By a pupil of Wren's," said Milo hopefully.

"Certainly not. By the master himself. Do you remember that poem — the one which suggested that Wren sited his churches so that ships coming up river could see — how does the line go? 'A coronal cluster of steeples tall'. I'm certain that's why he chose this precise spot. Our spire may not be tall, but it must have been one of the first which the sailors saw."

"This has always been a seafaring parish?"

"Indeed yes. Many quite well-known sailors are laid to rest here. You are interested in local history?"

Petrella said, "I think I ought to introduce myself." He did so.

"Do I gather that you are here on business?"

Petrella explained what had brought them there. The Reverend Sabine said, "What you suggest is perfectly possible. I never lock the gate, or the church for that matter. It sounds risky, but in fact I have never lost anything." He was leading the way out as he spoke. "The boys could have run straight down the lawn here, past my boat-house — that, incidentally, I *do* lock up — and dived straight into the river. If they are local boys, I don't doubt they can swim like fishes. They spend half the summer in and out of the water."

The bank of the river had been built up here against the winter floods and was capped with a flat wall of stone.

"At half past four this morning the tide would have been just on the ebb. There'd have been another two foot of water. It would have been a safe dive for a boy."

"I expect that's what happened," said Petrella. "It would fit in well with the point they were picked up at. Thank you very much. I'll come back some time and have a proper look at your church, sir."

"You'll be very welcome," said the Reverend Sabine.

As they were walking back up East Bank Street, Milo said, in a voice which he tried to keep carefully non-committal, "I suppose you noticed, sir—?"

"If you mean," said Petrella, "that the Reverend Sabine seemed to know the time the boys dived into the river, a point which I had *not* mentioned — "

"That's it, sir. Didn't you think it was odd — ?"

"I didn't think it odd at all. I imagine that everyone in this neck of the woods knows exactly what happened last night. Every detail of it. You have to remember that Lower Dock is not simply a neighbourhood or a parish. It's a family."

The red-haired young lady suspended her bossing of the hopscotch players long enough to catch his eye and wink at him.

Barry and Rex were drinking in the private bar at the back of the East Indiaman. They were as pleased with themselves as any two young men who had done a good night's work for which, in due course, they would receive a fair reward. They had both had a number of drinks, but neither of them was drunk.

"Christ," said Rex. "Here comes Soapy. What does *he* want?"

A small thin man, with the look of a bookmaker's runner, was pushing through the crowd towards them.

"Pretend we're not here," said Barry. He swung his chair round and presented a broad back. Soapy was not upset. He annexed a third chair, dragged it to their table and sat down.

"I want to talk to you, boys," he said.

"We're not boys," said Barry. "We're girls in drag."

"You ought to be ashamed of yourself," said Rex, "accosting two young ladies in a public house."

"I've been brought up respectable," said Barry, "and I intend to stay that way. Now you are here, could you lend me a touch of powder for my nose, dearie?"

Soapy said, "Very funny." He didn't sound amused. "That was a nice job someone pulled at Plowmans last night. I see in the papers he claims he lost twenty thousand quids' worth of stuff. Mind you, I expect he's laying it on a bit, for the insurers."

"I expect he is," said Barry. "Why are we supposed to be interested?"

"I thought you might be, seeing I happened to be down East Bank Street early this morning and saw you two run past."

"That's right," said Rex. "We often take an early morning run. We're in training for the Olympics."

"And I suppose you always run carrying a couple of bloody great satchels each."

"It's part of the training schedule," said Barry, but his eyes were wary.

"The same as your early morning swim — like you told the fuzz when they picked you up."

"That's right," said Rex. "It's a special pentathlon event. The other three events are putting the weight, tossing the caber and kicking people who butt in where they aren't wanted."

As he said this he shifted his chair slightly away from the table.

Soapy said, "There's no point in getting tough. I know what you done with that stuff. I want it. I'll give you a fair price for it. But I'm going to have it."

"Just suppose," said Rex, "for the sake of argument I mean, just suppose we had any idea what you were talking about, and just suppose we told you to get stuffed."

"I don't think you mean that."

"Why not?"

"Because if you took that attitude, I'd feel obliged to go and see the gent concerned myself. Of course, I'd have to say I got the tip from you. I don't think he'd be best pleased."

The two boys looked at each other, and then rose simultaneously to their feet. Soapy shifted his chair back. He didn't think they were going to attack him, but his right hand was on the taped hilt of a knife which lived in a leather sheath strapped to the outside of his right leg and which could be drawn quickly through his trouser pocket.

The boys seemed more amused than angry. Rex said, "Why don't you do that?" Barry said, "I'm sure you'll forgive us if we push off now. Athletes like us have to get to bed in good time."

Soapy sat staring after them. His suggestion ought to have scared them. He was worried that they should simply have been amused.

The Reverend Sabine answered the bell himself and stood gazing down enquiringly at his visitor.

"My name's Lidgett," said Soapy. "You don't know me."

"Are you the one the boys call Soapy?"

"Some of them do. It's a sort of nickname."

"I didn't imagine that it was your baptismal name," said the Rector. "What can I do for you, Mr. Lidgett?"

"I wanted to have a word with you."

"I have fifteen minutes to spare before the monthly committee meeting of the Women's Institute."

"That should be enough," said Soapy.

He followed the Rector into his study. The open spaces between the bookcases were crammed with photographs. One of them showed a much younger Sabine pulling an oar in a racing eight.

"Oxford, many years ago," said the Rector. "Won't you sit down."

Soapy perched himself on the edge of one of the upright chairs and cleared his throat. He found some difficulty in beginning. However sure you may be of your facts it is difficult to accuse an ordained clergyman of being the head and organiser of a ring which exports stolen goods.

The Reverend Sabine gave him no help. He listened impassively to what Soapy had to say. When he had finished, he said, "You seem to have been telling yourself some extraordinary story, Mr. Lidgett. What do you propose to do next?"

"I can tell you what I'm *not* going to do — unless I have to. I'm not running off to the police."

"I asked you what you *were* going to do," said the Reverend Sabine gently. "Not what you weren't."

"I've got a proposition. You cut me in for twenty per cent and I'll keep my mouth shut."

"I call that very generous," said the Reverend Sabine. As he spoke he was unlocking the drawer of his desk. Soapy wondered what he was looking for. It turned out to be an indexed notebook.

As he turned over the pages he said, "I've been a very long time in and around South London parishes. My first living was at the Elephant. Then I had a spell farther east at Catford. Then I ended up here. All rough areas. I enjoyed every one of them. And I made a lot of good friends." His fingers seemed to have settled on the letter "P." "Peddie. That was the one I was looking for."

"You know Jim Peddie?" said Soapy. There was a very slight catch in his voice.

"Jim's the younger brother. The one I was thinking of was Peter Peddie. The one they called Peter the Painter."

The Reverend Sabine had found the number he wanted and reached for the telephone.

"Look," said Soapy. "I think maybe you didn't quite understand what I was getting at."

"I understood you perfectly," said the Reverend Sabine. "You wanted to cut yourself in for a fifth share of some illegal profits you imagine I am making, and were threatening to report me to the police unless I co-operated. Am I right?"

"I didn't offer no threats," said Soapy. His voice was agitated.

"It sounded very like one. Oh — is that you, Lisa? Father Sabine here. Is Peter with you? I see. And I could contact him there this evening? How is everything with you? I was sorry to hear about Ronnie. Yes, I saw it in the papers. Come over and have a cup of tea and we'll talk about it."

He listened for a few moments to what the woman at the other end was saying and then replaced the receiver. Soapy was staring at him with a look of fascinated disbelief.

"Was that Mother Peddie you were talking to?"

"That's right. I shall be having a word with Peter this evening."

Soapy passed a tongue over lips which seemed suddenly to have gone dry.

"What are you going to tell him?"

"I shall tell him," said the Reverend Sabine, without any trace of humour in his voice, "that you have been annoying me. That sounds like Mrs. Partridge and the committee of the Women's Institute. I'm afraid you'll have to go now, Mr. Lidgett."

"I've had an idea," said Detective Sergeant Roughead. "Suppose Captain Crabtree was a real person."

"The idea had occurred to me," said Petrella. "And we got the checkers at Central on to it. It was complicated by the fact that 'Captain' could be a military or a naval title. To say nothing of the fact that lots of people call themselves 'Captain' without any real right to do so. They made a pretty fair job of it. There wasn't anyone round here who fitted in remotely with the sort of person we're looking for."

"Suppose he's dead."

"If he's dead, he can't be running a smuggling racket."

"It was just an idea I had."

"If you have ideas like that," said Petrella, "you work at them in your own time. Try the Free Library. It's got a useful section on local history.

When he left his house in the Cut that morning Soapy Lidgett had an uncomfortable experience. He spotted a business acquaintance on the other side of the street and hailed him. He was certain that the man heard him, but instead of coming across to talk, he dived down a side street and disappeared. Another man whom Soapy had met brushed straight past, apparently without seeing him.

Matters came to a head in the East Indiaman, when he went in for his midday drink. There was a party of four men, with half-filled glasses, seated at a table at the far end of the room. Soapy walked across to join them. One of the men saw him coming and said something. All four gulped down their drinks, rose to their feet and departed without a word.

Soapy was so upset that he left without ordering a drink for himself. He had an uncomfortable feeling that if he had done so the landlord might have refused to serve him.

He knew, now, what had happened.

The word had gone out against him.

Milo said, "I think I've found him, sir."

"Found who?"

"Captain Crabtree."

"All right. Let's have it."

"I've copied it out. It was in Palgrave's *South Bank*

Worthies. Charles Hannaford Crabtree. Came of humble parentage. His father was reported to have been a pork butcher, who amassed a considerable fortune at the time of the Great Plague. I thought that sounded rather gruesome, sir."

"Cut out the commentary, Sergeant. Just let us have the facts."

"Yes, sir. Charles was educated at the school in the Charterhouse and joined the navy as a gentleman volunteer in 1680. He attained the rank of Post Captain in 1703 and left the navy on the death of his father. Being the only surviving son he inherited the family business, which he expanded greatly into the importing and exporting side. He became a generous benefactor of all local charities and died in 1742, greatly respected by all who knew him."

"Importing and exporting," said Petrella thoughtfully. "It might be worth following up. I'd like to know more about him."

"I'm afraid that's all there is."

"Palgrave was only a collator. He usually gives references. See where he got his stuff from. Then have a look at the original works."

"Suppose they aren't in the library."

"The Library of the British Museum," said Petrella patiently, "has a copy of every published book. Don't they teach you anything at Eton?"

When Soapy left the East Indiaman he walked slowly in the direction of his house. He needed time to think. It was a few minutes before he got the impression that he was being followed. There were plenty of people about in the High Street. It was impossible to be sure.

He dived down a side turning, covered twenty yards almost at a run and then stopped. Nobody seemed to be following him. Fifty yards farther on the road he was in turned to the right. Then it turned to the right again and he found himself back in the High Street.

As he emerged, a young man bumped into him. Soapy

leaped back. The young man looked surprised, said, "Sorry I'm sure," and crossed the road to the opposite pavement. Here he was joined by a second young man, who said something which made them both laugh.

Soapy kept an eye on them as he moved off. They made no attempt to cross the road, but seemed to be keeping level with him on the opposite pavement. They were not in sight when he reached his front door. He let himself in, bolted the door behind him and stood for a moment, sweating.

He could hear his housekeeper, Mrs. Catterick, grumbling to herself in the kitchen. She seemed upset.

"Turning the place upside down," she said.

"Who did?"

"Those two men. I ought to report them. They got no right."

"*What* men?"

"Inspectors they called themselves. From the Gas Board. Had half the floor up."

Soapy held on to the door jamb to support himself. He said, "Just what did they do?"

"I dunno what they did. That's up to them, isn't it? They know their job, I suppose. Tracing a leak they said."

"And you let them do it?"

"What did you expect me to do?" said Mrs. Catterick with a show of spirit. "Throw them out? Where are you off to now? Your dinner's in the oven."

"I'm going out," said Soapy.

Milo presented his card and was shown into the great circular reading room at the British Museum. He said to the attendant, "Have you really got every book here that's ever been written?"

"Not on the shelves," said the attendant indulgently. "That's just a selection. Might be a hundredth of what we've got in store. You'll need one of those forms." He explained the procedure for obtaining books.

Milo handed in his completed form at the central counter and sat down at one of the desks. He had never imagined such a room. Maybe a hundred students, some with a dozen or more books in front of them. What obscure and esoteric subjects could they be reading up? The grey-haired matronly woman? The attractive girl with horn-rimmed glasses balanced on the end of her pert nose? The old man with a face like a goat?

Petrella had been hoping to get away early to take his wife out shopping. Three times he thought he'd made it, three times the telephone had thwarted him. This time it was Station Sergeant Cove.

"It's *who*?" said Petrella irritably.

"Lidgett, sir. Soapy Lidgett."

"What does he want?"

"What he says he wants," said Sergeant Cove impassively, "is police protection."

"He must be joking."

"You wouldn't say so. Not if you'd seen him. *And* he wants the Gas Board to inspect his house, to see if someone's left a bomb under the floor boards."

"I suppose I'd better find out what it's all about."

"Please yourself," said Sergeant Cove. "Speaking personally, I wouldn't worry if someone did Soapy up in a sack and dropped him in the river."

Soapy started talking as soon as he came into the room. Sergeant Cove had been right. The man was scared silly. Out of a jumble of words he gathered that he had been followed and threatened and that his house had been visited.

"Who by?"

"It's them Peddies."

At this Petrella did sit up. Peter and Jim Peddie and their families were a by-word in South London for genial brutality. They operated from Catford and were not Petrella's personal headache, but he knew their reputation.

"Why would the Peddies be bothering you?"

"I don't know. Honest to God, I don't, Inspector. I never done nothing to them."

"They wouldn't be bothering you unless you'd bothered them somehow."

Soapy shook his head. "Someone's been telling lies. That's all I can think."

"What have they actually done?"

It didn't seem to amount to much. People wouldn't talk to him. Men on the other side of the street. Gas Board looking for a leak.

"I don't see that we can do anything on that sort of evidence. If they start something, we'll crack down on them quick enough."

The telephone on his desk buzzed at him. He picked up the receiver, listened for a moment and then covered it with one hand.

"You'll have to run along. Have a word with Sergeant Cove. He'll get the man on the beat to keep an eye on your house." As soon as the door had shut behind him, he said, "Go on, Sergeant."

"I thought you ought to have this right away, sir. *Captain Crabtree was buried in St. Barnabas Church.* He'd contributed pretty handsomely in his lifetime and they gave him a private tomb. The book says, 'Students of mid-eighteenth century memorial sculpture will be interested in this tomb which stands against the south wall of the Lady Chapel. It shows the deceased recumbent, with his head on a pillow adorned with his personal armorial devices and his feet on a representation of a ship of war.' Hullo?"

But Petrella had gone.

He parked his car twenty yards short of the gate as the clock of St. Barnabas Church struck six.

At that hour, the streets were empty and quiet. The latch clacked loudly as he raised it. There was no one in the churchyard, or in the church. It occurred to Petrella, as he walked down the aisle, that if his suspicions were well-founded, it would have been sensible to have brought a couple of men with him. Too late now.

Captain Crabtree's tomb filled a lot of the floor space in the tiny Lady Chapel. Prostrate on his bed of stone, the face of the sailor-merchant looked up at him. Some forgotten craftsman had chiselled those life-like features, the masterful nose, the pursed lips, the triple chins, folding into a heavy neck.

There'll be some catch that holds the lid shut, thought Petrella. But it was only the weight of the lid and the recumbent figure which kept it down. Using all his strength, he raised it six inches.

It was enough for him to see that the interior was completely empty.

As he lowered it, the Reverend Sabine said from behind him, "You must be stronger than you look, Inspector. I know very few men who could lift that lid single-handed. If you want to look inside I could give you a hand, and we'd get it up all right."

"Thank you," said Petrella. He was still getting his breath back. "I could see that it was empty."

"Quite empty, alas."

"What happened to the Captain?"

"His coffin was stolen many years ago. The thieves would have been after the lead lining. No doubt the bones were dropped into the river. It's very handy for the disposal of unwanted objects. An undignified ending for one of our great benefactors. But I don't imagine that the Captain minded."

"I don't suppose he did," said Petrella. "What I was wondering about was whether this very convenient receptacle had been used for quite different purposes since."

"I can see that you have some theory about it. I suggest we move into the vestry and discuss it there. We shall be more comfortable."

The vestry, being on the north side of the church, and possessing only a single narrow window, was already in half darkness. The Rector switched on an overhead light and closed the heavy door behind him. He said, "Please sit down and tell me what is in your mind."

"I was interested," said Petrella, "in a comment which was reported to me some months ago. It was about a collection of stolen coins. One of the young men who was thought to have stolen them, said that the coins were quite safe, 'because Captain Crabtree was looking after them'. We were puzzled as we knew no one of that name in the district."

"But now you have solved the puzzle."

"I think so, yes."

"You have concluded that the thieves were using his empty tomb as a cache."

"A temporary cache, before they continued on their way out of the country. It is the second stage of their journey which would need careful organisation."

The Reverend Sabine smiled. It was a broad, relaxed smile, with no artifice about it. He said, "Break it to me gently. You concluded that I was the organiser."

"It seemed a possible explanation."

"Might I guess that Mr. Lidgett — Mr. Soapy Lidgett — has been talking to you?"

"He saw me this afternoon. And made certain allegations. I thought the least I could do was to put them to you."

"Suppose for a moment, Inspector, that Mr. Lidgett's fantasies were the sober truth. Would it shock you?"

The question was so unexpected that Petrella found himself fumbling for an answer. "Shock me?" he said at last. "No. It wouldn't shock me. Crime doesn't shock me. It's my business. You wouldn't expect a doctor to be shocked by disease."

"Let me remind you," said the Rector, "that the Roman Catholic Church, which is, in many ways, more logical than our own, decided some years ago that if religion was to be brought back as a genuine force into the lives of the people, priests must work much more closely with their flocks. They formed a guild of worker priests. Young men who spent their days in the factories and plants, in the mines and quarries, working alongside their own people."

"I think I read something about it," said Petrella. "But I haven't heard of it lately. Was it not a success?"

"On the contrary. It was too successful. The young priests became entirely imbued with the ideas of their parishioners. Ideas which were often Marxist, sometimes criminal. They undoubtedly exercised a great influence, but the Vatican could not accept the risks involved."

"You mean that the flock might corrupt the shepherd."

"They were young men. Young men are susceptible. It is only in very rare instances that a priest can descend from his pulpit, for six days in the week to live with and for his people, and reascend it on Sunday to give them the spiritual guidance which they need."

"I should have thought it was impossible."

"Curiously enough one of my ancestors seems to have achieved exactly that feat. He had a cure of souls at Cooling in the marshes. It was a small poor parish and the greater part of his people lived entirely by smuggling."

"And he helped them?"

"He did not help them. He led them. When the goods were landed, they were brought straight to the church. There was a convenient cache actually underneath the pulpit. But — and that is the point — it was from that same pulpit every Sunday that he preached the higher duties of Christian charity and faith."

Petrella said, "And he could do that although he was encouraging crime. As any man who acted in the way we have been discussing would also be encouraging crime. How could he square that with his conscience?"

"He would do so without difficulty. He would reflect that the people concerned would steal anyway and that all that he was doing was enabling them to obtain a fair reward for their labours."

Petrella was only half listening. A minute before he had thought he heard a footstep. Now he was certain. There was more than one man outside. He cast an eye round the vestry. The window was too narrow to permit of exit. It opened almost directly on to the river. As the Rector had said, very handy for the disposal of unwanted objects.

"You must look, too, on the positive side of the picture," said the Rector. "When I first came here the total congregation of this church was three old ladies. Now we have a regular attendance of over a hundred, many of them young people, an active parish council, an enthusiastic choir. *If this had been achieved by the methods that you and Mr. Lidgett are suggesting, would you not feel inclined to agree that the end justified the means?"

"No," said Petrella firmly. "I would not." He was certain now that a number of men had come into the church. He could hear the murmur of voices and even a quiet laugh. "Nor can I let this matter rest where it is."

"If I might advise you, in your own best interests, I think — I really do think — that you should regard the whole matter as closed."

Petrella stood up. He said, "Am I to understand that as a threat?"

The Reverend Sabine peered up at him in mild surprise. "A threat?" he said. "Why in the world should I threaten you? My meaning was, simply, that if you were to publish your theories to anyone else you would be in grave danger of being laughed at. Guardians of the law must never be laughed at. It is the one thing they cannot stand. And let me give you a further reason. Even if your theory was correct, it would be out of date."

"You mean," said Petrella slowly, "that if Captain Crabtree's tomb was used in the manner we have discussed, it will not be so used again."

"I mean that the matter would be out of my hands. I learned this afternoon that I have been appointed to the office of Archdeacon of Southwark. My work from now on will be very largely administrative. My successor here has already been nominated. He is, I believe, a thoroughly worthy young man and an enthusiast for the Boy Scout movement."

"I see," said Petrella.

"And in any event," said the Reverend Sabine, with something approaching an unclerical grin, "can you imagine that the word of Soapy Lidgett — and I can assure you that he would be your only witness — would have stood up against that of an Archdeacon elect of Southwark?"

Petrella thought about Soapy as he had last seen him. Even if he hadn't vanished altogether he would certainly refuse to open his mouth. It was an impossible situation. He would have to keep a close eye on the Reverend Sabine's successor though.

He said, "I take your point, Rector."

The Rector said, "I shall have to be getting along. Perhaps you would care to stay on for a little and listen."

"Listen?"

"To our choir practice." He led the way out into the church. The choir stalls were full of men and boys.

"I am sorry to have kept you waiting, gentlemen. Shall we start with the first of our evening hymns." He nodded to the organist, who played a soft chord.

"The day thou gavest, Lord, has ended," said the Reverend Sabine.

The Last Tenant

FRED JURY AND Johnny Tredgett would have described themselves, if they had thought of the word, as seasonal workers. They were prepared to tackle any job which called for muscle rather than brain power. Sorting and humping packages at the Crossways Goods Depot was their favourite occupation for the cold wet months of winter and early spring. With the turn of the year they liked to be out and about. They were not skilled enough to tackle the more sophisticated building trades but there was always rough work to be done; demolition, rubble shifting, drain laying and foundation digging. The local foremen knew them for good workers, with the bonus of a head for heights. They were seldom out of a job for long.

On this lovely April morning they were perched on a remnant of brick wall, sixty feet above the pavement, demolishing what had once been a snug little turret room at the top of a block of offices at the corner of Endless Street and Barton Street.

All that was left of the inner wall of the room was a fireplace with an imitation marble mantelshelf painted dark green and a mirror set in the wall above it. The three outer walls had already been demolished.

"Be a bit careful with that," said Fred. "Personally, I could use it myself. Go nicely in the front room."

Johnny slid the point of his pick into the plaster beside

the mirror. A lump came away but there was solid brick-work behind the plaster.

"Odd old way to fix a mirror," he said. He probed again. More plaster fell. The glass remained immovable.

He said, "If we can't shift her we'd better bust her, right? Don't want to be all day about it."

"Of course," said Fred. "Naturally, if you're looking for seven years bad luck, go ahead and bust it. Don't mind me. Just go right ahead. Bust it."

"That's a lot of bullshit," said Johnny, but he lowered his pick.

"My Uncle Arthur smashed a big looking-glass. Just after the war. Nothing went right for him after that. First his brother died. Then he got into trouble with the National Insurance for trying to steam the stamps off his brother's card and stick them on to his own. Then he got piles."

Fred, who had started scratching away at the other side of the mirror, said, "Take a look at that, will you."

The glass, it was now clear, was set in an iron frame. It was clear too, why they had been unable to shift it. The frame was hinged to a metal upright which was itself set in the brickwork. He said, "It's a sort of cupboard door really. The catch must be on your side."

Some more careful work with the point of the pick and the secret of the mirror was revealed. A small square of wood, painted the same colour as the plaster, came away. Under it was a keyhole in the iron frame.

"All we've got to do," said Johnny, "is get those bricks loose. We won't have no more trouble then." It took ten minutes to loosen the bricks all round the frame. Then they started to lever it out. As they did so, the foreman, who had climbed up behind them, said, "What are you two layabouts playing at? You ought to have had the whole wall down by now. God Almighty!"

He was staring at something Fred had picked out of the brick-lined cavity behind the looking-glass door.

Detective Chief Inspector Patrick Petrella was walking

to work. It was exactly a mile from his new flat to Patton Street Police Station and in fine weather the walk made a good start to a day most of which had to be spent inside his office. He was humming to himself as he walked. It wasn't just the weather. The wheels of existence seemed, for once, to be turning smoothly. There were encouraging reports on the progress of young-Petrella-to-be. A girl, this time, he felt sure. The rougher elements in his manor seemed to have declared an armistice for the moment. There was enough petty crime to keep them all from getting bored, but nothing which called for lengthy reports to Division or District. He had no reason to suppose that this happy state of affairs would last, but his years in the police service had taught him to live in the present.

In the charge room three men were awaiting his arrival, under the eye of Station Sergeant Cove. Two were tough cheerful youngsters in their working clothes. The third was an older man, a foreman he guessed. Stacked on the counter was a pile of cardboard boxes.

"Thought you might like to look at this little collection," said Sergeant Cove. "These boys just brought it along."

The largest of the boxes, an open shoe box, was crammed with banknotes, ones and fives in bundles.

"Haven't counted them yet," said Sergeant Cove. "But there must be more'n a thousand nicker there, wouldn't you say."

"A lot more than that, I should guess," said Petrella. He eased one of the bundles of fivers out of the box. They were packed so tightly that it was a job to get them out. There were forty notes in that bundle. Fred and Johnny watched him hungrily.

"Two hundred here. Must be three or four thousand altogether. What's in the other boxes?"

"Valuables," said Fred.

"Joolery," said Johnny.

It was good run-of-the-mill stuff. Gold chains and knick-knacks. Rings set with small diamonds and rubies. Wrist watches. Gold pens and pencils. Lighters, cigar cutters.

Everything looked new and unused. There was a necklace made out of linked gold coins that Petrella seemed to remember.

He said to the foreman, "We'll have to check these things in our lists. I've got a feeling that necklace is part of the stuff that was lifted from Adamsons last month. You did quite right to bring it along. We'll list it and give you a receipt."

The foreman said, "If any of it should be unclaimed, it was these boys who found it. They were knocking down the back wall of the very top room — "

"Easier to show me than talk about it," said Petrella. "Come on." The truth was he was glad of an excuse to get out into the sunshine again.

Ten minutes later he was wondering if he had been sensible. He had a fair head for heights. The real trouble was that there was nothing to hold onto.

"Easier if you sit down," said the foreman sympathetically.

"How on earth do you *work* up here?" said Petrella.

"Nothing to it, once you get used to it," said Johnny, balancing on a narrow ledge of brickwork and holding his pick in one hand.

After a minute Petrella felt better. He hauled himself up on to his feet, edged forward and peered into the cavity over the fireplace.

"How do you suppose it worked?" he said.

"Small square of wood," said Fred. "Fitted into the plaster, over the lock. Pick it out and undo the lock, always supposing you had the key. Then the mirror swings open."

It was a neat job and the steelwork looked new. Petrella said, "Who had this office, anyway?"

The foreman scratched his head and consulted his memory. "This'd be the turret room, wouldn't it? Fifth floor. Leo Hinn. Called himself an export agent."

"I wonder what he exported," said Petrella.

Later that morning he asked the same question of Mr. Tasker, the solicitor at the Oval.

Mr. Tasker said he thought it might have been hides or furs or something of that sort. Hinn wasn't a regular client.

He'd arranged the letting for him about two years ago. After some searching he found a thin folder of papers. There were two short hand-written notes on flimsy writing paper, with no address at the top and signed with a sort of hieroglyphic seeming to be made up of the letters L and H.

"He always signed his letters like that," said Mr. Tasker. "I had the devil of a job finding out where he lived. I finally tracked him down to a room he rents from a Mrs. Tappin in Pardoe Street. Number 46."

"Did he have a lease?"

"Of the office you mean? Certainly not. If you have a lease, you pay stamp duty. He was quite happy with a letter from the landlords telling him he could have the room and what rent he had to pay. I initialled it on his behalf."

"Who are the landlords?"

"At that time it was Fullbrights. A very decent old outfit. When Charlie Fullbright died last year they sold out to Lempard. Rather different sort of type."

"Different?"

"I don't mean bent. An eye to the main chance. All Lempard ever wanted with this particular building was to knock it down. Can't blame him really. Shockingly designed. Full of big hallways and corridors and a lot of air space taken up with turrets and battlements. He reckoned they could put up a modern building on the site with twice the lettable area. Offices on top, shops underneath."

"If he wanted to pull it down, I suppose he had to get rid of the tenants first?"

"That's right," said Mr. Tasker. "That's just what he did. He got rid of the tenants. It's a technique. You start by buying out the ground-floor tenant. You don't re-let. You just allow the ground-floor office to deteriorate. Maybe you board up the windows. The other tenants get a bit edgy. Perhaps another one pulls out. That gives you an excuse to lock up the main entrance. If there are only three or four tenants left, well, they can use the side entrance. Then the lift goes wrong. Of course, they're going to repair it, but it takes time. So the old gent who has the office on the third floor has to climb the stairs three or four times a day. It's surprising how quickly people take the hint."

"I see," said Petrella. It sounded dirty, but not quite criminal. "And he got them all out."

"He thought he had. Somehow he'd overlooked little Mr. Hinn, tucked away in his turret room. He was easy to overlook. Five foot nothing and no weight at all. As I was saying, Sam Lempard forgot about him. He made all his arrangements to pull the place down, signed up the builders, borrowed the money and was ready to press the button when someone said, 'Hold on a moment. What about old Hinn. Can't start work whilst he's there.' Talk about a row! He sacked his lawyers. Mellors and Rapp were acting for him at the time. Made out it was their fault, which was a load of nonsense. Then he tried to bully little Mr. Hinn. He wouldn't be bullied. Then he tried to buy him and he wouldn't be bought. Next he served a notice of dilapidation on him. There are agents who specialise in that sort of thing."

He mentioned a name and Petrella nodded. He knew them well.

"That was when Mr. Hinn came to me. I told him to ignore the notice. Tear it up. No court would enforce it. Not with the building in that state and going to be pulled down anyway. He didn't only tear up the notice. Dear me, no. He served a counter-notice on Sam Lempard, under the Landlord and Tenant Act, asking for a new tenancy. Ha! I enjoyed doing that for him."

"You say Lempard sacked Mellors. Who was acting for him?"

Mr. Tasker made a face and said, "Eric Duxford, who else?"

"Who else," agreed Petrella.

"He was in a corner. What with lay-off payments to the builders and interest on the money they'd borrowed, the delay must have been costing him a thousand a week and old man Hinn could have hung him up for three months, no question. Once the court heard the whole story — which I should have been delighted to tell them — he might even have got a new lease."

"So what did Lempard do?"

"I guess he did the only thing he could. Offered Hinn a really large sum of money. Too big for him to refuse."

"You *guess* that's what happened. But you don't know?"

"I don't know, because that's the last I saw of Mr. Hinn. He cleared out altogether. If you do find him, you might remind him that he hasn't paid my bill yet."

"When I find Mr. Hinn," said Petrella, "I shall have quite a lot of questions to ask him."

Samuel Lempard described himself as a property consultant. He had a handsome set of offices in Kentledge Road with a convenient rear exit into Kentledge Mews, where he kept one of his three cars. This enabled him to dodge importunate or indignant clients. He seemed unsurprised to receive a visit from Detective Chief Inspector Petrella. Word of what had happened on his building site that morning must already have reached him. He said, "It's a queer do. What do you make of it, Inspector?"

"It's a bit early to be certain," said Petrella. "We haven't had time to check out all the stuff yet. One bit, at least, is on the 'Recently Stolen List'. If it all turns out to be stolen goods, we shall have to assume that Mr. Hinn didn't confine his activities to dealing in hides and furs."

"A fence, eh?" said Mr. Lempard. "It doesn't surprise me a lot. He was a shifty little bastard."

"And took a bit of shifting," said Petrella.

Mr. Lempard's face showed a mottled red and Petrella could see the veins in his neck swelling. He said to himself, "By God, he *has* got a temper. He can't think of it, even now, without coming to the boil." The flush subsided slowly. As soon as Mr. Lempard could speak he grunted out, "So you heard about that, eh?"

"I heard about it. And I want to hear more about it."

"Where the hell do the police come into my business?" He was still angry.

"Not your business. Mr. Hinn's business."

Sam Lempard thought about it. Petrella imagined he could read his thoughts. Was there anything in it for him? He'd paid out good money to little Mr. Hinn. There'd been a boxful of notes in the cache behind the mirror. A lot of it was probably his money. Was this a chance to get some of it back?

In the end he said, "I don't see why I shouldn't tell you. You heard how he stuck me up. Straight blackmail. Prompted by Geoff Tasker, I don't doubt. In the end I paid him two thousand quid, in notes, and he signed the necessary document."

"A surrender of his lease."

"That's right. Duxford drew it up. Hinn came round here the same evening and signed it."

"What happened then?"

Mr. Lempard looked surprised. He said, "I don't follow you. He got out, of course."

"But what happened exactly? Did he clear all his stuff out and hand over the keys?"

"Now you come to mention it, that was a bit funny. Duxford and I went round the next morning. We found the door locked."

"So?"

"We broke it down."

"Wasn't that a bit irregular?"

"I don't see it. We'd paid the money. We could do what we liked with the place."

"And the furniture?"

"There were a few sticks there. Not what I'd call furniture." Mr. Lempard looked round complacently at his own massively furnished office. "A desk, two or three chairs, a bookcase with a few trade catalogues in it."

"What did you do with it?"

"We sold it. No point in paying storage charges."

The scholarly Sergeant Ambrose said, "We've placed all the stuff. It's the proceeds of three shop-breakings. We had

the proprietors round here with their records and they were
able to identify every piece. Adamsons, in the High Street,
Alpha Jewellery Sales in the Cut, and Hingstons. All the
watches and pens came from Hingstons."

"You mean we've got it all back?"

"No such luck. About a quarter of Hingstons and a third
of the other two."

Petrella thought about it. It was beginning to add up. He
said, "The M.O. people tipped Mick the Pat for all those jobs,
didn't they?"

"I have the relevant report here," said Sergeant Ambrose.
He could always produce the relevant report. Petrella wondered what they were going to do when Sergeant Ambrose
was promoted, as inevitably he would be, and removed to an
office desk at New Scotland Yard. "It was a definite identification. Method of entry. Timing. Method of neutralising the
alarms."

Petrella grunted. The *modus operandi* files were useful at
pointing the finger of suspicion. They were never conclusive
enough to justify an arrest. He said, "Irish Mick's a violent
character. But I wouldn't have thought he went in for
murder."

"Do you think Hinn's dead, then?" said Sergeant Blencowe,
who had been listening to the conversation.

"It must be a strong possibility. The first idea was that
he'd scarpered. That doesn't hold up. He was fencing Mick's
stuff for him. That's clear. If he'd got cold feet and decided
to scarper, he might have left the rest of the stuff behind,
but he'd surely have taken the money."

"Unless he had to get out so quick he couldn't reach the
money. If Mick thought he was being short-changed he'd have
been after him with a pick helve."

"For God's sake!" said Petrella. "The money wasn't
buried six feet down in the middle of a blasted heath. He'd
only got to open his patent looking-glass cupboard and put
the stuff in his pockets. I think we'll call on his last known
address. You can come with me, Sergeant."

Pardoe Street was composed of small semi-detached houses

which had been undistinguished when they were built and were now sliding into slumdom. The door of Number 46 was opened to them by a thin woman wearing an overall and carrying four empty milk bottles impaled on the fingers of her left hand. Mrs. Tappin, Petrella guessed.

He introduced himself and said, "I believe Mr. Hinn had rooms here. I suppose he isn't in just now?"

"Haven't seen him for more'n a month," said Mrs. Tappin. As she spoke she clanked the milk bottles on her fingers like castanets. Sergeant Blencowe watched her, fascinated.

"I suppose you've re-let the room."

"Can't do that. Paid up three months." Clank, clank —

"Then no one's been in it for a month."

"Just his friends."

"Which friends?"

"Two men. Big men." Mrs. Tappin demonstrated their size with a rattle on her castanets.

"I think we'd better have a look round."

"I expect that's right," said the woman. She deposited the milk bottles expertly on the top step. "After all, it's more'n a month. He might be anywhere by now, mightn't he?"

"He might indeed," said Petrella.

Mrs. Tappin led the way up three narrow flights of stairs. The first flight had a carpet on it, the second linoleum, the third nothing at all. She extracted a key from the mysteries of her upper garments and unlocked the door on the left of the landing and opened it. They all looked in.

"His friends seem to have been untidy sort of people," said Petrella mildly.

The place was in chaos. Drawers pulled out, furniture overturned, the carpet rolled back, books tipped out of shelves, pictures wrenched from their frames.

"Well, now," said Mrs. Tappin, "why would they want to do that?" She didn't seem unduly surprised. A life spent letting rooms in Pardoe Street must have made her a difficult person to surprise. She picked up one of the chairs and stood it carefully on its feet. "I expect they were looking for something."

"I guess they were," said Petrella. He took a photograph out of his wallet. "Would that have been one of the men?"

"Could have been," said Mrs. Tappin. "I didn't notice him all that clearly."

"Had he got an Irish accent?"

"He might have had. I wouldn't want to swear to it in court."

"She recognised him all right," said Sergeant Blencowe. They were back at Patton Street. "She didn't want to say so, in case Mick came back and duffed her up. What a character! I must try it when I get home."

"Try what?"

"Playing tunes with milk bottles. Amuse the kids."

"You're not going to have much time for playing with your kids in the near future," said Petrella. "You're going to do a check-up on Mr. Hinn. Former places of work, family, pubs and eating places he used. Have a word with the Social Security. And try the Russian Orthodox Church down in Little Baltic. It's a long shot but Tasker said his family originally came from Lithuania or some place like that. You know the form."

Sergeant Blencowe agreed, gloomily, that he knew the form. It was not that he objected to hard work. But he knew Little Baltic, a huddle of factories, slaughter houses and skinning shops which stank even in cool weather and were full of men who jabbered in their own God-forgotten lingo.

The next thing that happened was the arrival at Patton Street of Irish Mick. Petrella had had dealings with him before and had once described him as honestly dishonest. He was a huge man (by Mrs. Tappin's units of measurement ten milk bottles in height and eight round the waist). He maintained a large family by his efforts at shop-breaking, being, for all his bulk, remarkably clever with his fingers and adept at inserting himself through the smallest of gaps.

Sergeant Roughead brought him up. He said, "Mick wants to see you, Skipper. He thinks we've got some property which belongs to him."

"It's the money you found, if it's the truth I've been told, at the premises of Mr. Hinn."

"Quite true," said Petrella. "We did find some money there. Quite a lot of money. You say it was yours?"

"He was minding it for me."

"Was he minding the other things as well?"

"Now what other things would those be?" said Mick, looking at Petrella out of guileless eyes of Irish blue.

"One or two little trifles. Someone seems to have removed them from jewellers' shops without going through the formality of paying for them."

"The world is full of dishonest craytures," said Mick. "I wouldn't know anything about that sort of thing. It's the money I was interested in."

"Have you any sort of proof it belonged to you?"

"Something in writing, you mean. Mr. Hinn couldn't write his own name. It's a known fact."

"If there's nothing in writing — " said Petrella. Mick made a very slight movement with his head. Petrella understood it. He said, "That'll be all for now, Sergeant." Sergeant Roughead removed himself unwillingly. He was a student of human nature and Mick was one of his favourite characters.

When the door had closed and Sergeant Roughead's footsteps had died away down the passage, Mick leaned forward, his large hands on Petrella's desk, and said softly. "If you'd care to spend five hundred pounds of that money."

"What would I buy with it?" said Petrella equally softly.

"I'll sell you the Pole."

Detective Superintendent Watterson said, "He's got a nerve. Five hundred pounds."

"For the Pole."

"For the Pole," agreed Watterson.

The Pole, sometimes referred to as Augie the Pole, was a man that both Watterson and Petrella would have given a lot of money to put away.

Neither of them had ever set eyes on him. He was a denizen of Little Baltic. He was an unknown quantity. He was a name.

It was a name which a number of people had cause to loathe and to fear.

There had been protection rackets before. Shopkeepers and restaurant proprietors had sometimes paid sums of money under threat that their premises would be disrupted if they refused. More often they had jibbed and asked for police protection. This had led, sooner or later, to a noisy finale and the temporary closing down of the racket. The Pole did not attack premises. He attacked families. Your wife was alone in the house whilst you went out to work. Did you fancy coming home at night and finding her unconscious on the floor with two black eyes and a broken rib? Or maybe you had children. Odd things could happen to children, particularly to young girls. One or two people had complained to the police. Nothing had happened to them, or their families, for several months. The Pole was a patient man. Then he had sent out two of his countrymen. They came, in the early dusk, wearing silk stocking masks and carrying axe-handles or cleavers and they broke up things and people. How many preferred to pay? Petrella had no means of knowing. The Pole never appeared himself. He sent his friends. Their best hope was that some day they would catch one of them red-handed and he might be induced to talk.

"If Mick could put a finger on him," said Petrella, "and give us some solid evidence, it'd be worth paying for."

"Paying for, certainly," said Watterson. "But five hundred pounds!" Petrella knew that the pounds disbursed to informers were counted in tens and twenties. Twenty-five was the most he had ever paid out himself.

"It's not as though it was coming out of police funds," said Petrella.

Watterson said, "That's all very well. Sooner or later someone's going to lay claim to that money. We can't just throw it around as if it belonged to us."

The next claimant arrived that afternoon, in the form of a stout little lady, tightly cased in old-fashioned black. She had read the story of Fred Jury and Johnny Tredgett's discovery. She was, she said, the lawful and only wedded wife of

Leopold Hinn. She laid her credentials on the table. They seemed to establish her identity.

She had parted from Leopold some years before, but there had been no divorce. Therefore, he could not lawfully have married again. Therefore, if he was dead, and had left no will, all his goods belonged to her.

Petrella said, "There are two difficulties. The first is that we don't know that he's dead. The second is that we have no means of being certain that the money you are talking about belonged to him."

"Of course it belonged to him," said Mrs. Hinn. "It was found behind a looking-glass in his office. It said so in the newspaper."

"Certainly. But he had been there for less than two years. It could have been left there by a previous tenant."

Mrs. Hinn said, "You are talking nonsense. No one would leave such money behind them, unless they were dead. I shall speak to a lawyer. He will make you give up the money."

A third claimant announced himself by telephone on the following morning. It was Samuel Lempard. He said, "I've been talking to my solicitor. In fact, he's here with me now. He says that when Hinn gave up — what's that?" Petrella could hear someone prompting him in the background. "Surrendered, yes. When he surrendered the lease he specifically surrendered the contents of the office as well. He's reminded me, that's how we were able to sell the furniture."

"And the document he signed actually says that?"

"In black and white."

"Have you got it there?"

"Right on my desk."

"I'd better come and look at it," said Petrella.

He was on the point of leaving when Sergeant Blencowe appeared. He said, "We've had a get-well card."

It was a dirty piece of paper, in a dirty envelope. The words on the paper had been printed in capital letters, in purple ink. It said, "Mick keeps his stuff in his mother's house in Gosport Lane. It's under the coal in the shed at the end of her garden."

Holding it in his hand, Petrella walked across to one of his
filing cabinets and took out a folder. It contained half a dozen
letters, all on dirty scraps of paper, all printed in capital
letters in purple ink. They were threatening letters which the
recipients had brought round to Patton Street.

"It's the Pole all right," said Sergeant Blencowe. "If he's
shopping Mick, he must have known Mick was ready to shop
him. When thieves fall out, eh?"

"Check up on that coal-shed first. You'll need a warrant.
If you find the goods there, pull Mick in." He thought about
Mick. "You'd better take a driver and another man with
you."

"Mick won't give no trouble. But if the stuff is on his
mum's premises, not on his, how are we going to charge
him?"

Petrella said, "He won't let his mother stand the racket.
He's fond of her."

He was thinking about Mick as his driver inched the car
through the thick traffic in Kentledge Road. He was thinking
about his two brothers, nearly as big as Mick, and about the
small white-haired woman who was the mother of the three.
He had a weakness for the Irish. He wished they had taken up
Mick's offer when he made it and gone after the Pole. It
would have been a lot more satisfactory that way round.

The policeman on point duty recognised the car and held
up the traffic for them whilst they turned into Kentledge
Mews. They squeezed in behind a large blue station-wagon
parked in front of an unmarked door which, Petrella assumed,
led up to Mr. Lempard's office. The door was locked.

He walked round to the front of the building and took
the lift up to the first floor. Here he found Mr. Lempard and,
lounging in a chair in front of the electric fire, his legal
adviser, Eric Duxford.

"Good of you to come round," said Mr. Lempard. "Have
a drink?"

"Not just now."

"Show him the paper, Duxford."

Eric Duxford uncoiled himself from the chair. He had a

long white face, made longer by a pointed beard. He smiled thinly at Petrella. He had been a thorn in the flesh of the South London police for twenty years.

"I think the wording is quite clear," he said. "It's at the top of page two. 'In consideration of the remission of any rental then due and a release from all obligations arising from his tenancy or occupation of the room on the fifth floor of Radnor House in Endless Street the tenant surrenders to the Landlord the said room and all fixtures fittings furniture and other contents thereof.' "

Petrella took the document across to the window and read it through slowly. He was particularly interested in the last page, which was some inches shorter than the other two. Ignoring Mr. Duxford's outstretched hand he walked across to Mr. Lempard, holding the paper so that the last page only was visible, and said, "You say that Mr. Hinn signed this in your office one evening."

"So he did."

Petrella could see the tell-tale flush creeping up again.

"And I see that you witnessed his signature."

"That's right."

"Which means that you actually saw him writing his name."

"That's right."

"Then why hasn't he done so?"

There was a moment of absolute silence. Mr. Duxford said, "I don't understand you, Inspector — "

Petrella swung round on him and said savagely, "I advise you to keep out of this," and swung back on Mr. Lempard.

"I'm going to ask you once again, and I advise you to be very careful about what you say. Did Mr. Hinn sign this document in your presence?"

Mr. Lempard seemed to be finding some difficulty with his breathing. In the end he said, in a voice so thick that they could scarcely make out the words, "Of course he bloody did. I told you."

Petrella pointed to the straggling letters "L. Hinn", stretching in an almost illiterate scrawl across the paper. He said,

"I suppose you thought that was how Mr. Hinn would write his name."

"Really, Inspector," said Eric Duxford. "I'm not sure what you're insinuating. It's well known that he was practically illiterate — "

"All that was known about him," said Petrella, "was that he chose to initial documents with a personal hieroglyphic. Quite a common practice in some countries. When he *did* have to write his name on an official paper for instance, he was perfectly capable of doing so." As he spoke he was laying on the desk in front of the lawyer the documents which Mrs. Hinn had produced. These were a form of application to the Home Office for naturalisation dated two years previously, a ten-year-old passport in their joint names and a certificate of marriage. Mr. Duxford stared at them, his face nearly as white as his client's.

"You will observe," said Petrella, "that not only does he write his name in a characteristic but perfectly legible hand, but he also spells it in the Nordic way, Hynn."

Both men looked at Mr. Lempard, but he seemed to be incapable of speaking.

Petrella said, "I must warn you that a very serious charge may be made against you. A charge of forgery. Mr. Duxford will advise you about your rights."

Mr. Lempard stared at him without speaking. Petrella could see his lips moving.

"What first gave you the idea that it might be murder?" said Watterson.

"It was a tiny thing," said Petrella. "When I told him he was likely to be charged with forgery, I'll swear his first reaction was relief."

"Try explaining that to a jury."

"And why did he cut off the bottom of the last page? Obviously because there were bloodstains on it."

"Always supposing he did cut it off."

"And look at those two tiny spots, close to the signature.

There. One of them looks almost like a full stop. If you hold them up to the light you can see a sort of reddish tinge."

Watterson held the paper up to the light and said, "*If* they're spots of blood the Laboratory will tell us quick enough. But suppose they are. What does it amount to? They could have come from a cut finger or a nose bleed. They don't add up to murder."

"I'm not sure that it was murder," said Petrella. "My guess would be that Mr. Hinn agreed to the money that was offered to him — or said he was going to agree. The document was got ready and when he went round to sign it that night he changed his mind. Perhaps he thought he could squeeze a bit more money out of the situation. Lempard's a big man and he's got a hair-trigger temper. I think he hit Mr. Hinn a lot harder than he meant, and found himself with an unsigned document and a dead man on his hands."

"Since you've been gazing into the crystal ball," said Watterson sourly, "perhaps you can tell me what he did with the body?"

"If the first part's right, there's not much doubt about the next bit. He'd pick the little man up, carry him down those private stairs and put him into the back of the station-wagon. He'd need a bit of luck there, but it was dark and there wouldn't be many people about in the Mews at that time of night."

"And then?"

"Drop it in the river, dump it in Epping Forest, bury it in his own garden."

Watterson thought about it. He said, "It's full of ifs and buts and guesswork and precious little hard evidence. I can tell you straight away that the Director won't underwrite a murder charge on the strength of one hunch and two drops of blood." He thought about it some more. Petrella waited patiently. He knew his man.

Finally Watterson grunted and said, "All right. *If* the Laboratory says these spots are human blood, we might have enough to justify a few precautionary measures. Lempard's house is in P Division. I could ask Haxtell to have it watched."

"I don't think he'll try to bolt," said Petrella. "He's got too much sense."

Many of his guesses were shortly to be proved right, but over this one he was wrong.

A month later, as proceedings leading to a charge of forgery ground slowly forward, with reports from handwriting experts and statements from Mrs. Hinn and others, Lempard decided to leave. He had made a number of discreet preparations and on a rainy night towards the end of April he drove to Heathrow Airport, unaware that a car was following him and that a telephone message had gone before him. The proceedings at the airport were brisk and, for Mr. Lempard, uncomfortable. He could offer no explanation of why he was carrying ten thousand pounds in Swiss notes under the lining of his suitcase and a quantity of small but very valuable diamonds embedded in two cakes of soap in his sponge bag.

A search warrant was now felt to be justified. The body of little Mr. Hinn was discovered, four feet down, in the rose-bed at the foot of Mr. Lempard's well-kept garden and Mr. Lempard was charged with his murder.

Mrs. Hinn's claim to the money was conceded. Grudgingly and after considerable pressure, she gave up ten per cent of it to the finders, Fred Jury and Johnny Tredgett, who spent most of it in a celebration party which ended with both of them in the cells of Patton Street Police Station, charged with being drunk and disorderly and assaulting the police.

Petrella took very little part in these final transactions. By that time other matters were occupying his attention fully.

Mutiny at Patton Street

IT WAS HALF past six and it was getting dark when the knock on the door came. Mrs. Milton, the wife of Fred Milton the bookmaker, was just lifting the kettle from the gas-ring to make tea. She called through to her twelve-year-old daughter, Sylvia, "Go and see who it is, love."

Sylvia put down the magazine she was reading and got reluctantly to her feet. Nurse Patricia had just slapped the face of young Doctor Fosdyke and it was clear that young Doctor Fosdyke, who was tall and dark and had deep blue eyes, wasn't going to take it lying down.

Mrs. Milton heard her daughter's high heels tittupping down the passage, heard the door open and then heard something that sounded like a scream quickly cut off. She put down the kettle and hurried back into the living-room, in time to be knocked down by a back-hand swipe across the eyes.

From the floor, she saw a second man come into the room carrying Sylvia. He had one arm round her body and a big hand clapped over her mouth and nose. Both men were wearing masks made out of nylon stockings.

The man who had hit Mrs. Milton, and who seemed from his build and general appearance to be the younger of the two, sat down and stretched out his legs. He said to Sylvia, "One scream out of you, and I'll kick your Ma's head in. Understand?"

Sylvia nodded. The man who was holding her let her go

and she slipped down on to the floor and sat there, sobbing quietly.

The young man swung one well-shod foot and hooked over a small table. A china dog, a glass vase and a framed photograph of Mr. and Mrs. Milton on their wedding day crashed together on to the floor. The young man then picked up the table, swung it round his head and pitched it into a dresser full of crockery.

Mrs. Milton had climbed back on to her feet. She was still dazed. She said, "What — " and stopped.

"Yes?" said the young man politely.

"Why are you doing this?"

"You'd better ask your old man when he comes home."

"Fred's never done nothing to you."

"That's right. He hasn't done what he ought to have done. He hasn't paid his dues. This your daughter?"

"Yes."

"How old is she?"

"Twelve."

The young man got up, walked across to Sylvia, put one hand down, grabbed the front of her dress, and jerked her up on to her knees. The dress ripped down the front.

"She's a big girl for her age, isn't she?"

Desperation in her eyes, Mrs. Milton bolted for the kitchen door. The young man pushed out a leg and tripped her. She fell forward, hitting her head on the door as she went down.

"Like I was saying — " said the young man.

In the room upstairs old Mrs. Milton, who was nearly eighty, had got out of her bed when she heard the smash of glass and china. She was not a fast mover. First she tottered across to the window and drew up the blind. Then she padded slowly back to the electric light switch by the door. She knew what she had to do. Up, down. Light off. Light on. A second terrifying crash downstairs. Off, on. Darkness, light. Off, on. Darkness, light.

Mrs. Robbins, who had the house which backed on to the Miltons', saw the agreed signal and ran for the telephone. When the two squad cars reached her house, she gabbled out an explanation. Sergeant Blencowe said, "On foot from here. You two with me, three round the back. Sharpish."

The older and larger of the two intruders put up a fight. It lasted for three seconds. Blencowe had a daughter of his own and was in no mood for picking daisies. He hit the man once, very low and, as he doubled up in agony, jerked a knee under his chin. The younger man had run for it and was half way out of the kitchen window when Lampier caught hold of one foot and started to twist it. As the man was forced over on to his back, Lampier brought the sash of the window down across his throat.

Fred Milton arrived as they were tidying up. The two men had been taken to Patton Street and Mrs. Milton was away being patched up in the Casualty Department of the local hospital. Sergeant Milo Roughead gave him a brief account of what had happened. When Mr. Milton had got over the first shock he said, "You'll put these men away?"

"For a long, long time," said Milo. "In fact, with a bit of luck, we might be able to pick up the rest."

"If you can do that," said Mr. Milton, who was short and fat, but not lacking in courage, "it'll be worth it. Almost."

"It'll be worth it quite," said Milo. "We won't need to bother your wife until the morning, but we'd like your daughter to come along and make a statement. I could drive her in my car."

"All right, Sylvie?" said Mr. Milton.

Sylvia thought it was quite all right. The Sergeant was tall and dark, like young Doctor Fosdyke, and had deep blue eyes. She was feeling better already.

"The older of the two," said Petrella, "is a man called Dimitri Ossupov. On this occasion he was a conscript, rather than a volunteer."

"That's his story," said Superintendent Watterson.

"Agreed. We've only his word for it. But I've got a feeling he might be telling the truth. He was in the leather business and was bought out by Augie the Pole. He got the money back to his family, who live on a farm near Cracow. I expect the Bank of England would be interested to know just how he did it. Anyway, he was planning to go back there and settle down to do a little farming. He was more or less ordered to come out on this last job to keep an eye on young Stanislaus. He's Augie's kid brother."

"I see."

"What I was thinking — "

"I know what you're thinking," said Watterson. "I could put it up to the legal boys. Evidence by an accessory. It's not a line they're too keen on. It might be worth it in this case."

"If it puts Augie away," said Petrella, "it will surely be worth it. He's a nasty customer."

Dimitri said much the same thing to Sergeant Blencowe. He seemed to bear him no ill-will for loosening two teeth in his lower jaw.

"He will be mad," he said. "Quite mad. That young brother of his, Stanislaus. He was ver' fond of Stanny."

"No accounting for tastes," said Sergeant Blencowe. "I thought he was a nasty little sod."

Dimitri considered the matter and nodded his head in agreement. "He is a nasty little sod, yes. But not as nasty as Augie."

It was at the third of these discussions that the proposition finally took shape. Blencowe reported it to Petrella.

"*If* we could guarantee to get him out of the country, he'd stand up in court and give us the works. Enough to put Augie and Stanislaus and two or three of the worst of his friends away for a long time. It's a lovely set-up they've got down there in Little Baltic. It's not just money from honest citizens like Milton. That's almost a side-line. They collect a regular levy in cash and kind from their compatriots who work down there. Skin money, they call it."

"Skin money?"

"That's right. You've got a choice. Which would you rather part with? Your money or your skin? Remember that body we pulled out of the river a month ago. There wasn't enough of him left to identify him. Dimitri says it was a new arrival from Lithuania who refused to pay up. They flayed him alive before they put him in the river."

Petrella took a deep breath and said, "It's time we finished them."

He was in his office late that same afternoon, writing an urgent recommendation to Division to this effect, when his telephone rang. He had two lines. One went through the Station exchange, the second was a direct line. The number was known to a few very private informers who wanted to talk off the record.

"Detective Chief Inspector Petrella?"

"Yes."

It was a thick, gravelly voice. The laboured enunciation, with equal stress on each syllable, suggested a foreigner who had learned most of his English out of books.

"I have a suggestion to make to you, Inspector. Tomorrow morning Stanislaus Volk and Dimitri Ossupov will appear before the Magistrate for a further remand. They will be transported in a police tender. There will be a driver and a policeman in front. There will be only one man in the back. This will be thought sufficient, since they will be handcuffed."

"Any other arrangements you'd care to suggest?"

"The man in the back will be you. Stanislaus will succeed in slipping off his handcuffs. They will have been inefficiently fastened. At a moment when the vehicle is halted by the traffic he will hit you, hard enough to put you off balance and will make his escape. He will be out of the country by that evening."

"Haven't you forgotten Dimitri?"

"Dimitri you may keep. I have no further use for him."

"That's very generous of you. But if you don't mind, I think we'll keep both of them. The general opinion is that Stanislaus will get ten to fourteen years. He shouldn't have touched that girl."

The voice at the other end said, in the same deliberate tone, with the words well spaced out, "I think you would be well advised to consult your wife before you finally make up your mind."

Petrella was aware that someone else had come into the room. He sat, gripping the telephone and staring at it. The voice said, "You understand what I am saying?"

"Where does my wife come into it?"

"She does not come into it. But she might advise you to co-operate. We have taken charge of your son."

Petrella tried to say something, but no words came.

"If you want him back with his skin on you will follow out my instructions to the letter. Neither you, nor your wife, will say anything of this to anyone."

There was a click as the receiver was replaced and a purring sound on the disconnected line.

Petrella made three attempts to put the receiver back on the hook. He had some difficulty in unclenching his hand. Finally he left the receiver lying on the desk, got to his feet, stared at Sergeant Roughead, who was standing beside the desk, and left the room without saying a word. Milo heard him running down the passage.

Milo replaced the receiver, took it off again and dialled. A voice said, "Father Amberline here."

"It's me, Father. Milo."

"What can I do for you, my boy?"

"Patrick's new flat is just round the corner from your Vicarage, isn't it? Could you get round there quickly. There's been some trouble. I think they're going to need help. Don't say I told you. But hurry."

"I was planning to call on Mrs. Petrella anyway," said the Reverend Amberline. "I'll go over right away."

It took Petrella fifteen minutes of panic and frustration to reach home. First he discovered that both police cars were out on duty. Then he wasted further minutes looking for a taxi. Then he started running.

When he arrived breathless, the front door of his flat was open and he could hear voices from the sitting-room. One was the comfortable bass of Father Patrick Amberline. The other he scarcely recognised as that of his wife. She was lying back in a chair and there was a long livid bruise down the side of her face. When she saw Patrick she tried to get up, but the priest put a hand on her shoulder. He said, "Concussion. Nothing worse, I think. I've sent for the doctor. She oughtn't to move about too much until he's seen her."

She said, "They took Donald. They came in here and knocked me down and took him. I'd have killed them if I could, but I had nothing to do it with."

"We'll have him back," said Father Amberline. "Never fear. Just rest easy now."

"Yes," said Petrella. "We'll have him back." He seemed to be thinking. "Would you look after things here, Father? There's a lot to do."

"Surely, surely."

There were a few signs of disorder. A table had been knocked over. The telephone had been torn out of the wall. In the corner was a building estate which Donald, an ambitious four-year-old architect, had been constructing when the men arrived.

Petrella took a last look round the room. There was an expression on his face which Father Amberline, had he been a Spaniard himself, might have recognised. It was the cold composed look of a matador facing a dangerous bull.

Outside it was beginning to get dark. Petrella found a taxi and dismissed it at the end of Archer Street. When Mrs. Sullivan saw who it was, she tried to slam the door. Petrella pushed it open, not rudely but quite firmly, and went through into the kitchen.

Mrs. Sullivan pattered after him. She said, "You've put away my son, Patrick. Is it me you're after now, then?"

Petrella ignored this. He sat down in a chair in front of the stove and said, "I want to talk to Michael and Liam."

There was something in his voice which Mrs. Sullivan evidently found hard to understand. It was not threatening. It was certainly not placatory. It was the flat voice of someone asking for something which was going to happen anyway.

"I might fetch them," she said, "if you'd tell me what you want with them."

"I'll tell you when they get here," said Petrella.

Mrs. Sullivan looked at him once again. Then she picked up a shawl and started to wrap it round her head.

"Quickly, please," said Petrella.

Mrs. Sullivan went out, closing the door behind her. Petrella sat quietly staring into the red heart of the fire.

Michael and Liam Sullivan were big men, though not as tall or as broad by a few inches as their brother Patrick. They drifted into the room, treading softly, and stood looking down at Petrella.

Petrella said, in the same flat voice, "Three weeks ago your brother Patrick was charged with theft. The charge arose from the discovery of stolen articles concealed, very cleverly, under the floor of the coal-shed behind this house. We should never have found them, in fact we'd never have suspected they were here, if we hadn't had a direct tip-off."

Michael Sullivan said, "Ah," and sat down on the edge of the kitchen table which creaked under his weight.

Petrella said, "I am assuming that you have no idea who gave us this information."

Mrs. Sullivan said, sharply, "Careful what you say, now." She could feel the tension that was building up.

Petrella ignored her. He said, "I'm prepared to sell you that information."

There was a long silence. Then Liam said, "It's not normal, if I understand correctly, for members of the police force to say where their information comes to them from."

"This is not a normal occasion."

"You mentioned selling. What price exactly had you in mind?"

"In return I want what your brother Patrick once offered me. I want to know where I can find Augie Volk."

"Augie the Pole is it? You want enough to put him away?"

"No. I want to know where to find him tonight."

The two big Irishmen looked at each other. Finally Michael nodded and Liam said, "He has a place he and his boys use. It's not in his name. It's an old meat packing station. It lies behind the Foundry, in Lower Dock. He should be there tonight."

Petrella said, "Thank you," and got up. Michael said, "You were going to tell us — "

"I've already told you," said Petrella.

By eight o'clock he was back at his desk writing a note. It covered two pages in his neat handwriting and was addressed to Superintendent Watterson. He was finishing it when he heard footsteps in the passage. He looked up as Sergeant Roughead came in, followed by Sergeant Blencowe and Detective Lampier.

Petrella said, "What on earth are you doing here? You're all meant to be off duty."

Milo said, "It did just occur to us that you might be needing some help."

"What put that idea into your head?"

"Something Father Amberline said to me."

"I see."

"Then we heard from Sergeant Cove that you'd drawn a gun from the Armoury. So we put two and two together and came along."

Petrella put the two sheets of paper into an envelope and sealed it. He said, "I don't know what answer you got when you put two and two together. But whatever it was, it was wrong. I'm going out tonight to do a job. If I'd needed any help, be sure I'd have asked for it."

He put the envelope on the mantelpiece, walked to the door and held it open. The three men trooped out ahead of him.

Downstairs they found Station Sergeant Cove looking unusually wide awake. Petrella said, "Let me have the keys of the smaller car, Harry. I'll be back in about an hour. Thanks."

He went out, leaving the four men staring after him.

The night was clear, but the moon was not yet up. Petrella drove carefully, using the smaller roads, keeping north of the Causeway and heading down towards the river. The light reflected up from the dashboard showed his face composed and passive. When his instinct told him that he had gone far enough he stopped, backed the car into a gateway, switched off the engine and lights and got out. He could hear cars passing along the main road but everything round him was silent. He locked the car and started to walk, padding along quietly over pavements damp with the mist which came up from the river every evening.

When he turned the corner and found that he was in Lampe Lane he had his bearings. Lampe Lane led to Stable Dock, so called because it had once been used to land pit ponies brought down from Yorkshire for the Kent mines. Both the dock and the light railway which served it were now unused, but they formed a back-stop which would prevent him from overrunning his objective.

The first turning off Lampe Lane was Colinbrook Street which ran along the frontage of the foundry. The next must be Palance Street. The meat packing station would be the last of the three gaunt buildings on the river side of the street. He remembered that a passage had been marked on the map running down west of the packing station and leading to the wharfside.

He approached with caution. The first two buildings were derelict. The third was occupied. There was a glimmer of light filtering out through the clouded glass and grime of one of the ground-floor windows. Something else, too. The sound of men's voices from the lit room.

On one side of the main door a notice, barely decipherable, said *Henders Bros. Canning and Packing. Deliveries at Rear.*

Petrella thought about it. The rear would be deserted. It was a lot to hope that it would offer any point of entry. But it was the best chance. He slipped and skidded down the passage, which was an inch deep in filth, and came out into the open space behind.

The main part of the packing station was joined at one end to an extension which was one storey higher and carried two chimneys. Outlined against the night sky, paling with the coming of the moon, it looked like the hulk of a ship, its bridge and funnels cocked up at one end; a ship run ashore and left to rot.

The ground-floor windows and the windows of the first floor were heavily barred. The double doors, presumably designed for deliveries, looked as though they had not been used for years.

It was whilst he was studying them that Petrella heard footsteps coming down the passage. More than one person. There was no easy way out. On one side a spike-topped wall marked the edge of the old wharf and to the right an equally high wall blanked off the railway line. He squeezed himself back into the doorway, cursing as he did so. If he had to use his gun all surprise would be lost. What had started as difficult would become starkly impossible.

There were three men. It was not until they were quite close to him that Petrella recognised them.

"We thought we'd find you round here somewhere," said Sergeant Roughead.

Petrella said, in a voice to which relief had added almost as much venom as the fright which had preceded it, "I told you not to come."

"That's right," said Milo cheerfully. "You told us not to come, but we decided to come anyway. In the army it's called mutiny."

Petrella struggled to find something to say. Before he could start Sergeant Blencowe said, moderating his normal bellow to a hoarse whisper, "We brought Len along. If anyone can get into this place he can."

Milo said, "Do you think you can do it, Len?"

Detective Lampier examined the back of the building, which was becoming clearer each minute as the moon edged up.

"Piece of cake," he said.

He tested the drainpipe which ran up the far corner of the building. Then he started to climb. He might have been going up a staircase. When he got level with the first of the unbarred windows at second-storey level he held the pipe in one hand and swung himself across to the sill. There was a soft tinkle of broken glass, a moment's pause and Detective Lampier's slender body disappeared through the window.

"Lovely," said Milo. "He picked up the knack from his old man, did you know? He was the finest cat burglar in London, Len said. Didn't give it up until he was over sixty."

"I'm not sure — " said Petrella.

"We're not going in that way," said Milo. "He'll get that door open somehow. It's only bolted or barred."

It took ten minutes to do it, but finally, reluctantly and with assistance from both sides, one of the double doors was forced open enough for them to slip through.

"We'll leave it like that," said Petrella. "We may have to duck out quick." He was using his torch as he spoke.

"Back stairs over here," said Lampier. "Lead all the way up."

"What's at the top?"

"Sort of storeroom. Raw hides I guess, by the smell. There must be another staircase at the other end."

"We'll go up to the top, across and down the second staircase. That should bring us out in the front hall. Before we go, I've got something to say. One piece of insubordination you can get away with, but not two. From now on, if I tell you to do something — whatever it is — you do it and you do it without arguing. Is that understood?"

"Quite understood, Skipper," said Milo, who seemed to have appointed himself as spokesman for the three. "You say jump, and we jump."

Lampier led the way. They climbed the back stairs, crossed a long attic room between mounds of strong-smelling skins, and went through an unlocked door onto a landing. Then they went down. They took their time and made very little noise.

The room from which the light was coming faced the foot of the stairs. They stopped to listen. There were at least three men talking. Two normal male rumbles and one curiously high-pitched voice. Petrella knew that it was the first two seconds that were going to make the difference. He said, "Blencowe and I will go in as close together as we can. You two follow and fan out. Anyone makes a wrong move, hit him at once."

Then he started to turn the door handle, very slowly indeed.

The voices went on talking.

As soon as he felt the door give, he kicked it open and jumped through.

There were three men in the room. It was furnished as an office, with a big safe in one corner, and a roll-top desk. One man, the oldest of the three, was sitting on a swivel chair behind the desk. The second, an enormously fat man, was balanced on a stool at a table covered with the remains of a meal. The third, and youngest, was squatting on the edge of the table.

There was a moment of paralysis. Then the young man started to reach inside his coat. Before he could do any more, Blencowe had hit him. A swinging blow which knocked him off the table. As he went down he hit his head with a crack on the edge of the safe.

The other two men had not moved. Either the surprise of the attack or the sight of the gun in Petrella's hand kept them nailed to their chairs.

The man behind the desk had a flat white face, two small black eyes like currants in a suet pudding and a stubble of grey hair, shaved closely over his skull in the German fashion. When he opened his mouth he showed a lot of gold. He said, "You had no right to do that, Inspector."

Petrella recognised the voice which had spoken to him on the telephone. He said to Blencowe, "We'll have the handcuffs on both of these men. Hands behind their backs. Then search them. The one on the floor, too."

The search produced a gun from the shoulder holster of the man on the floor, which Blencowe took charge of, an eight-inch black-handled skinning knife in a leather sheath from the fat man and nothing from the Pole.

He said, "This is irregular; you have made no charge."

"There will be a number of charges," said Petrella. "Owning a gun without a licence, for a start. And a general charge of extortion, conspiracy and kidnapping — against all of you."

"You have no proof of a kidnapping."

Petrella looked directly at the Pole for the first time since he had come into the room. He said, "That is the next thing I mean to attend to."

There was an un-lit table lamp on the desk. Petrella pulled it out of its socket and jerked out the long flex. He said to Lampier, "Hobble his ankles, leave him enough slack to walk, but not to run."

He gave his own gun to Milo, and said, "The three of you can keep an eye on these two. That one may be shamming, I don't know. If either of them makes a move you don't like, shoot their feet off." Then he got behind the Pole, jerked him onto his feet and said, "Walk."

"I refuse — " said the Pole and gave a sharp gasp. Petrella had driven the point of the knife into his back.

"Word of advice, chum," said Blencowe. "I should do what you're told and do it quick."

The Pole shuffled to the door, and took a quick look back. The young man was still on the floor. They had rolled him over when searching him and the swollen bruise on his forehead was visible with blood oozing slowly out of it. The fat man was perched on his stool with his hands behind his back. The sweat was standing out on his forehead. The Pole shuffled out into the passage. Petrella followed and shut the door carefully.

The fat man started muttering to himself.

"Something bothering you?" said Blencowe.

"What's he going to do to him?" The piping voice made him sound like a frightened little girl.

"I should think he's planning to cut little bits off him with that knife," said Blencowe. "What do you think, Milo?"

"That'd be the main course," said Milo. "He wouldn't get round to it straight away. For starters, I guess he'll pick off his fingernails."

"What he might do," said Lampier, "I read about an Indian who did this, he might cut out his knee-caps."

The scream, when it came, was two rooms away, but it was so loud that it made the fat man jump. With his hands manacled behind his back he was unable to save himself and toppled off the stool. Blencowe and Lampier hoisted him carefully back again.

"The point is," said Blencowe, "suppose he passes out

before the Skipper can get the info he wants out of him, there'll only be one thing for it. He'll have to come back and start on our friend here."

The fat man said, "It's no good doing anything to me. I don't know where the boy is."

"And who said anything about a boy?" said Milo gently. The fat man looked at him. His lips were moving but he seemed unable to speak. Milo said, "Augie made a mistake there. The Skipper's half Spanish. It's the Spanish half that's operating just now."

The second scream was muffled, as if it was made through folds of thick cloth.

Petrella ran up to the landing on the first floor. The door at the top was locked, but he had a key. His hand was shaking so badly that it took him a minute to get it into the lock. Then he opened the door and switched on the light.

In this room dressed hides were stacked in bales which covered most of the floor space and were piled high against the walls, with a narrow passageway between them. Petrella went to the far end and started shifting the bales. Behind them was a low cupboard, bolted on the outside.

Donald was curled up inside the cupboard. He was asleep. When Petrella picked him up he said something that sounded like "Mummy". Petrella carried him back down the stairs and into the hall and said, "Sergeant Blencowe."

He had hardly raised his voice, but Blencowe came running. He grinned when he saw Donald. Petrella said, "Come and give me a hand."

Augie was lying on the floor of a small bare room. His ankles were shackled to the radiator.

Petrella stooped over him, still holding Donald, and jerked the flex free. Augie stared up at him. His lips were drawn back from his teeth and a trickle of saliva had run down from the corner of his mouth. His small black eyes were alive with hatred.

"Take this thing back to the office," said Petrella. "He can walk if he wants to. There's a telephone on the desk. We'll need another car."

Blencowe dragged the Pole to his feet and started frog-marching him down the passage. Donald had opened his eyes. His face puckered, for a moment, as if he was going to cry. Then he said, "Put me down. I want to walk."

"All right," said Petrella. "Stand on your own feet. I've got a little tidying up to do here. Then we'll all have a ride home in the car." He found a piece of sacking and was rubbing it over a patch of something damp on the floor.

Blencowe pushed the Pole into a chair beside the fat man and had his hand on the telephone when both windows splintered at the same moment, and the shotguns opened up.

Two sawn-off shotguns, at close range, throw a lot of shot. Lampier had hurled himself flat on the floor under the window and was out of range. Blencowe was protected by the desk. Milo, who was opening the door to let Petrella in, collected half a dozen pellets in his right arm. Most of the rest of the contents of both barrels went into the Pole and the fat man and tore them into bloodstained pieces.

Over the shocking roar of the explosions they heard a car starting up.

"There's not much doubt about it," said Superintendent Watterson. "It was the Micks. They must have got wind of the fact that Augie shopped their brother and gone down there to even the score. I doubt if we shall be able to prove it. No one saw the car, and the guns will be in the river by now."

"Do we want to prove it?" said Commander Ratto. He had taken over at District from Baylis, who had departed, unregretted, a month before. Watterson was finding him a distinct improvement. "I take it we're not shedding many tears over those two beauties. I'm sorry Sergeant Roughead picked up some of the strays. What were our men doing down there, by the way?"

"Information received," said Watterson cautiously. There

had been elements in the story as reported to him which he had found puzzling. "They wanted to see what was in that safe. One of them went for a gun. Blencowe knocked him down and he hit his head a smack on the safe. Lucky not to fracture his skull. He was out cold during the whole episode. As soon as he's out of hospital we'll be charging him with illegal possession of a firearm."

"Right," said Ratto. "Put Blencowe in for a commendation and I'll back it. What about the stuff you found in the safe?"

"Some of it's identifiable stolen property. The rest of it seems to be bits of jewellery and rings and watches. Mostly old and some of it foreign. I think we shall find it's stuff that Volk extorted from his fellow countrymen. He wasn't a very nice character."

"He didn't die a very nice death," said Ratto. "Have you had the autopsy report yet?"

"I've got it here," said Watterson. "Faulds did it for us. He's something of an expert on wounds. He says that he's always surprised at the damage a shotgun will do. Some of it looked like extensive burning and cutting."

Ratto was reading the report. When he had finished he said, "Yes. I imagine you get all sorts of freak effects when a thing like that is loosed off at close quarters."

"I imagine you do," said Watterson.

There was something else to be said.

"About Petrella," said Ratto. "I understand he's given notice of resignation. Do you know why?"

"It's his wife. She lost the child she was expecting. It upset her badly. Patrick wants to take her right away."

"Surely we could organise that for him without losing him altogether? I haven't seen a lot of him since I came over, but he struck me as a very good man. Too good to lose."

"He's one of the best officers I've ever had working for me," said Watterson. "If things had gone differently, I'd have tipped him to end up as Assistant Commissioner."

This was handsome of Watterson. His own promotion to

Chief Superintendent had come through that morning and he was young enough to hope to climb to the top of the ladder himself.

"Do you think we can talk him out of it?" said Ratto.

"I think so," said Watterson. He added, after a pause, "I hope so."

Sale